# The Case

by

## Leopold Borstinski

# Nevada 1979

# 1

YOU COULD SAY this all began twenty years ago when I stepped off the plane. She stood there at the foot of the steps, her strapless black ball gown fluttering in the breeze. Just before then, I'd been in Vegas for a couple of days paid break to take photos for Eliza Rothstein, a jealous broad obsessed with the belief that her husband, Aaron, was shtupping a call girl from out of town. I told her not to worry and I'd check things out. Two hundred dollars a day plus expenses. Rothstein was rich and I knew I could get away with it. The thought I was taking Aaron's dough to break up his marriage didn't cross my mind. Besides, I knew Aaron wasn't shtupping a call girl.

He was shtupping Rachel, Eliza's closest friend, but I wanted a holiday and Aaron had taken Rachel to play the wheels in Vegas. So I went along for the ride. Aaron had set up a cozy apartment on the upper east side for the two of them, overlooking the park. If I hadn't wanted a holiday so bad, I'd have rented a place on the west side and used a telephoto lens. The case would have been that simple. Aaron was shrewd in business – he owned enough water utilities to drown the nation – but he let his dick do the walking whenever a blonde with big blue eyes and breasts to match came into his line of vision. And anyway, Rachel and Aaron were the worst kept secret in Manhattan. But Eliza was so dumb, she didn't understand why the guy who collected her trash was called Giuseppe. So I took the greenbacks and headed west.

Vegas is the only town where hookers and Frank Sinatra both feel at home, only they're surrounded by a million wannabes, hoping the next spin of the wheel will give them the big break. I didn't mind visiting it for a few days, but after a couple of weeks, I missed the sun so bad my ulcer started playing up.

Aaron's money meant he could afford to stay at the Tropicana, the swankiest joint in Vegas. I was on expenses so I took a room on the fifteenth floor. By the time I arrived at reception, Aaron and Rachel were already tucked up for the night, so I wandered around the casino for some relaxation. I knew I wasn't going to bump into them because Aaron hadn't flown over here for the wheels, if you see what I mean. He was after some silky sheet action rather than blackjack and watered-down beer.

Anyway, I checked out the poker tables and watched a drunk lose his shirt at the wheel. Jeez, I could tell he was a loser from the moment I saw him. The lush was playing with his chips like a kid plays with his food. His first time at the wheel. Even the green baize felt his virginity every time he put the fifty buck chips on it. Pathetic. The kind of guy that gives a casino a bad name. And that's saying something.

After a couple of hours, I'd drunk enough vodka to knock out the ghosts and stumbled back to my room, number 1526. As soon as I put my head to the pillow, I was out until morning. By the time my eyes opened, the maid had already tried to clean my room. Fumbling for my watch, I saw it was half ten. I slouched out of bed and lurched into the shower. The water woke me up; I shaved and headed straight for reception.

THE FIRST TRICK was to find their room and figure out how to get some evidence without taking a photo of them in the sack. As much as I liked Aaron, I had no real desire to see his dick in action. And besides, I didn't want to put Eliza through the pain of seeing her husband sticking it into her best friend. A lighter touch was needed here.

Aaron was a schmuck with broads and I did the only bit of gambling in my whole stay in Vegas. I walked up to reception and asked which room Mr. and Mrs. Rothstein were staying in. Only Aaron would have been so stupid to use his real name. He probably paid for the hotel on one of his credit cards too. Aaron truly was that careless. Sure enough, the honeymoon couple hadn't left the bridal suite this morning. I smiled, said thank you to the big-breasted grin that gave me this information, tipped my hat, and ambled into the dining room for breakfast.

My breakfast always consists of the same thing. Glass of orange juice, eggs sunny side up, two slices of granary toast, and a cup of strong coffee-no-milk to wash it down with. Today was no exception. By the time I saw the bottom of my cup, I was alone in the breakfast room. In Vegas, you go to sleep at six in the morning and breakfast is a burger at the bar before you start playing again.

I tilted back the cup to swallow the last dregs. A few granules caught the back of my throat and I began to choke. Aaron and Rachel entered the room: I didn't know them as well as I thought. If I hadn't been choking, I might have had a chance of hiding behind my Vegas Tribune, but I was out of luck.

When he first saw me, Aaron's face would have been great to describe, but I was banging my fist on the table in the vain hope of stopping myself from choking. Besides, by the time he arrived at my table, he was fuming.

"What the hell are you doing here, Jake?" His tone of voice told me he wasn't pleased. I looked him straight in the eye, once my coughing fit had ended. "If I told you I was on vacation, would you believe me?" He glared at me for a couple of seconds and fumed some more. "Are you spying on me?" Aaron had grasped the situation in a matter of minutes. He impressed me – or I would have been impressed – if by this time he hadn't got his hand around my throat.

INSTINCTIVELY I LUNGED out, catching him in the groin. Shame. I was aiming for his solar plexus. It did the trick. Aaron landed on the floor, having whipped his hand off my throat and onto his dick. This was not the way I planned it to happen. I now had to deal with Aaron writhing on the ground at my feet and Rachel, the love of his life, rushing over to find out why her gold mine was on the floor. Until now, she had stayed by the entrance.

"Sorry, Aaron. It was an instinct thing, y'know?" I didn't expect an answer and none came, unless you count a muffled wheeze.

"My dearest. What has he done to you?" Even when Rachel is having an adulterous relationship, she still maintains her upper east side accent. What a gal. I admire that in a woman and my own dick started to itch. There was something about her. Her perfume, the way her Italian dress kissed her body. I stopped looking at Aaron and turned my attention to Rachel. Tipping my hat, I said: "I'm Jack Adkins, but my friends call me Jake."

"Well, Mister Kiss-ass, I'm calling the cops. You've just assaulted Mr. Rothstein and I saw it all."

"The name's Adkins. A-d-k-i-n-s. And you can call the cops, but Aaron won't press charges. Right, Aaron?" The wheeze on the floor nodded in agreement.

Rachel's forehead furrowed. "You've met this ape?"

"Jake's a friend. It's okay," Aaron rasped. Rachel's head flipped between me and Aaron. Like most broads, she didn't get it. "It was an instinct thing," Aaron added by way of explanation.

Rachel slumped into a chair at a neighboring table. Her head nestling in her hands. I could see why Aaron had fallen for her. Eliza's beautiful in a classic sense, but this kid had sex written all over her body. Tattooed across her hips were the words 'ball me.' Word about town was that only two men had: a millionaire Texan named Hank Something, who had made his money out of elastic bands and her childhood sweetheart, Maurice. He was the first but couldn't satisfy her appetite… for greenbacks. Aaron made three. He had everything Rachel wanted: a big bank balance and a dick to match. I felt sorry for him. I've said it before and I'll say it again: he's smart, but he ain't got smarts.

Aaron picked himself off the floor and stood to his full height of five foot nine. His jacket had fallen open and, as he did it up, I could see he was carrying a piece but didn't let it show.

"I suppose you're wondering what's going on?" Aaron had regained his composure and was trying to gain control of the situation.

"Yep," I replied, not knowing whether he meant what he and Rachel were doing in the city of dreams or what the Colt was doing stuck in his waistband.

"It's like this, see? There's nothing going on for you to worry about, okay? Nothing you need to worry Eliza about. Rachel wanted to check out the tables in Vegas 'cause she'd never been before and I said I'd show her the sights. Okay?"

"Right. And I'm Abe Lincoln I s'pose?"

"Don't get sarcastic with me, Jake. There's nothing going on. Nothing. If you go back to the city and tell Eliza anything, I'll see that they revoke your license."

"If there's nothing going on, why are you threatening me?" It seemed like the right thing to say at the time, but thinking back I should have kept my mouth shut. Aaron leaned back to throw a punch at me and, just at that moment, a bullet whizzed past his head, missing him by less than an inch. I hit the deck, throwing Aaron down with me. I rolled over and dragged Rachel to the floor, covering her body with mine. Jeez, this was supposed to be a simple case of wandering dick. By now, Aaron had taken his gun out and was pointing it at the breakfast room entrance. The snub nose quivered in his shaking hand.

And that was that. Waiters ran into the room after a couple of minutes. Aaron tried firing at them, but the asshole had left the safety on. Lucky really, otherwise he'd have been looking at ten to twenty. The maître d' called the cops and they took us taken to the station.

2

LIEUTENANT RODRIGUEZ WAS not the brightest man in uniform. Which is saying something. He had been promoted to increase the number of racial minorities of senior rank. Me? I don't care what color a man's skin is. A wop cop's still a cop to me. I told him the three of us were visiting Las Vegas together and that we couldn't see where the shot came from or who fired it. Aaron had to hand over his snub nose, but that was no bad thing. He had already shown that when it was needed, he might as well hold his dick in his hand. Aaron promised to make a payment to the Police Benevolent Fund and we walked out of the station in under five hours. A personal best. Aaron didn't see it that way.

When we got back to the hotel, Rachel was all set for heading back east on the next plane out of town, but Aaron was having none of it and we headed straight for the bar while he tried to settle her mind: "The guy must have been a crackpot. It could have been a champagne cork popping. Or anything."

"That doesn't explain the bullet lodged in the wall, does it?" I countered, fueling Rachel's desire to head home. Aaron stared at me as if to say, Shut up about the goddamn slug. You don't think I don't know it was a slug?

There's a time to speak and a time to be silent. This was one of those times. Rachel went to powder her nose. Aaron ordered a dry vodka martini straight up with a twist for her, a Scotch on the rocks for himself, and a double vodka on the rocks for me. Aaron checked toward the ladies' bathroom and said: "I don't want to talk about it, okay? We'll have to deal with this when I get back to New York. When are you leaving?"

I sighed and whispered between my teeth: "I'm not going back just yet. First, you know why I'm here and we're going to have to deal with that before you get back to the city. Before she comes back from the john. Second, you'd better tell me why you were carrying a piece and who was trying to kill you. That can wait a couple of hours."

Aaron's eyes looked at the john again. Without looking back at me, he spoke. "Eliza would've found out sooner or later. Now it can be sooner. Rachel's got a great ass and she makes me happy. We laugh, y'know. Eliza's a pain and she makes me cry. What choice is that for a man of my age? What?"

"And the rest?" I hadn't bought that story, but I wanted to cut to the chase before Rachel had a chance to adjust her pantyhose.

"There is no 'rest.' Anything else is my business, not yours. I love you, Jake, but don't go sniffing round in my affairs. I'm warning you, understand?" Aaron turned his head to face mine. "As one friend to another."

Then his face turned to a smile. I could smell Rachel behind me as she walked past, placing her arm around Aaron's neck. "Darling, I've had enough of Vegas, why don't we go home now?"

"No, we're here for a vacation and we're gonna have a fuckin' vacation. Right?"

"Jake, tell him. I'm scared. I want to go home." Her pouting lips made me want to sink my tongue in her mouth. She was putting on her little girl act. If it wasn't working on Aaron, it sure as hell was working on me. But I knew that whatever reason Aaron actually came to Vegas for, he hadn't got it nailed yet and there was no use arguing with him.

"Sorry, babe. No can do. Besides, Aaron knows best." I lied, hoping that she'd buy it. She took a sip of her martini and it calmed her down. "I'm going to back to the room. You coming?" she asked Aaron while looking at me.

"Not just yet, I'll be up in five. There's something I want to say to Jake first."

"Okay, honey, don't be too long."

"I won't." Aaron patted her butt as she turned to walk out of the bar. I hadn't checked it out until then. Those buns were firm and round. Man, I wanted a piece of that.

AARON WAITED UNTIL Rachel was out of earshot. "Jake, I've got some business to take care of tomorrow. Will you look after Rachel for me while I'm gone?"

"Sure. But you do understand we've got some talking to do, don't you?"

"Yeah, yeah, but right now there's a great piece of ass waiting for me in my room and I'm not gonna disappoint her." Aaron stood up and dashed across the room. Who could blame him? If I'd been in his loafers, I'd have done the same thing.

I stayed at the bar and finished my drink. Two hours later, I stumbled out of the bar, still thinking about Rachel. I was feeling horny, but all the hookers at the Tropicana were old enough to be my mother. And I didn't want to fuck my mother. So I shimmied back to my room and fell asleep.

By the time I woke up the next morning, Aaron had already left the hotel and Rachel gave me a wake-up call.

"What time is it?" I asked, having fumbled the receiver onto the floor, picked it up, and slammed it against my ear.

"Half nine. Aaron said you'd look after me today."

"Yep, sure did." My mind, still half asleep, started to think up all sorts of ways I'd like to look after that woman. Most of them didn't involve my moving from the bed; those that did involved a dining table and a pat of butter. "Have you had breakfast yet?" I asked. "A little toast with Aaron about an hour ago."

"Well, you can watch me eat mine. Meet me in the Acapulco lounge in thirty."

"Okay. In thirty minutes then."

"Yeah." I jumped out of bed, showered, shaved, and washed in less than fifteen minutes. I was sat at a table for two by the time Rachel arrived. She turned up ten minutes early.

"HOW ARE YOU?"

"Still shaken a bit from yesterday," she replied.

"I don't want to know," I countered. She looked at me quizzically and I realized I'd revealed more than I'd wanted to with that remark. Like an angel with an apron, the waitress took our order. I had my usual and Rachel had coffee. Even though she'd already eaten, she could have had anything on the menu. After all, Eliza was paying for the damn thing.

As I was eating, I could tell Rachel was watching my every move. By the time I'd finished my coffee, she had turned her napkin into a catamaran. "What shall we do today, then?" I looked deep into her eyes and thought of nothing but her perfume. I made a mental note to find out what it was.

"When's Aaron back?"

She lowered her eyes and played with her hair. "I dunno. He didn't say. Only that he'd back in time for dinner tonight."

"Did he say where he was going?" Having lost eye contact I snapped back into private dick mode. I needed to figure out what Aaron was up to. Yesterday's breakfast was still sitting in the pit of my stomach. And I'm not talking about the undercooked eggs either.

"No, but I overheard him speaking to a guy on the phone before we came down for breakfast."

"What did he say?"

"Not much. He just checked on the time for the meeting and that was it." I could tell the broad was lying; her eyes kept shifting from left to right, but wouldn't look into mine.

"How d'you figure it was a guy and not a dame?"

"Aaron wouldn't have dumped me for the day to see another woman," she replied, indignantly. She was probably right. Whatever business Aaron was involved in, the chances were that it was business. Not even Aaron would take a dame to Vegas to fuck her brains out and then leave her to ball some other babe. Aaron might not have smarts, but he's not a complete schlemiel.

"So what else did he say?"

"Not much, like I said. Only he was going to see this guy at nine and that it could last all day… stop quizzing me, I don't like it." That I could believe. Rachel was used to giving the orders and she didn't like it when I turned the tables on her.

"Sorry," I lied, "I'm just worried that Aaron's in trouble. If he is, I want to help. That's all."

We sat, silent for a spell, and the catamaran became a swan. "Where d'you learn to do that?"

"Art school. I took a class last year. Gave me something to do in the afternoons."

"Yeah?" For the moment, I couldn't think of anything to say. And then I realized what I needed to do. "How d'you fancy a walk on the Strip?" The walk wasn't important, I was just hoping that as we checked out the no-hopers taking a break from their gambling, Rachel might loosen up. I needed to find out what Aaron was up to. Whatever it was – and I had some ideas already – I knew he was in over his head. Aaron wasn't the kind of guy to carry a piece and, despite the many deals he struck, I'd never known anyone to actually want him dead. There'd been Bernie Schwartz, of course. He was all mouth though. I'll tell you his story some other time. For now, my task was to find out what was going on with Aaron and who the hell he was meeting.

3

IF I'D HAD any sense, I would have got up early and followed him, but I'd drunk too much the night before and besides, I liked Aaron a lot, but not enough to lose any sleep over him. He'd done me some favors along the way and, in turn, I'd helped him out of a few jams.

Rachel agreed to the walk, muttering something about wanting to get a gulp of fresh air. She was sick and tired of the air con in the hotel. This made no sense as her apartment in New York had air con. I said nothing. We left the Tropicana and headed east.

"Tell me more about your art class," I asked. It worked. Rachel was happy to talk about herself for the ten minutes we took to reach my favorite hotel again, the Vacation Villa. For no good reason other than Rachel didn't want to walk anymore, we popped inside to have a coffee.

As we sauntered into the coffee lounge, I was shocked at what I saw, but I didn't let it show.

"What are you looking at?"

"Nothing, I thought I recognized one of the punters, that's all," I said, deadpan. Aaron was sitting with his back to us, talking to an olive-skinned greaseball in a three-piece green suit. And I mean green. Like an apple.

My brain whirled round inside my head. I needed to find out precisely what was being said, but I knew if we stayed, Aaron would

have a bullet in his brains before lunchtime because his companion
was a made man. Today was not going to win any Best Day of 1976.
Shit.

Grabbing Rachel by the elbow, I tried to swivel her round.

"What're you doing, you ape?"

"The punter… it is him and the last time I saw him he said he'd
break my arms if he saw me again. Sorry, babe, we've gotta leave.
Now." By this time Green Suit was looking our way and we were
starting to make a scene. Or rather Rachel was starting to make a
scene. Aaron turned round to check out the commotion and for the
second time in two days, there was total anger in his expression. I
was not helping his blood pressure. Aaron stormed over to us, at
which point Rachel pulled herself away from me and went straight
to the bar. Not to Aaron but to the bar – like she knew not to screw
things up for Aaron.

"You stupid fuck! What the fuck are you doing? For Chris' sake,
all you had to do was keep that bitch company for one day." Aaron
pointed to Rachel as he screamed this. I looked him straight in the
eyes: "We'd just been going for a walk…" I trailed off because I knew
that the truth was unbelievable. But Aaron calmed down almost
immediately.

"Okay. Now you're here, you can help me."

"How?"

"I want you to pretend you're my bodyguard. A heavy. Don't act
like a gorilla, but make sure Frankie sees you're carrying your gun."

"Okay, but what's going on, Aaron?"

"Can't say now. I'll tell you later. Promise."

WE WALKED OVER to Frankie and Aaron made the
introductions. We sat down and I ordered a black coffee. Frankie
spoke as though nothing had happened and I didn't exist.

"You're getting heat from Michael and you want me to act on
your behalf. Why should I intercede in this matter?" That one line
told me all I needed to know. Don Michael Lambretti was the head of
one of the five families and Aaron was going to cut a deal with

Frankie – or rather I should say Frankie 'The Hammer' Pentangelo – to save his bacon.

Frankie was Lambretti's nephew. A wise guy. There were a million stories of how Frankie got his nickname. My favorite concerned a Joe who had run up a hundred-grand marker with a bookie named Vince, who was working under the don's protection. The joe's real name was Fred or Barny or whatever. Anyway, the story goes that Don Michael didn't approve of this bum treating him like JP Morgan and wanted to teach him a lesson – as well as send out a message to the other Joes. Don Michael was not pleased and he let Frankie know it. Frankie was only twenty at the time and, quite rightly, wanted to show Don Michael what a good guy he was. So, in his naïve way, he could only think of one thing to do. He invited Barny over to his apartment to talk about a numbers racket. While he was sipping his seven-and-seven on the rocks, Frankie Pentangelo slammed a hammer into the top of his head, killing him instantly. He dumped Barny's body into the Hudson and got an alibi. Four days later, the body washed up on the New Jersey side. The cops used dental records to identify him – Frankie had sliced off the guy's fingertips. He was brought in for questioning, but Frankie had done a thorough job and the cops had to let him go. And that is the story of how Frankie Pentangelo, nephew to the great Don Michael, got his nickname of the Hammer.

Aaron's response to Frankie's question was slow, thoughtful, and with more than just a trace of fear: "If you don't help me, I'm dead. Don Michael wants to 'invest' in Five Counties Water to get hold of white money. He's talking about taking fifty-one percent of the shares. I can't afford for him to do that. If you help me here, I'll give you…" Frankie raised his hand in the air to stop Aaron's gushing.

"You think too highly of me. Now, I will not sit in the coffee lounge of the Vacation Villa and state that I know this man is a don. And I'm not going to say I even know him. Besides, the information I have is that there's already a contract on your head and that someone from Chicago nearly pushed the button on you yesterday. On that basis, I must tell you that my answer is no."

AARON HAD TEARS in his eyes. I was in awe of Frankie. This man had the power to save Aaron's life and he didn't give a damn. He wasn't even interested in what his consideration would be. Aaron pulled himself together and started right back at Frankie. "If you help me and call off the contract, I'll give you a controlling stake in Los Angeles Water. It clears at least half a billion a year. Profit."

Frankie sat there silent and put his hands together like he was about to pray. He was weighing up the deal; half a billion personal profit a year against sticking his neck out for a New York Jew. The silence lasted about a minute and I could tell Frankie had made up his mind within the first ten seconds. He wouldn't have agreed to the meeting if he hadn't intended to do something. He was just showing Aaron that his gratitude would need to be immense for this accommodation.

"The certificates for Los Angeles Water will arrive at my attorney's office by tomorrow morning. I appreciate the donation. As for the other matter, let us just say you need not worry about any hostile takeover of your Five Counties business. Make the call now to get those certificates on an overnight flight. When you return to the coffee lounge, I shall be gone." And with that, Frankie sat back in his chair and sipped his coffee. I did the same and Aaron jumped up and walked, slightly faster than normal, to the kiosks to make the call.

Frankie turned to me and said, "Get out of my face." I got up and walked over to Rachel, who was tucking into her second dry vodka martini straight up with a twist.

"You knew?"

"Yeah, but Aaron told me not to tell you… you're a nice guy, y'know that?" Rachel put her hands through her hair and pushed out her breasts. The drink was getting to her and her body was coming on strong.

Aaron returned and stood next to me. He looked at where Frankie had been sitting, but the Hammer had disappeared.

"It's all taken care of."

We stayed so that Aaron could have a drink, which he gulped down in one. Then we headed for the door. Quite what happened next will always be a blur. A guy with sunglasses and a gray suit stood at the entrance to the lounge. From what I remember, he pulled out a gun and pointed it at Aaron, who grabbed Rachel to use as a shield. The hood fired three shots. The first hit Rachel's shoulder. I grabbed her and yanked Aaron onto the floor. The second shot spat out of the barrel and whipped straight through her chest and out the other side, missing me by about an inch. Instinctively, I hit the deck, taking Rachel with me, but the third slug landed between her eyes. The splatter spread across Aaron, myself, and the bar. Two early morning drinkers vomited immediately.

That was it. Aaron noticed all the blood and brains on him and screamed, thinking bullets had splattered through his body. But he was clean. Me too. Rachel was dead after the second shot, according to the autopsy. We spent thirteen hours in the precinct house but neither Aaron nor myself knew what the guy looked like and, even if we had, we weren't going to say.

There's not a lot else to add. Rachel was a sexy broad, with big tits and a lovely ass who screwed her best friend's husband. Given time, I could have fallen in love with her. One final thing, I never found out what scent she was wearing.

# NEW YORK 1961

$$4$$

BY THE TIME my plane landed back at JFK, I'd had time to settle my stomach. As I stood at the top of the steps leading down from the shuttle, Simone Lambretti was waiting for me. To say I was surprised to see her would be an understatement. The last time I'd seen her, she'd shown me her stomach. But that was okay, she was only four at the time. Simone'd snuck into her father's office when I'd been summoned there for a meeting. That was eighteen years before, back in '61.

I recognized her through the papers. I don't think a month'd gone by since her sixteenth birthday when she'd been out of the press. Much to her old man's annoyance. The reason I was in Don Lambretti's office had nothing to do with Simone, however, and a lot to do with some difficulties he was facing. One of his 'associates' had thumbed through the phone book for a gumshoe and dialed my number. When an associate of the don calls you and asks whether you'd like to meet with the don this afternoon, you take a cab and to hell with the expense.

Lambretti lived upstate in a mansion hidden from the road by a wood. A single dirt track led to the copse where the house was. Kids were playing out front and, leaning against the front door posts, were two hoods packing pieces. It was the middle of summer and these goons were sporting long black coats.

As my cab stopped out front, one of the goons sprang up and rushed to open the door. "I've come to see Mr. Lam—" I began to say, but before I could finish my sentence, the goon had grabbed me from the cab, paid off the driver, and hustled me inside. This was not a good way to start a business meeting.

THE INSIDE OF the house was cluttered. Filled with the kind of crap only an extremely rich man with very little taste could accumulate. Stag heads mounted on the walls. Paintings of old men with their horses. The one thing I was certain of was that none of the guys in the pictures were Lambretti's family – this Italian-American had WASPs on his walls.

The goons hustled me into the library. I stood in the middle of the room and as I swiveled round, the gorilla shut the door on his way out and I heard him turn the key. In the room were rows of dusty leather-bound slabs set against the walls and two high-backed reading chairs. I grabbed one of them and dragged it so that its back was against one of the walls. I sat down, sinking into the upholstery, and waited.

One lifetime later, the door unlocked itself and Lambretti entered, closely followed by two of his henchmen. Instinctively, I stood up and went over to shake his hand. Lambretti looked at my outstretched hand as though it had shit on it. I smiled and put the offending item in my pants pocket. Lambretti glided over to my chair and sat down, beckoning me to do likewise. Without taking his eyes off me, he motioned for the goons to leave the room. They nodded, departing without saying a word. We were alone.

"So Mr. A-d-k-i-n-s, thank you for coming to see me at such short notice," he intoned, slowly, coldly; as though his interest in the niceties was to set me at my ease rather than because there was even a grain of truth in his gratitude.

"No problem. It is an honor that a man such as yourself should have even heard of me, let alone—"

Lambretti held his hand up to silence me. He wasn't interested in my ass-licking.

"Never mind. I did not invite you here to exchange pleasantries, Mr. Adkins. May I call you Jake?"

"Sure can, all my friends call me Jake."

"I am not proposing to be your friend, Jake. Instead, I am proposing you carry out a job of work for me."

"I guessed as much," I retorted, hoping to show that I was quick-witted and the kinda guy who wouldn't let him down.

"A very fine guess, Jake. The task I have in mind for you should be relatively simple to accomplish," he smiled, "even for someone of your… shall we say… talents."

I scrunched up my face quizzically, not knowing whether he was complimenting me or not.

"Jake. All I ask that you do is to do nothing. Or rather carry on doing what you are currently doing. Nothing more."

AT THIS POINT, the French windows burst open – had I mentioned there were French windows? – and little Simone rushed in, jumping onto her dad's knee, and lifted up her smock. Lambretti's eyes warmed and he said sweet nothings to his kid, before telling her to leave him and daddy's friend to their conversation. I had never really thought of Don Lambretti as a 'daddy,' you know?

Anyway, once the French windows were securely shut and Lambretti had sat back in his chair, I asked, "I'm sorry, but I don't understand. What do you mean?"

"You are on a case at the moment, are you not?"

I thought long and hard. I had a couple of choices. First, I could lie and pretend I wasn't on a case and that they'd got the wrong guy. The chances are I'd end up at the bottom of the Hudson. Second, I could tell the truth and admit I'd been following a broad for a couple of weeks. This blonde spent her whole time sashaying between beauty parlors and Fifth Avenue boutiques. Her life was a million miles from daddy Lambretti and his hoods. Third, I could admit that I was on a job and that I was tailing Dawn Pasquale, but that as nothing was happening, I had called it quits.

"Yes, I am. I've been tailing a broad up and down Fifth Avenue. It's good money but I'm gonna call it quits."

"No, you are not. I will double whatever you are being paid now if you agree to my request that you carry on."

The john who'd got me to tail Pasquale was a well-to-do heel who was paranoid she was out sucking some other guy's cock. Instead, she was sucking his credit cards dry. But the way I figured it was this: he was paying me two hundred a day plus expenses. If I told Lambretti I was earning three hundred, the don would give me six hundred to do the same job, making a grand total of eight hundred dollars every time the alarm clock went off. And whichever way you look at it, that's a lot of greenbacks.

"I'M ON THREE hundred a day, plus expenses. I'm happy to help you, but what will I say to Jimmy the Greek?"

"That is the second time you have lied to me today," said the don flatly, "The first lie was that you were going to tell Jimmy that you were going to quit. As I understand, this is the first solid piece of work you have had in four months and you are desperate for the money. Which leads me to the second lie. You are only being paid two hundred a day. But I will pay you six hundred because I want you to do the job and I know that you will only feel cheated if I offer four."

I could tell that my face was twitching nervously. "I cannot trust a man who never lies, especially a man in your circumstances. Lying to me once in that situation is acceptable. Lying to me twice is not. Lie to me a third time and you will incur my displeasure. Do we have an understanding?"

We sure as hell did. When the don was displeased, the object of his anger was normally found at the bottom of the East River with rocks tied to his feet and a bullet between his eyes. That was not one of my life goals.

"Yes, we have an understanding. But what am I going to say to Jimmy the Greek?"

Lambretti was silent for a spell, thinking, his eyes downcast and his arms resting by his side as they had done for the entire time since he sat down.

"You will work for me for a week. You will tell James Popoudopolos that Dawn Pasquale is doing nothing for him to be suspicious of and that the case is closed."

"Okay."

"And as of today, you will stop following her. Is that clear?"

"Yes."

"One final thing before you go… have you taken any notes or have any other records of your spell following the blonde?"

"Um, let me think… nothing much. Just her timesheets and stuff."

"When my assistant drives you back to your office, you will give him any paperwork on Miss Pasquale. Do you understand?"

"Yes, I do."

And with that, he stood up, walked over to the door, and opened it. He mumbled something to one of the goons, who nodded and took me to his car. The journey back to the city was quiet. I don't think Cheech could say anything more than 'No' in English and I didn't feel like getting to learn the Italian for 'sleeps with the fishes.'

We got to my office and the goon came with me to get the papers. They were all in the file marked 'Popoudopolos.' Me? I hate paperwork, but that's why I pay a secretary to come in, look after the phones and generally tell me when I should be meeting who and where.

Without a word said between us, the goon walked out of my office and that was the last I saw of him. I called up Jimmy the Greek and broke the news to him. He was okay about it – after all, I told him that everything was fine and that his darling Dawn was a stand-up broad. But there was one thing bugging me. Why would the great Don Michael Lambretti give a shit about that babe, Pasquale?

■      ■      ■       ■       ■      ■      ■

# 5

I LEARNED THE answer one week later. In the morning, a
package arrived containing a roll of in-god-we-trusts to the tune of
forty-two hundred bucks. In the afternoon I got a call from Jimmy
that Dawn had been shot dead at lunchtime.

When I tootled over to her apartment to see what I could find
out, I discovered the great Detective Superintendent Paul 'Rickshaw'
Thomas at the scene. I say great; he was great to me because he'd got
me out of more than one jam with the commissioner downtown, but
he was just a humble super to everybody else.

"What's up?"

"You tell me, you're the cop, right?"

"Funny. Real funny. What do you care about another dead broad
in this big city?"

"Always with the questions. You a cop or something?"

"Still with the funnies."

"So what's the story here, officer?"

"Not much to see, move along."

Thomas winked at me and we moved around the corner, away
from the front door of the apartment so's we could have a more
private chat.

"Shot dead. Point blank range to the back of the head."

I grimaced because that was not a nice way to go; it implied a
professional hit.

"Tell me about it. And there's more. She wasn't alone. She was found, um, on top of a fella, see?"

"Dead also?'

"Yeah but with a smile on his face, if you get my meanin'."

For a second or two, I imagined the two of them dead with the coroner trying to prise them apart so that they could be buried in different caskets. Then my reverie was interrupted by Rickshaw laughing at me. Clearly, he could read my mind.

"Doesn't bear thinking about, does it? To put you out of your misery, I said she was on top of him, I didn't say he was inside of her. Schmuck." One bullet, two bodies, and a happy Don Michael. Quite a day's work for some lucky guy.

I smiled at Rickshaw's words, but I couldn't figure out what Dawn was doing sleeping with this guy. From what I'd heard, Jimmy the Greek was all the man that Dawn would have needed in her life – and that didn't just come from Jimmy himself, although he did proclaim it from the rooftops at every opportunity. After a day or two's solid gumshoe work, I'd started to build up a picture of Dawn's lothario Pete.

Word in the Big Apple was that our man came from Cincinnati and had only been in the city a matter of weeks. A couple of long-distance calls told me the guy was a low-level goon for a local enforcer. Nothing clever, nothing fancy, but a regular beater-up of neighborhood pond scum – and nothing much more. I couldn't fathom Pete's connection with Dawn because she had never been to Cincinnati and this was his first visit to NYC. Time to hit the streets again.

FIRST STOP WAS a trip to Jimmy the Greek to find out what he didn't know he knew. When he came to the door of his Bronx row house, there was no light on inside. He let me in and he shuffled into his living room, a broken man, slumped onto a chair and I sat opposite him. We were silent for a spell and I broke the monotony of his inability to communicate:

"Shall I make us a cup of java?"

"What? Yes… Yes, why not?"

I stood up and wandered into the kitchen, opening every cupboard door until I found the coffee grounds. Then I messed about with the percolator until everything was brewing. Finally, I took the milk out of the refrigerator and opened the cupboards up again until I found the sugar for Jimmy.

"How'd you take it?" I shouted out to him.

"No milk, no sugar, thanks," was the reply, so I put my newly found prizes back in their place and waltzed back into the living room with two cups of dark brown liquid.

"So tell me…" I began, "what made you think she was having an affair?"

His doleful eyes looked woefully at me, salty liquid forming around the corners. He sniffed.

"The way she was behaving the last few days before I called you."

"In what way, Jimmy?"

"She was touching me less."

"And she was making phone calls."

"Phone calls? What's so unusual about that?"

"The number of them and, what raised my attention, the way that she put the phone down almost every time I entered the room. Made me think that she wanted to hide the call from me."

"Did you ask her about them?"

"No." He looked down at the floor again and sniffed, rubbing the moisture away from his eyes. I needed him this side of morose to get what I needed.

"Do you know if they were local calls?"

"Local? I dunno. Do you think they were local?"

"Just asking. I've got no clue what numbers she dialed – but I might know a guy who does. Leave it with me."

"Okay. Anything else?"

"Not for now."

"I'm going back to bed. Let yourself out." So I did.

◆ ◆ ◆

# The Case

I SWUNG BY Rickshaw's desk at the precinct later that day, mainly to catch up because bumping into him had reminded me I liked his company, but also to see if I could get access to Jimmy the Greek's phone records. The answer was a big zero but Rickshaw knew me well enough to leave the right bits of paper face up on his desk when he went for a leak. Sure enough, there were daily incoming and outgoing calls to Cincinnati, so Dawn and Pete had something brewing before he hit town last week. But what?

Traveling back to my office, I tried to think of the different games that could have been playing out in front of Jimmy – and what possible connection they had with Don Michael. There was nothing direct to connect all these people, so I figured there must be a third person in the mix who hadn't shown themselves yet. Apart from the hitman, of course.

What would make Don Michael call a hit on Pete and not want any witnesses? Because he could have just paid me to keep my mouth shut and I surely would. I'd slash my mother's face for a Jackson and everyone knew it. My conclusion – Don Michael didn't want me to even see who was performing the hit. And why would that be? Because the hit was personal, otherwise any old out-of-town hood could have pulled the trigger. So if it was personal, I'd be looking at family or a friend of Don Michael's who lived in Cincinnati. The field of suspects suddenly got very narrow indeed because Don Michael was not a man who traveled round the country picking up friends. He stayed in the state so that he would not make himself susceptible to detainment by the FBI under the RICO laws. And quite right too. If you are going to be responsible for one of the five Mafia families in New York, you are not going to want to be interrogated by J Edgar's finest.

One of the bonuses of being an investigator is that we held phone books from each of the major cities, so a quick check in the Cincinnati L-R volume indicated there were only three Lambrettis residing legally. There was Mr. and Mrs. R Lambretti and Mr. P Lambretti. You don't need lexicographical skills to figure out which one of the three was Pete. Back then, phone books gave addresses as well as phone numbers, so I scribbled down the details and booked a flight to the Queen City.

◆ ◆ ◆

YOU CAN TELL a lot about a city by the way it welcomes you at its airport. This town wouldn't piss down your throat if your heart was on fire. I had to wait twenty minutes to catch a cab to my hotel – such a great town that you can't even pay people to drive round it. Fabulous.

I crashed in my room and after breakfast the next morning, I waited fifteen minutes for a taxi to take me to Mr. P Lambretti's residence. And what a residence it was. The pillars at the front were making a statement in themselves – and that was once you'd trekked along the path from the front gate built into a privet hedge to the main building itself. Mr. P had been doing extraordinarily well for a lowlife thug – or he had a rich friend.

The guy who opened the door to me clearly believed I was wasting his time even though he was obviously paid to open the door to strangers such as myself.

"Yes?" The single syllable was stretched out on his lips like a body on a rack. It contained at least three separate notes to my count.

"Is Mr. P Lambretti in, by any chance?"

"And you are?"

"I'm the guy asking if Lambretti is in."

He looked at me like I was scum and said nothing. I could tell that an aggressive, assumptive tone was not going to work on this gatekeeper.

"Word on the street is that he's been shot dead in New York and I wanted to find out if the rumor was true,"

"Dead? Dead, you say?"

"Yeah… so is he in?"

"No. Dead… and his voice trailed off as the butler allowed the reality of the statement to sink into his brain.

"When did you see him last?"

"What? Um… last week. He stayed as long as he could after Miss Lambretti left, but then he…"

"Miss Lambretti?"

"Yes, Miss Lambretti," he said with a simple assertion as though this was the most normal thing in the world. I whipped out a black-and-white of Dawn and showed it to him. He nodded recognition and scrunched up his face, trying to understand why I'd have her photo in my jacket pocket when Pete was the one who'd copped it.

"Can I come inside?" I asked by way of non-explanation. He opened the door wider and stepped aside to let me past the threshold. As impressive as the pillars were, the marble vestibule was something else; a sweeping curved staircase led to the second floor and two imposing doors led off the vestibule. I guessed one was a sitting room and I was right because a few seconds later, George and myself were sitting in that room having a fireside chat, although the fire wasn't lit.

He told me how Pete and Miss Lambretti had been living in the house on their own ever since Mr. Lambretti had died about a year ago.

"So when you say Miss Lambretti," I asked after a while because I really wanted to get to the punchline, "what exactly do you mean?"

"I don't understand the meaning behind your question," responded George and I believed him as my question was particularly vague.

"Well… Pete wasn't the only person to be found dead, to be honest."

"Not Dawn as well?"

"I'm afraid so, George. I'm afraid so."

"Oh God…"

I gave George time to compose himself again. He was definitely saddened by the whole situation; the tears were not from a crocodile.

"The thing is they were found dead together."

"Ah, I see," replied George almost immediately.

"What do you see?"

"Well, let's just say they had a special relationship."

"Special is the word."

"Yes. If you think I am very calm about this matter, you must understand that we have got used to them over a long period of time. I nearly threw up the first time I walked into Pete's bedroom with his breakfast to find Dawn in there, naked, with him."

I pondered this thought for a while, letting it melt into my mind. "And let's be clear, shall we? Dawn and Pete were…"

"Brother and sister. Yes."

THE CONVERSATION FELL away and I stirred my cup of coffee and sipped it slowly. George carried on sitting opposite me, probably enjoying sitting in the chair instead of serving in these rooms.

"So why did Dawn leave for New York then?"

"Not sure, to be honest. They had an argument. I could hear the shouting but couldn't work out any of the words. Next thing, Dawn had grabbed her bag and some clothes and plain walked out the house."

Out of the house and into the arms of Jimmy the Greek, which was very convenient, given that she had spent less than two weeks in Manhattan before bumping into the moneylender in his local bar in the Bronx. Sounded to me like there was much more to this whole situation than a brother and sister lovers' argument. The fact that Don Michael was involved, and what appeared to be a large number of the Lambretti family, meant that I was beginning to get quite nervous about delving too deeply.

I stayed in Cincinnati for one more day, mainly to scout around the house and to try to find out what the two of them might have been arguing about, but when they were outside the house, they were just brother and sister to the local community. On that basis, I could only imagine that Don Michael had heard wind of the unusual family situation and decided to put an end to the entire affair. And the simple truth of the matter was that Don Michael had paid me to look the other way as he killed Pete and, presumably, Dawn just happened to be in the way. Having been paid once to ignore the situation, I figured it was time to go home and ignore the situation from the comfort of my own bed.

When I arrived back in the Big Apple, I spent some time talking to some Bronx guys I knew. Word on the mean streets was that Pete had been operating a sideline business for himself. A small amount of heroin was being shipped in from Sicily by Pete the Lothario and he was making a tidy profit by selling the little bags of brown dust cheaper than other members of his family. Great for short-term profitability; bad for long-term chances of survival. So Dawn must have realized this was bad for the family and left Cincinnati to avoid the inevitable fallout. Unfortunately for her, she kept in touch with the dope, because of their unholy union, and, in the end, she got hers. Dawn had the right idea about the heroin but an amazingly bad idea about adult sexual relations.

Moral of the story: don't deal drugs in your own family's backyard and always trust the instincts of an enormously fat Greek man.

# Chicago 1949

# 6

DAWN'S DEATH PLAYED heavily on my soul. Not because I thought her incestuous relationship chimed with anything I'd come across, but because the *ménage à trois* reminded me of Ed Schwartz, my erstwhile business partner and closest friend in the world. Well, he held that honor until he got a bullet in his skull.

Before I found myself in the depths of Korea, Ed Schwartz and I worked the beat in Chicago. When I say "worked," I mean we had PI licenses and when I say "the beat" I mean we took any case that was going provided we were getting paid – preferably up front.

Anyway, Ed and I had an office with our names on the door in a building where it was pretty swanky to have gold lettering anywhere really. There were two desks in our room – one for each of us with matching chairs – and an anteroom where Cheryl Dupovnik, our secretary, sat typing and generally keeping the riffraff out until they looked like clients.

So it was one August day that a dame walked in that Cheryl allowed inside our hallowed turf. Her name was Mrs. McCready and her cream silk skirt suit did little to hide her hips or breasts. Ed and I were suitably entranced by her tale of woe; her husband was cheating on her, she was certain of that. And while that wasn't good, she wanted us to understand that what really mattered to her was that Mr. McCready didn't get his hands on Daddy Roebuck's packing case fortune. Her father had found himself in the wonderful position of furnishing Uncle Sam with gun packaging during WWII and had established a strong presence in the civilian packing industry afterward as a result.

Bottom line: Mrs. McCready was stinking rich and when she divorced her husband, she wanted to make sure he didn't get one stinking dime of her old man's money.

We figured this sounded like a fabulous opportunity and suggested that she pay us one hundred dollars a day to follow him around and capture some photographic evidence that could later be relied on in court. Mrs. McCready didn't blanch at our price and we knew this would take us quite a while, so instead of being a quiet summer, we banked ourselves a winner.

Thanking Mrs. McCready for having the foresight and confidence to speak with us, Ed shepherded her out the door and we made plans, having secured a week's money in advance.

OUR FIRST THOUGHT was to blow the entire bundle, but Cheryl grabbed the greenbacks out of our hands because she knew we had bills to pay. Besides, we'd blow the whole stack on a horse – and she wanted to get paid every week over the summer. Sensible girl, that Cheryl. I always said I should have married her.

Now, you might well be forgiven for thinking I've spent most of my life following dames around in order to take photos of them in clinches with some lucky randy lad and you'd be pretty much on the money. Most cases most years have been jealous spouses – of either sex. The one thing they all share is they know that the other one is cheating on them, but the only way they can truly believe it is if some schmuck like me uses a camera on the situation.

Ed took the first shift. Mrs. Gravy-Train had given us her husband's work address and the location of their home, along with a brief itinerary. Ed started at about six in the evening and the intention was for me to take over at six in the morning or so, but after he grabbed his car keys from his desk and his jacket from the back of his chair, I never saw him alive again.

Instead, just after one, I received a knock on the door. An insistent rat-a-tat that can only originate from a detective's hand. Bolt upright on my couch, I almost tripped on the Bourbon bottle by my foot as I jumped up and went to open the door.

"What's up, officer?"

"Hi, Jake." The irony of my question was not lost on the sergeant standing in front of me. Sean and I had known each other since we were kids and, despite sitting the exams, he had never been promoted to detective – much to the annoyance of himself and, more importantly, his wife.

"Wanna come in?"

"Love to, Jake. Love to."

Something about his tone made me wake up a little faster than I wanted.

"Bit early for house calls, Sean?"

"I know…"

"So…?"

"Sit down, Jake."

"Oh Jesus! What's happened? What's happened to Ed?"

I figured it had to be Ed, as there were only three people who'd have got Sean to make his way to my troubled neighborhood in the middle of the night: Cheryl, Ed, or my ma. Chances were that if it had been Cheryl, Sean's manner would have been different. If it was my ma, Sean would've waited until morning. That left Ed.

"We found Ed in his car about twenty minutes ago. Dead."

I slumped down onto the couch. I had intellectualized it was bad news about Ed, but I was expecting it to be that he was found in the drunk tank somewhere or he'd got into a brawl. Both were frequent occurrences. This was the first time he'd died on me.

SOME BEAT COP had been walking round his block on the lookout for trouble when he noticed a guy asleep in his car. When he got closer, he could see the blood splatter on the windows, glistening in the moonlight. Finding Ed was far from asleep, plugged with what looked like a single shot to the head and multiple shots to the torso, he called for backup. How many? Sean didn't have the precise number right now, but a lot.

I went into the bathroom and threw a large amount of water on my face to sober up and hopped into Sean's blue-and-white to go to the scene.

When we arrived, police tape was already up and two of Chicago's finest were holding the crowd at bay. The two guys were stopping the three dog walkers from letting their pooches take a shit all over the evidence. And that was respectful too.

Ed's body was in one hell of a mess. Chunks of his brain were still dripping down the inside of the windows and small pieces of torso were splattered over the front and rear passenger seats even though Ed had been shot while behind the wheel. Given the sheer volume of blood, this was definitely the primary scene.

I looked at Sean and he looked back at me, eyes trailing to the ground. He shook his head and sloped off to give me some time alone with Ed.

After a couple of minutes quiet contemplation, I turned round and went over to Sean.

"You know I have to ask you a few questions." A statement, not a question in itself.

"Sure thing. Shoot." Then I winced at my own unintended joke. Sean winced too.

"When did you last see Ed?"

"In our office at around six, maybe six thirty. Cheryl will know. Then he left."

"Where'd he go?"

"On a case."

"Who's the client?"

"You know I can't tell you that. Look, it was the first day of the case and, before you ask, no, Ed didn't have any enemies – apart from every single person he put inside when he was a cop and everyone he's taken a photo of ever since in a marital dispute."

Sean just stared at me.

"Best I can offer you is that if anything turns up in the case that even smells as if it might be to do with Ed, I'll drop a dime soonest."

Sean nodded, aware that was probably the best deal on offer tonight.

"That only leaves the widow."

"Let me take care of that. You can question her some other time, okay?"

"Sure thing. We'll be over in the morning shift, so just make sure you do it by then."

"I'll head off now if you're done with me."

"For now, Jake. For now."

Sean got one of his boys to drop me back to my pad, so's I could grab a change of clothes and snatch my car keys from the kitchen table. By the time I reached Ed and Veronica's, the clock was showing seven – it had been a long night.

7

VERONICA OPENED THE door only a few seconds after I pressed the doorbell.

"Hey, you!"

"Hi, Veronica."

"What're you doing here?"

"Got some news. Can I come in?"

"What? Sure."

Veronica turned round and I caught the door before it closed on my nose. She sauntered to the living room and I followed her to sit down on their two-piece sofa. Veronica sat next to me and placed her hands daintily on her lap. I placed my hands on hers because I knew the next few minutes were going to hurt her a lot.

"It's about Ed."

"What?"

"He stayed out last night to follow an errant husband and was found shot in his car in the small hours of the morning."

"What?"

"Ed is dead."

"You're kidding me."

"No. No joke. This is real. This is what has happened."

"Oh my good God."

"Yes."

"Stay with me."

"Sure thing."

I smiled and reached over and hugged her long and hard. We remained that way for minute after minute, both receiving some comfort from each other's body. Both not wanting to stop as that would mean the world would turn again. But eventually, we did.

The day was filled with mixed emotions – the shock of knowing Ed was no more, hung over me like the shroud that would cover Ed's face nine days later.

There was another emotion at play too: absolute and total relief. With Ed gone, I was now the sole owner of *Adkins & Schwartz Investigators*, our PI business, but the relief came from the fact that Veronica and I had been seeing each other every time Ed had taken a night shift for the last eight months – apart from the night of his death, that is. So Ed's death would certainly change the dynamic in Veronica's house.

I stayed with Veronica for several hours until Ed's family arrived. I couldn't face dealing with the Schwartz clan today. Not today of all days. And I couldn't face being in the same room as Veronica and not be able to touch her. Then I made my excuses and left the house to the sound of Ed's ma wailing in grief. Just another day in Mrs. Schwartz's world. She enjoyed wailing like a banshee did Ed's mama.

When I got home, I poured myself three fingers of Scotch and drank to the man's memory, because I knew I'd feel too guilty drinking to his memory in front of his mother or wife at the shiva. I stayed hiding in my apartment for the rest of the day, and then I visited Sean the next day, the Tuesday.

THE CORONER HAD issued his report but there were no surprises; the bullets which had riddled his body were the cause of his death. What the report never said in these circumstances was who pulled the trigger. And that was what I wanted to know. The good news was the initial indication gave the shooter as a single person who Ed had wound down his window for. That meant either they were wearing a uniform or they were known to Ed. The fact

Ed's gun was still in its holster beneath his jacket showed he had not tried to defend himself. It had been quick.

The chances someone was impersonating a cop or a GI were pretty slender, which meant it boiled down to an unknown assailant known by Ed. They got up close and personal, but who would have known he was sitting in a car in a random street in the city. The answer, of course, was no one, but there was someone who would have easily found him in a random street in a car in the city – Mr. McCready.

I wasn't the only one to reach the same conclusion, because, by the time I trolleyed over to McCready's house, he was gone. Sean had picked him up an hour or two earlier and he was answering questions in the station house. Thirty minutes after the interrogation began, it was over. Way before I could get to the station, McCready had confessed to the murder, although his motive was wafer thin.

According to the transcript of the interview, McCready said he was afraid for his life because he'd seen the same car behind him as he'd driven all around the city. So when he noticed it was parked on the other side of the street from his mistress's apartment, he thought it might be her husband and went outside to deal with him. He walked over, having taken his gun out of his jacket pocket, and the guy opened his window. Without looking too closely, McCready started blasting away. Only after he'd run out of bullets did he realize he'd shot the wrong guy. Ed was a complete stranger to him.

And that was the end of Ed.

THE NEXT QUESTION in my mind was why didn't Mrs. M mention her husband carried a gun in his jacket pocket – that may well have changed our approach somewhat. I mean, if we'd known he had a rod we'd have used a telephoto lens not a Chevy across the street. Mrs. McCready seemed none too distraught when I visited her that afternoon, given her husband was still awaiting a court appearance to get bail. Something at the back of my mind told me she might not stump bail for the chump. After all, she wanted to divorce him; he'd been found in another woman's bedroom and he'd murdered the guy Mrs. M had sent to spy on him. She had a right to be none too pleased.

When I'd settled down in their library – yes, the mansion was big enough to have a library – Mrs. McCready offered me tea, which I declined. She shrugged and asked the butler for a pot for one.

"How are you doing, Mrs. McCready, given all that's… happened?"

"Well, these things are a trial, aren't they?" she responded with a half-smile on her face.

"Sure are." I hadn't quite figured out how to ask her why she set my friend up to be killed by her husband, so I skirted some more until an idea popped into my head.

"I guess this means your divorce will be easier to come by."

"You know, I hadn't thought about that. But yes, there should be no contest – even if he is acquitted."

"I doubt if there's much chance of that. The bullets that killed Ed – Mr. Schwartz – were a match to his pistol and he's admitted it anyway. Open and shut case, if you ask me. He'd need an amazingly sharp lawyer to get him out of this hole."

She smiled at me, almost breaking into a laugh.

"Well I don't think he has the money for an amazingly sharp lawyer, now does he?"

"No?" I asked, already knowing the poor schmuck was being hung out to dry.

"Oh no. I couldn't possibly support a man who was a cold-blooded killer."

Now it was my turn to smile.

"And did you know he packed a pistol when you hired us?"

"Pistol? Of course not. I wanted some photos of the man in *flagrante delicto*. I didn't want anyone to get hurt, let alone murdered."

"For sure?"

"Why yes. The most I imagined happening was that Mr. Schwartz might end up having a conversation with Harvey and that might have been enough to get the matter set straight."

While she was clearly a greedy, conniving shrew, somehow I believed she just wanted to protect her family's money and nothing more. Besides, she had a cute nose. If it wasn't that her husband was in the slammer and Veronica might well have been warming my bed up for me, I might have made a move.

But I didn't. Instead, I went home and freshened up. Grabbed some toast and coffee and headed over to the widow, Veronica Schwartz.

I was pleased to find she was alone. His family had let her be for a day having sucked all the life out of the air in the house since the morning after Ed stopped breathing. Veronica had turned her back on her own ma and pop many years ago and the only support they'd show Veronica would be to tell her, I told you so. But they didn't hear about Ed's death for another six months or so.

VERONICA OPENED THE door to me and I walked straight in and hugged her as soon as we had closed the door behind ourselves.

"Everything's goin' to be all right, baby," I reassured her.

She dug her arms into my torso just a bit more but said not a word. We stood like that for two, maybe five, minutes and then I broke the hold we had on each other and sauntered into the living room and sat down in an easy chair. Veronica padded over to the drinks cabinet and poured me a stiff one. Then she sat down near me on the leather sofa.

"What am I going to do, Jake?"

"About what in particular?" With such an open question, I couldn't guess if she was thinking about the choice of coffin or what would happen between me and her. The latter I didn't want to deal with right now and the former I had no idea about – I'd never organized a Jewish funeral before.

"About Ed?"

"Um, I don't quite know what you mean. What do you need to do about Ed?"

"Why, bury him of course."

Inside, I breathed a huge sigh of relief. She just had no idea what to do about the arrangements.

"I can help you choose a coffin if you like?"

"What for? Coffin? What's there to choose? A box is a box. I mean, the police say they won't be releasing the body for another week at least and I need to get that man underground much sooner than that."

After much more conversation, it turned out that my ignorance of Jewish funerals was at the heart of my confusion. A Jew should be buried within twenty-four hours and certainly shouldn't be hanging around a morgue for a week or two, merely because the paperwork hadn't been put in place right by a Gentile coroner. And, for the record, everyone gets buried in a plain coffin – nothing fancy like those Catholics.

The next few days went very slowly, each day drawing out its dying breath from the moment the sun rose to the point when it was no longer visible on the horizon. I tried to spend as many of my waking hours with Veronica as I could; either in her bed, in her arms, or just in her presence. I wasn't used to seeing her outside her house as we had spent the time we had together hiding in her bedroom. Now, we could go anywhere and be seen in any place because she was the grieving widow and I was the consoling business partner.

Funny thing was the more time we spent together, the more we got on each other's nerves. Without the safety umbrella of a secret affair, we didn't seem to have too much in common or have much tolerance of the other's point of view. Now, it could just have been the grief speaking, but the truth was that neither of us was exactly grieving. If we didn't like him enough when he was alive to keep our hands off each other, there wasn't much chance we'd like him enough to cry about his death after he was gone.

The day after we'd buried him, Veronica told me she was going to sell up and move to California. The life policy Ed had paid into ever since he'd started sleuthing would give her a very comfortable nest egg and she couldn't think of anything to keep her in Chicago and she was right. Spending time in a sunny climate sounded a much better prospect than spending time with me. And we both knew it.

Two months later, Veronica moved and shipped out to the west coast. I stayed in the Windy City. The best time I ever had with her was the day after Ed's funeral. We spent the entire afternoon and most of the night in bed together, talking and making love as though the weight of the world wasn't on our shoulders. And it certainly wasn't on Veronica's.

# NEW YORK 1962

# 8

HEADING DOWN THE steps of the plane, with Simone Lambretti waiting at the bottom to greet me, was one of the more stressful moments of my life. But there had been moments of tension every time the iron hand of Don Michael had waved in the shadows.

A year after I met the don, a formally dressed gentleman entered my offices and asked for an appointment. His three-piece suit shrieked out foreigner and my guess was correct; he had one of the funniest English accents you've ever heard in your life, like an alto version of Queen Elizabeth herself. All clipped vowels and straight back. When he eventually died, I reckon they found a broom handle stuck up the dude's ass, if you get what I mean.

His name was Colonel Mustard and he was with the Brigadiers. Okay, I lied. His name was Colonel Mumford and he implied he was something to do with the Palace, but he wasn't particularly specific.

To be honest, the key fact I focused on the first time we met was that Lambretti had recommended him to me and that meant there was zero chance of failure on my part. And that focuses your mind, man.

At this point in my life, I had no secretary and my office was just a room in a serviced building – times were tough and sleuthing was not the game it had been a decade before. So I was pleased to see a strange face walk into my room because that translated as greenbacks in my eyes.

Mumford explained the matter he had to discuss was delicate and I assured him nothing he said to me would be repeated to anyone else. I was more confidential than a priest because I held a licensed firearm and would shoot anyone who asked too many questions of me. He raised his eyebrows at me in total disbelief.

"Colonel Mumford, I'm exaggerating for comic effect. But believe me when I tell you that I run a successful business by keeping confidences, not by blurting things out. Why else do you think the don would have recommended me in the first place?"

Mumford sat silent for a spell in the only other chair in my office. There was a metal, locked filing cabinet to one side of my desk, a filter coffee machine on a small table on the other, and a hatstand in the corner by the door. That was all I had by way of furnishings – apart from a small Chinese rug under my desk so I could take off my shoes and uncurl my toes.

◆ ◆ ◆

BY THIS POINT, I'd reckoned there was a woman in Mumford's story who either was playing the field or who needed following because he thought she was playing the field. I thought about the camera I kept in the bottom drawer of the filing cabinet for just such cases. But I was wrong. So wrong. Thinking back, I wish it had been yet another caught-in-the-act photo shoot.

"It's Sofia."

I was silent, nodding to encourage him to talk but not wanting to appear to hang on his every word in case he clammed up. My guess, Sofia was his wife and the story would unfold in predictable fashion.

"I haven't seen her in two days." Silence. Moisture appeared in the corner of his left eye. This Brit was showing emotion.

"Take your time, Colonel."

Silence.

"Does she often go off for days at a time?"

"What? No? Of course not. She's fourteen years old for Christ's sake, man."

Then it dawned on me. This wasn't a case of wandering hands; it was a case of wandering daughters.

"This is a job for the Missing Persons Bureau. Why are you here and not talking to them instead?"

"Are you mad? You fool, don't you understand? I received a note this morning."

"Do you have it with you?"

He pulled a folded sheet of paper out from inside his jacket and thrust it towards me. I reached across my desk for the note but he dropped it on the desk instead. Hard to tell if this was an accident or he was playing some stupid power game. Either way, I read the note: We have the girl. Get $500,000 or we'll return her piece by piece.

"Where and when did the note appear?" I asked with all the seriousness I could muster to reflect the significance of the note.

"This morning. It fell out of the newspaper that was delivered to my hotel room."

"Which hotel was that?"

"The Hilton on the Avenue of the Americas."

"And why did you go to Lambretti and not the cops? You didn't say."

Mumford looked coldly at me and then a shiver went down my spine as he looked straight through me.

"The situation is delicate. I am not here and neither is my daughter, so I can't involve the police."

"You're not here?"

"No. Let's just say that my work for the British Government is… confidential and officially I simply am not in the United States."

"Ah, I see."

"Exactly. And if I am not here and Sofia is not here then I can't go to the police to complain that my daughter isn't here, now can I?"

"Yes."

"So Mr. Lambretti suggested you would be able to help instead."

Mumford was a British spy who, for reasons best known to himself, had brought his daughter over on one of his sprees. Lambretti wanted me to find the kidnapped daughter of a British spy who had illegally entered the country, probably just to do a spot of shopping or something.

"I can see why he'd have done that." Now it was my turn to be silent.

"Have you considered using your network, shall we say, because if this has anything to do with your work, the chances are it's the Russkies. MI5 or MI6 is far more likely to be able to help than me."

"Can't be Comrade Boris, they wouldn't hold her to ransom. They would have merely slammed through the hotel door and shot me in the head, Mr. Adkins."

"Call me Jake and I take your point."

"What I need you to do is to find these fellows before they harm my Sofia and deal with them accordingly."

"Accordingly?" He was using long words and his accent was almost impossible for me to figure, so I didn't completely get what the guy was on about.

"Yes, deal with them. Mr. Lambretti didn't recommend you just so you could help me rescue Sofia. You need to kill the bastards who have taken her, goddamn it."

MUMFORD WAS LOSING his temper and I needed him cool as ice for him to be any help to me – so's I could help him and keep in Don Michael's good books. The other thing, of course, was that I was none too happy at the thought of having to shoot a bunch of bad guys, especially as right now I had zero idea why they'd nabbed the girl in the first place.

"Okay, okay. What exactly was Sofia doing hooking up with Simone Lambretti, then?"

"They both went to the same school in Switzerland and had kept in contact during the summer vacation." He translated the last phrase into American, much as you would explain a pencil to a two-year-old, but I chose not to take offense; the guy's daughter had been kidnapped after all.

"And who knew that you guys were going to be over here?"

"No one. It was just a vacation."

"No one?"

"Well…" I raised an eyebrow because we both knew that to make a transatlantic flight and to stay in a hotel meant there were loads of people who knew. Also, you can add on all the people who followed Mumford because of his work and you have a long list of potential kidnappers, even before you throw into the mix some random opportunists who happen to see a guy and his daughter wearing nice clothes walking down Fifth Avenue.

But after Mumford had thought for a while and taken the question seriously, there didn't seem to be any obvious suspects. Of course, there was the ransom note and the promise of another message.

"And what about the money?"

"What about it, Adkins?"

"Jake, please. People call me Jake. I mean, can you raise the money?"

"Well of course not. If I could raise the money, I'd just hand it over and get Sofia back. It is because I don't have the money that you and I are in the same room together. You really are exceedingly obtuse, aren't you?"

I let that one slide too. The guy was stressed and being verbally abusive, but that was part of the job – sucking in other people's angst.

"And did you keep the newspaper the note fell out of?"

"No, by Jove, do you think that was important?"

"I have no idea. I'm only asking. To cover obvious ground, find any clues there are to find."

"I see. So where do we go from here?"

"Good question. I think it's time for you to go back to your hotel room and for us to start some surveillance. Wherever we go next, we should find out how the note was delivered to you – who is delivering the note and maybe follow them back to their pit."

We hopped into a cab and hightailed it back to the Hilton to sit out the long wait until a follow-up letter appeared, probably the next morning. At the back of both our minds was the stone-cold fact that after twenty-four hours, the chances of finding a kidnap victim alive plummeted to near zero.

BACK IN MUMFORD'S room, we sketched out a plan for the rest of the day. For now, he'd stay put and I'd check out the hotel staff and anyone else I could find who might know something about something. Mumford was desperate to be doing some constructive task other than waiting, but I convinced him his best place was the hotel room – if only because in the unlikely event the kidnappers decided to call him, he needed to be by a phone. But to make him feel better, I got him to write down a list of people who would want to hurt him and had the resources to do so in another continent. We agreed those criteria should narrow the names down to something vaguely manageable as his day job meant a lot of people were pissed with him a lot of the time.

Meanwhile, I popped down to the front desk to talk to housekeeping or whoever else it was that looked after room service with a smile.

Frank was seventeen years old and had the swagger of a teenager with attitude. Luckily for him, this was slowly being smothered by the rest of the hotel staff who had no time for his youthful arrogance. By the time I was waving a Jackson in his face, he'd learned to answer my direct questions in a direct manner – otherwise, the bread would go back into my pocket. He also understood that if he lied I'd rip him a new asshole, so that meant we were able to hold a civilized conversation without any distractions.

"So you bring the breakfasts and papers up to the rooms on the fifteenth?"

"Yessir."

"And how does that work?"

"Huh?"

"What precisely is your routine? What do you do so that each guest ends up with the right food and the right newspaper?"

"Oh. There's a list of newspapers I'm given by Mr. Naughton and each tray is already numbered. So I take the list, check the room number, and grab the right paper from the piles on top of the trolley. Then I take the tray and knock on the door of the room. Easy."

"And has anyone ever given you something to put inside the newspapers?"

"Sure thing!"

My ears twitched and the hairs at the back of my neck stood up.

"A dude gave me a note to put in his girlfriend's *New York Times* a couple of weeks ago. That's how he proposed to her, schmuck." I sighed.

"No, I mean in the last couple of days. On the fifteenth. Capiche?"

The boy furrowed his brow as he imagined the money floating back into my pocket.

"No, nobody's given me nothing for the last couple of weeks, not on that floor... But yesterday I did have to leave the trolley for a minute when I was on the fifteenth. Some dude couldn't figure out where the ice machine was and I took him there 'cause he couldn't follow my directions."

"Really? When was this?"

"Yesterday, like I said."

"And what did he look like, this guy?"

"Tall, thin, black hair. Wore metal-rimmed glasses like he was smart or something."

"And his clothes?"

"Gray suit, blue shirt, bow tie."

"And had you seen him around the hotel before?"

"Um... no, don't think so, but I spend most of my time back of house. It's only room service when I get to see the guests."

"Would you recognize him if you saw him again?"

"Yes, I reckon."

"Okay, if you spot him, or find out what room he's staying in, let me or my friend know – we'll be in 1504."

Frank nodded, all the while keeping his beady eye on the greenback in my hand.

"Here's something for your trouble now." I raised my hand out for him to take the note. Frank put his hand out and touched mine to get at the note at which point, I put my other hand over his.

"But if you mess with me, I'll break your hand clean off."

His boyish grin fled his face. He nodded and I let go of him so's he could get to his cash and he walked extraordinarily briskly away.

# 9

BACK UP AT Mumford's, I explained to him we'd need to wait until morning if our Frank had actually been misdirected by one of the gang members. I holed up in 1506, adjacent to Mumford and we unlocked the connecting doors, in case things got ugly in the morning. Frank had told me he delivered the papers around five thirty to be certain of catching everyone before they woke up, so I set my alarm for five to give myself a chance to splash water on my face before the excitement of the day kicked in.

Mumford and I sat up talking for a while, but he was brooding over his little girl and I was tired of expressing fake sympathy. Don't get me wrong, I felt for the guy, but I didn't feel *that* much for him and he'd been pissing and moaning on the same subject for the whole day and I'd just about had enough – even if he was the client and the spirit of Lambretti was hovering over his shoulder. Enough was enough and I made my excuses and cut into the neighboring room.

I took a slug from a miniature bottle out of the minibar, sat down, and watched a bit of TV before the Ed Sullivan Show bored me into hitting the head and going to sleep.

I woke up with a start at a quarter to five, darted a glance at the clock, and lay awake in a cold sweat. Must have been quite some dream, but I had no memory of it whatsoever. I went into the bathroom, used a finger for a toothbrush, patted my hair down to make it look slightly less slept in, put my clothes back on, and stuck my ear to the adjoining door. Mumford was snoring loudly. I scooted over to the front door, listened but heard nothing. Then I looked out of the hawkeye lens in the door and saw less than I'd heard. Zip, nada, zilch.

I STOOD THERE with my eye glued to the wood of the door for a lifetime, every so often I'd lean in so close I could sense my eyelashes swiping against the surface of the lens, and then I'd pull back with a start – and commence again.

Eventually, I was rewarded with the briefest of sights – a flash of a bow tie and I knew it was time to party. There was some kind of talking going on and I thought I recognized Frank's muffled voice. A slip appeared under my door as Frank fed my room with the notification there was a complimentary newspaper.

Swiftly, I opened the door and looked in the direction Bow Tie had gone. Putting my finger to my lips, I looked quizzically at Frank, who pointed down the corridor. I gave him a thumbs up and edged along the corridor, my hand hovering over my piece, but I was not stupid enough to draw it on the man I was following.

I saw him turn the corner and ran to catch up. As I got to my left turn, I saw the stairwell door swing shut. Two choices: go into the stairwell and see if the guy goes into a room on a different floor or bet on him leaving the hotel discreetly. The truth is there is no way you can follow someone on an echoing set of stairs; not an option. So I had to guess if he was staying in the hotel or just a casual early morning visitor.

With a couple of seconds thought, I wait straight to the elevator and hit the down button. If Bow Tie was a guest, he wouldn't need to wait for a newspaper delivery to send a note to Mumford. So down I went, watching the dial slowly descend from fifteen down to the letter L, for Lobby.

As the elevator doors slid open, I caught Bow Tie leaving the hotel and jumping in a cab. Out of the doors myself and into a yellow box. There are very few times when you get to say a cliché and mean it. This was one of those times.

"Follow that cab!" I said and the cabbie smiled at me, nodded and screeched forwards.

"Careful!" I instructed with as fierce a tone as I could generate at short notice, "The idea is they don't notice us following them." Another nod and some much better quality driving ensued.

We headed east and took the Midtown Tunnel out to Queens. By this time, I had already negotiated with my chauffeur to enable him to stop freaking out about leaving Manhattan. Fear vs bread? Bread wins every time.

Five minutes later and Bow Tie had stopped his ride and opened a passenger door. Another guy – I couldn't see his face from that distance – hopped in and the cab carried on meandering its way to LaGuardia Airport.

Paying my driver an extra fifty so he'd hang around and wait in case Bow Tie and his buddy doubled back on me, I raced into the terminal building just fast enough to see them head straight for their gate: Logan. I went to the desk and bought myself a ticket, as well as a newspaper to hide behind during the flight, having made sure I was at the back of the plane. There was no time to phone Mumford; he'd have to wallow in his own juices for a while.

FROM THE BACK of the plane, I kept a good eye on Bow Tie and Buddy who were near the front. There were only twenty or so rows, so I was far enough away not to be seen but close enough to be able to keep tabs on them after we landed.

During the flight, they joked and chatted all the way so whatever they were cooking up was going to wait until they got into Boston.

A screech of undercarriage hitting tarmac, and a brief wait before the doors, front and back, opened up and we disgorged into the Boston night. Outside the airport, they grabbed a white taxi and I followed them in a more casual manner because New England is not Manhattan.

The journey was surprisingly short because we stayed in the docks, near the airport, and didn't head off into the city. This kept the fare low but there is nothing good about following two guys into a warehouse on a dock when you know they are involved in the kidnap of a teenage girl.

On the plus side, at least I knew they were the right guys. There'd been a slender chance I'd followed some random dude to Boston, only to find him heading back to his wife and a night watching TV with his dinner on his lap.

The door of the warehouse slammed shut and Bow Tie plus one vanished indoors.

I scurried round the outside walls, trying to figure out how to get inside without opening the front door and slamming it shut. Like most warehouses, this building was not constructed for multiple entries. That was the bad news. The good news was that I found a couple of windows at ground level and desperately peered inside.

Saw nothing. The room was totally dark, which meant, of course, that no one was inside. Both windows opened outwards, so all I needed to do was to get one open and crawl inside; they were man-sized windows.

From my inside jacket pocket, I pulled out a small set of metal implements, a private eye's tool bag you might say, and selected a steel file to jimmy the window open. I pushed the file near the handle and started to slide and move the file up and down until the latch mechanism began to give. Eventually, it pinged apart and the glass swung out, nearly hitting me in the face in the process.

File back in my tool bag, I slithered into the room and closed the window behind me.

# 10

THERE WAS A desk, some chairs, a few boxes, and a filing cabinet. The room was probably called the office, but paperwork was clearly not the number one priority in this organization. Sneaking over to the door, I realized I had no idea what was on the other side and no idea what I was going to do, apart from try to find Sofia.

The door was made of solid wood and a glow of light came from the crack beneath it, so there would be no cover of darkness once I turned the handle and looked the other side.

I flattened my ear to the door to listen for any noises, but I heard nothing. With my ear still stuck to the wood, I turned the handle, hovering in a half squatting position in case I needed to make a bolt for it.

Then I moved my ear away from the door as nothing appeared to be happening. All I could hear was a bunch of murmuring from a long way off. Peering round the door, I found out why the noise was muffled; this room was on a corridor with the top half of the opposite wall made of glass and the rest of the warehouse there for the viewing.

Sneaking and hunkering down, I popped one eye above the opposite wall to see what was happening. There were rugs on the floors and comfortable sofas with a group of men lounging on them, some laughing, some looking nervous. And there were other guys, arms folded, stood at the various exit doors that led to other parts of the warehouse on the far side of this charming scene.

Amid these dudes, all dressed in their finest, were a string of girls wearing nothing but their panties and bras. A brief look down the row told me they were all jailbait, but old enough to have teenage curves in the right places.

Staying exactly where I was, I watched as each man picked out a girl – by their looks or by grabbing their tits or asses – and then he was led out of this anteroom and off up some stairs to what I imagined was a similar layout to the one I was in, a windowed corridor with a series of rooms and curtains in front of each door to make them seem so much more homely than they were. Bow Tie whispered in the ear of one of the serious-looking guys and then went straight upstairs. Bow Tie's buddy stayed in the background, watching all that was before him.

But no sign of Sofia. My guess was that she was in one of the second-floor rooms but to find her I'd need some help. Some British help with a crazy accent and a stiff upper lip.

I SCOUTED ROUND the building some more so that I was certain there was only one exit – the door I'd seen when I first arrived. My cabbie was waiting for me, meter running and we scuttled off to a nearby phone booth. I called Mumford and told him all I knew. Without waiting for an invitation, he told me he was going to be on the next plane to Boston. Good news. I told him where to meet me and promised I'd keep watch.

We returned to the warehouse via a convenience store, so I'd have some snacks and a cup of acrid coffee, and I paid the fare and watched the white vehicle vanish into the darkness of the Boston night.

Mumford would be at least two hours at best and there was only going to be a whole load of fucking taking place in the warehouse, so I found a dry piece of ground in the shaded doorway across from the honky-tonk cathouse and settled in for the wait.

Three hours later Mumford arrived, hot-footing it out of his taxi, which sped away as soon as he'd placed both feet onto the ground.

There was a steely darkness to his eyes and a deadpan expression all over his face.

"In there," I said, pointing to the cathouse without forcing him to ask the only question he wanted the answer to.

"Let's go."

"Wait a sec. How are we going to play this?" I asked.

"We go in like customers and get as close as we can to Sofia. Then we kill every last motherfucker in that building and leave."

The simplicity of his approach was astounding, but it had a level of risk and uncertainty I was not entirely comfortable with. By the time I realized that it was too late. Mumford bowled over to the front door and knocked. I caught up with him just before the door was opened ajar and I repeated the password I'd heard earlier in the evening.

We walked in and, not surprisingly, we were gently but professionally frisked. Luckily, we both knew how to hide handguns from prying fingers.

Into the anteroom we went and a fresh crop of jailbait was brought out for our delight. None of them were Sofia and Mumford did the only sensible thing he could. He randomly picked one of them so he could be led up to the second-floor rooms and I did the same.

I HAD TO walk past Bow Tie to get to the stairs but he didn't appear to recognize me. The Asian girl, whose hand I was holding, wore white panties and bra and took me to the first door on the left after we walked up the stairs. Mumford was taken into the second room with three more further down the corridor.

I turned to close the bordello door and Asian Alice had already taken off what was left of her clothes and was lying on the mattress in repose for my coming. I smiled at her and shook my head.

Just at that moment, I heard gunfire: Mumford had wasted no time at all. I ran out the room, leaving Alice, who had pissed herself, on her bed.

Between opening the door and entering the corridor, I put the gun in my hand and started shouting at any adult I saw. Sprinting down the corridor, I reached the third door, which was already open, and looked inside. Mumford had plugged a hole in the back of the head of the john inside but the dark-haired girl cowering in the corner was definitely not Sofia.

Out of that room and Bow Tie was at the top of the stairs. I aimed squarely at his chest, used two bullets and he flew back down the stairs. On jobs like these, I always carried a Magnum.

Turning my head I saw Mumford leave the fourth room and head on to the fifth. Popped my head into the fourth to see a similar scene – a dead john and a freaked out underage hooker. This time the john was still alive but there was blood gushing out of his groin. Mumford had shot him in the dick.

And on into the last room. I'd heard one shot come from there before I got in. There was Mumford slumped on the floor, weeping. Bow Tie's buddy was lying in the corner, half slumped on the bed with a knife in his hand and blood spewing out of his neck.

Lying on the bed was a girl, Sofia's age, build, and height. It was too difficult for me to tell exactly what she looked like because there was blood streaming out of her neck, carotid sliced in two. She had fought to the end because one of her breasts was hanging by a thread and there were a couple of her fingertips lying on the floor in the lake of blood., where she had tried to ward off the knife.

I turned round and managed to get into the corridor before I threw up. Returning to the room, I put my hand on Mumford's shoulder. There was nothing else I could think of doing or saying that would make any difference in the world to him right now.

Back down the stairs, I found a phone and dialed 911 to call it in. A day of questioning and they let me go. Mumford declared diplomatic immunity and vanished into the shadows by the time they let me out of the station.

I still have nightmares from that night and when I met up with Mumford a few years later, he told me he did too.

# KOREA 1950

# 11

THE REASON I threw up when I saw Sofia's body was the sheer surprise and shock of seeing her there – like that. I'd seen worse bloodshed in Korea and I never threw up when I was over there. Pissed myself a couple of times, but never threw up.

I joined up at the beginning of July 1950, a few days after Truman declared war on North Korea and after the fall of Seoul. I wouldn't say I was particularly patriotic or anything, but the look in my mother's eyes when she heard Truman on the radio meant I had no choice but to join up. Those eyes screamed out to me that my father had died only five years before to protect and save us from the foreign hordes and now it was my turn. There was an inevitability to the whole affair, which makes little sense now but we were living under the specter of nuclear annihilation at the hands of the Soviets and we still felt the cold shadow of the last great conflict too.

So, off I trotted to the army with my ever-watchful mama trailing along to make sure I didn't just go over the border to Canada or, God help her, Mexico.

Basic training was as basic training is. I'd love to pretend that it made me a man, but it did not. Instead, it taught me how to fire a gun, kill the enemy, and hide in camouflage with my face in the dirt. And some marching songs. "I don't know, but I've been told…"

A HANDFUL OF weeks later and I was flying out to Korea. "Sir, Private Jake Adkins, at your service, sir!" and so on. You know the drill. The way I figured it the grunts were the ones most likely to be sent over the hill, so I made it my cause to find every way to not be that grunt. In this man's army that meant I had to get myself promoted at the earliest opportunity. Most of the lunks could hardly string a whole sentence together and it didn't take me that long to shine above the helmeted hordes on our side. With a war to be won, Uncle Sam wasn't too picky who he put in charge of his platoons, so I soon found myself as a sergeant with my own bunch of guys to order about.

A day or two after the Inchon Landing at the back end of September, a full month before we took Pyongyang, we were stuck by some river. It had a long name and all that mattered was that it was damn wide, had long reeds on the other bank, and was virtually barren on our side.

As soon as the first private stepped foot on the bank, a ripple of machine-gun fire strafed through his body and he fell to the floor, blood pouring from each bullet hole. Private Dachman bit the dust. Rest In Peace.

We ducked down behind the palm trees nature had kindly placed in a convenient location near enough to the bank.

I took out my binoculars and swept the other side of the river, desperately trying to spot the sniper or snipers, but nothing.

"Wilson!"

"By your side, boss."

"Call base. Let them know what's going down."

"Ten four that."

"And keep close."

"On your tail, boss."

Wilson was from Illinois and believed in God and Country. Tell him to do something and he'd walk across the whole of this sorry earth to get it done. But never ask him a question. Not even "What's your name?" Reliable, honest, dumb.

Most of the men under my command were boys, green-horned boys, but that often meant they had guts and an unbelievable ability

to not see the consequences of their actions. In many circumstances
that would be a very bad thing, but in love and war – well, war
anyway – not being able to see your impending death could be a real
boon. They'd cross this river for me even if we weren't able to knock
out the Koreans on the other side of the water.

We hid in the undergrowth by the trees and waited. No one was
going anywhere. After ten, fifteen minutes there was still no
movement, still nothing happening to give us even a slight clue
where they were stationed. I sent two of the smaller men to climb a
tree and see if they could spot anyone from on high.

The answer came quickly; two bursts of gunfire and they both
slammed back to the ground too damn fast. We dragged the bodies
out the way and caught our breaths. We still had zero idea where the
hell they were. The only thing we could be sure of was there were at
least two machine gun nests because both were killed at the same
time. The other thing we could be pretty certain was that they were
placed quite a ways back from the riverbank otherwise we'd have
been able to spy them by now.

Neither of these facts made me feel any better. Our orders were
very clear – keep going until we reach Pyongyang.

"Wilson. Call base. Tell them I want us to go half a click west and
avoid this mayhem. We're pinned down and there's no easy way to
get across here."

"Sir, yessir."

Crackle and squawk of the radio box and muffled conversation
with Wilson and HQ. Then he turned to me and quietly relayed the
message he'd received:

"Get your head out your ass, grow a pair, and get the men over
the river now and stop fucking about."

SIMPLE. WE WERE going to have to take the snipers out one
way or another. Asian vultures were already nibbling on the bits of
body that had been shot through from our boys and left on the bank.
I wasn't happy about the way things were turning out and I knew it
was going to get worse before the day was over.

I called the boys over in a huddle and explained the situation. They nodded and ground their molars, some of them, a little less gung-ho than the rest, realized that some bad shit was going to go down and they were in it up to their necks.

Georgie made a joke – something about shoving a machine gun barrel up a sniper's ass – which got a much bigger laugh than it deserved, mainly because we knew some or all of us were going to die crossing that expanse of water. Georgie was from Florida and always wore sunglasses. Just habit I guess.

We needed a plan. I needed a plan and one that was smarter than all of us running into the water, screaming and shouting and hoping that at least one or two of us managed to travel the thirty feet to get to the other side and take out the snipers with a couple of lucky bullets. That was the best plan available and I wasn't going to share it with the men just yet. Somehow, they expected more of me than that.

The way I figured it: the biggest problem we had was getting across the water without being seen. We couldn't fly over the river as there was no helicopter support. We couldn't float on the river as we weren't Jesus Christ and, besides, even if we had a raft we would be riddled with bullets before we'd stepped onto the damn thing.

The answer, therefore, was to go under the river. If we found some hollow reeds, we could send men swimming underwater to the other side without being seen if they started a little further down the bank where there were grasses to hide in.

Once they reached the bank, they could stay hidden in the reeds before the second part of my plan. This involved finding a way to get their rifles over the water without them becoming waterlogged. There's always a weakness to any idea and I'd quickly found my own Achilles heel. I thought for a while, staring into the middle distance.

Then it hit me. I was staring at a log, cracked and gnarled. But cracked. We'd put the rifles inside half of that log and cover them with leaves and twigs and shit. The swimmers would pull the log, which'd float, along with them using some string – or bootlaces if we needed to. If the whole activity was done at night, or even around dusk, we might stand a good chance.

I told the men my idea and asked anyone if they foresaw any problems. It never hurts to hear practical people spot practical problems, especially if you're going to ask them to do something crazy in your name. But everyone thought it was the best plan they'd heard all day. The time was around three so we had a few hours to wait before the big push.

# 12

WE ALL SAT around, gazing into space, lying flat on our bellies, and generally staring out beyond the river and into the reeds and trees on the other side. Somehow, we all thought if we looked enough then something would appear. That somehow the enemy would just give up hiding, stand up, and wave at us. Or something.

Anyway, we all kept our eyes peeled hoping to catch some sort of glint in the scope of a rifle or the lens of a pair of binoculars, but nothing.

The light started to fade and I could feel the men around me getting twitchy. They weren't good at waiting; they were much better at doing. Over the past hour, I'd worked out who needed to be sent across. The decision was hardly inspirational. Two of our number, Vince and Sylvester, were state champion swimmers so that was a decision made. Before I spoke with them, they knew they were the ones. Stood to reason. An appropriate log had been found, gouged hollow and camouflage for the top had been procured. Again, this wasn't exactly rocket science as we were surrounded by trees, branches, twigs, leaves, and all manner of green and brown vegetation. We had US Army string in our provisions so the rifle float had been made ready within thirty minutes of the plan being hatched.

Now was the time for action. Vince and Sylvester went off some ways down the bank, through the trees so they couldn't be spotted. A few minutes later, we saw a log floating diagonally across the river and we knew they were underneath. Slowly, slowly.

Inch by inch, the log headed towards the other side. The water was flowing to our right and Vince and Sylvester were swimming against the current so the log floated upstream. But there was no way you could see any string coming out of it. The boys had done a brilliant job of hiding those rifles in plain sight.

Five or six feet ahead of the log, you could make out two reeds sticking out of the water – their air supply. The grass was only just above the waterline and you'd have thought they'd choke on the water as it splashed into the hollow lifeline, but they did not. Slowly, slowly.

The pair were no more than ten feet away from that reedy bank when it happened. Gunfire ripped out onto the water. Their two bodies floated to the surface, large red circles of blood pooling around them, and the log floated away, turning, and heading downstream. What a fucking waste.

The only good news was that we could see where the flashes of gunfire had come from because dusk was rapidly heading into night. Previously, I'd warned the men not to return fire because I knew it would give away our positions just as the Koreans had given up theirs.

"Wilson. Call it in."

WILSON NODDED AND went to tell base what had just gone down. When he came back, his face was ashen like he'd just eaten something made of cockroach. The news from HQ was clear and simple. I was to lead the platoon with a full-on assault. If we threw enough GIs at a handful of Koreans eventually the Koreans will die and we will be the victors. Those of us who survive, that is.

Made no sense to me whatsoever. What was the point of killing our boys when we could just as easily go all the way around them and even sneak up from the back – if we ever came this way again? Our aim was Pyongyang, not a couple of dudes in a tree.

"Pass me the walkie talkie, Wilson."

He dialed base and I told them I thought their plan was dumbass at best and stupid at worst. If they wanted to send our boys to certain death – those snipers were good, man – then they'd better find someone else to do it. I felt good after venting the tension out of my body and I'm sure the corporal at the other end of the phone felt good as he immediately demoted me back to private and got me to pass the phone back to Wilson. Or should I say Interim Sergeant Wilson McCloy?

Wilson listened to the corporal. The guy didn't feel as good as I had imagined because there sure was an awful lot of shouting going on into Wilson's ear. He kneeled there like a Trojan, taking it all through what became gritted teeth, as he realized he was going to send the boys across that river and few, if any, would make it to the other side.

Eventually, the conversation ended and he put the phone back in its holder. Wilson looked at me. "Sorry, boss."

"Don't worry about it. And now you're the boss. Sorry straight back at you."

The corners of his mouth curled upwards in an attempt to smile and acknowledge my response, but he had weightier matters on his mind and I left him to his thoughts and walked away.

Wilson took about twenty minutes to hatch his plan. Out of politeness, or because he knew I was good at plans, he talked it through with me first before issuing orders to the men.

Phase one involved two pairs of men shooting at where the machine gun fire had come from. This would last around thirty seconds. Halfway through, all but two of us would head into the river and get as far across as we physically could. If this was working the four shooters would keep on with the cover fire. If it wasn't working, they'd join the main body of boys in the water and try to get across.

The other two were there to try to pick off any spotters the Koreans had and to look after the radio equipment. Truth was they must have had at least one spotter to be able to figure out where Vince and Sylvester were. I should have thought of that but I hadn't. Their blood was on my hands, but it had long since floated down the river, along with their bodies.

The two we were leaving behind – Mallory and Anyon – set themselves up by trees nearest the bank to give themselves some cover but also to ensure there was the least amount of shrubbery between them and the gun placements.

The rest of us waited for the off, spread along the line of the river, hoping that we'd not get picked off like the others. I positioned myself on the far right of the crew. I figured the further away I was from the snipers, the better chance I had of surviving and maybe even getting across and doing some damage to those motherfuckers.

THIS MEANT THAT by the time we were all ready for the push, I had made sure I was a solid couple of hundred feet away from center stage. This was Wilson's show now and I didn't want to look like I was stealing the limelight.

Wilson had the bright idea of spreading us quite thin to make the snipers' job harder, which made sense and helped me be even further from the action than I'd planned.

A short peep from Wilson's whistle and the mayhem began. First, the snipers were strafed with bullets, and then a second peep from that whistle and we all hurled ourselves into the water and scrambled to get across in one piece. Because we were so spread out, those in the middle had reacted first to Wilson's command and we quickly formed a chevron, as our feet got wet and the bullets started to whizz past our ears.

The center section became a pile of bodies strewn across the riverbed, blood, and body parts splattering out of the water as the Koreans lobbed grenades at us, as well as sniping away. Limbs, intestines, and gunk floated past and into me – I'd stupidly chosen the wrong end of the line and was downstream from the main action.

Those center stage were dead. There wasn't much light left but you could see that there was no one in the water and, if they had got to the other side, they'd have been assaulting the snipers by now.

As for the rest of us? Well, the pair of shooters stayed on our side of the bank, either because they believed the plan was working despite the evidence in front of their own eyes or, more realistically, they didn't fancy their chances in the shooting gallery in front of them. I certainly didn't blame them.

The other flank was the next to be assaulted by the snipers, presumably because they were ever so slightly nearer the far side of the bank than my right flank. Whatever the reason, they became dog meat just as fast as the middle tranche.

At this point, I was only two steps away from the bank. Almost made it.

Like the guy running next to me, I threw myself forward and rolled into the reeds. Steadied myself and Sanders and I both headed for the nearest tree to see what we could see.

The fire coming from the ends of the sniper's rifles was in plain sight and we picked both off in a matter of seconds. Any spotters who had been up in the trees sure weren't there anymore, but we didn't know that then. So we stayed close and low and waited.

And waited, but nothing happened apart from one more GI sitting next to us, who'd made it to this side. Gingerly, we started scouting out the area and found four dead Korean bodies: two snipers and two spotters. The oldest looked about sixteen, the youngest hadn't started shaving yet.

We called out to the others and they joined us a few minutes later with the radio equipment and such. Wilson had been one of the first to fall; he'd led from the front the way army lunkheads do.

Later, much later, after we reached Pyongyang, they decided to pin a medal on me for surviving the assault on those boy snipers, but I never made it past private. Couldn't take orders, see, and that's important in any man's army, especially with Uncle Sam.

I saw more guts and bodies and blood that day than at any other time I've spent on this planet, but nowadays I'm still haunted by the memory of Sofia's fingers in the pool of her own fluid and not by a bunch of GIs sprinting across a river fifty clicks south of Pyongyang.

# ATLANTIC CITY 1979

# 13

ANYWAY, THERE I was walking down the steps of that plane with the Lambretti girl, Simone, waiting at the bottom. She knew what I carried in my hand and by that point, I had guessed it was about the most valuable attaché case in America, if not the world. There was blood on that case. Literally.

As I looked down to make sure I kept safe footing on the steps, I noticed some splatter on the top and side. Not sufficient to cause anyone concern, but enough for me to see it and wonder whose blood was coating the leather exterior.

As I surveyed the scene before me, I thought the whole situation was completely crazy. Here I was, a retired investigator, holding some case that too many people had died for already and I knew – deep in my gut – this was going to be the longest walk of my life. Too much depended on my getting this into Simone's hands. Too many people, too many agencies, had been chasing this thing around the country for it to be as simple as a stroll down a plane exit.

When Don Michael first spoke to me about this after I came back from Nevada, we went through the usual shenanigans, hopping between different cars parked in a number of different underground garages so the Feds couldn't follow us. I was frisked every time we swapped cars and so on. This was the time when the FBI had started to make real inroads in attacking the head of the Cosa Nostra and the don was taking no chances. He didn't want to spend the rest of his life behind bars just for the sake of meeting me and giving me a job.

Why did he meet me in person? Good question. Basically, he didn't want anyone else to hear what he had to say to me. Call him paranoid, but he reckoned that if no one heard him give an order then the order didn't happen – or at least it couldn't be proved in a court of law, officer.

BEING BACK IN the don's library after all these years, reminded me of little Simone running in to bare her belly. The furniture was almost identical to before. Same oak desk, same bookcases, but a different chair. This one looked considerably more modern and I could tell it had better lumbar support. We were all getting older, for sure.

The great don's hair was silver gray and the number of wrinkles around his eyes had skyrocketed. But the piercing darts in those eyes remained exactly the same. Only a fool would have treated the don with anything but the utmost respect and an overwhelming assumption of an incredible intellect. For that was Don Lambretti whether in his twenties, fifties, or his eighties. The man could think and the man knew, all right.

His genuine disdain for me had not diminished with age either and he proceeded to lambast me with my ignorance and inadequacies until he tired of this sport and focused on the real matter at hand.

"My dear boy, I'd like you to collect a special package from an acquaintance of mine in Atlantic City."

"Sh… Sure. But why me, Don? After all, there are younger and more agile men than me you could get to courier your parcel."

The don raised one eyebrow at me for a second and then smiled; probably the only time he smiled at me in his life.

"Why yes, there are many who are younger, faster, and smarter than you, for sure." He allowed those words to hang in the air and then descend like a cloud of thick cigar smoke.

"BUT WE UNDERSTAND each other, don't we?" Now it was my turn to offer a half-smile to him. Yes, I understood that if the don asked me to do him a favor then I should immediately do it to the best of my ability. And if the don asked me to do him a favor, usually people wound up dead as a result of that favor. Yes, I understood.

"Besides," he continued, "your ignorance is your strength. Because you know next to nothing of my business, you cannot tell anyone anything of any value to me." And then a genuine smile spread across his face which, due to the inelasticity of his skin, stretched into a fairly unpleasant grimace.

"Even if someone were to torture you, you couldn't give up any information, because you know nothing. You. Know. Nothing." The final three words were said slowly, emphatically, and those cold darts had returned to his irises.

I nodded because he was right. I knew nothing and that was the safest way for me to stay. However, the idea people might want to torture me just to get hold of a parcel was not sounding like the walk in the park that package collection usually involved.

"As ever, I will pay you a daily stipend until the work is done. A day there and a day back should be more than sufficient, but I am a generous man, a kind man, and a pessimistic man. We will pay you seven days in advance because nothing happens the way we plan it.

"When you fly back, call my house and arrange with Simone for her to meet you at the airport. Then our business will be complete."

"I understand, Don."

Lambretti explained that the man who held the parcel was named Dakila Valdez, a Filipino guy, who'd been living in the US since he fled the Marcos regime a few years before. His English was acceptable, but he was only a mule. He had no better idea what was in the parcel than myself and it would stay that way for the duration of my trip.

The don passed me a slip of paper with Valdez' address and, with a flutter of his hand, I was dismissed, so I walked out of his office quick as sticks and handled the payment details with Lambretti's accountant. Well, it was a guy who was paying me from an enormous roll of ten-dollar bills, so he had to have been the money man.

Then back in the car, driving around underground car parks in the tristate area and back to Manhattan and my midtown one-bedroom apartment.

THAT NIGHT I packed a small carry-on bag as I knew I was going to be in Atlantic City overnight and, if the don's prediction was right, probably longer.

Before I went to sleep, I phoned my travel agent and got her to book me an open-ended flight to AC for maximum flexibility.

The following day I took a taxi to the airport because I was flush with the Lambretti dough, and waited patiently by the gate for our departure.

As much as the job filled me with terror – the don and I only appeared to cross paths when blood was shed – I was still looking forward to visiting Atlantic City. I hadn't been there in years and I always kept a faint smile in my heart for that town.

The plane journey itself was uneventful and, because of the distance, wasn't anything much more than a hop-on, hop-off experience. That suited me down to the ground as I was never big into flying and had got worse over the years.

Valdez was holed up on the wrong side of the tracks. I could have guessed that before I even stepped on the plane. A recent immigrant in AC was never going to have a luxury apartment with a doorman and marble reception area. And Valdez certainly did not.

THE RUNDOWN TENEMENT building was as inviting as a whore with crabs, but I pressed his apartment buzzer just in case he was in. The trouble with these situations is that you never know how willing the other party is to hand over the goods. I was in no state for a chase down the fire escape and Lambretti knew that so I was hoping this was going to be a nice and easy trade – the parcel for the don's pleasure. And there was the five hundred dollars in an envelope I was supposed to offer him as well.

Naturally, I got no response from the buzzer, but the concierge was so concerned about security, I pushed and the front door opened.

Valdez lived in 4F and the elevator was in bad need of repair. I looked around the lobby and saw only needles on the floor, piss stains on the wall, and an unpleasant odor similar to stale puke. Then in the corner, I spotted the stairwell and ambled toward it, knowing I had three flights to walk up once I'd got past that door.

The stairs were a grubbier version of the lobby and I made sure I didn't make the mistake of touching the banister rail as I climbed up. One, two, three flights later, I was wheezing, leaning my back against a wall, and struggling to get my breath back. I sure was in no fit state for a chase down the fire escape. In fact, I was in no fit state at all. I waited for about five minutes until my lungs were back to normal and pushed the stairwell door onto the fourth floor.

As I walked along, the carpet felt like it was sticking to my shoes. This place had seen better days – and had better days. If this building had always been a flea pit, it would have had linoleum flooring, but the carpet once had a deep pile and a shine to it. Just not today or any time recently.

I found apartment F by using my eyes and knowledge of the alphabet; knocked on the door but no response. Hardly surprising as I was an unexpected visitor and there had been no reply when I hit the bell downstairs ten minutes before.

I banged on the door in the vain attempt to get Valdez to open up, but I knew he wasn't in and so did he.

Two options – walk away or use my shoulder. The latter seemed better as going away meant I'd have to use my shoulder later on or spin some yarn to the super that neither of us believed and I didn't have the energy to lie to a janitor.

I leave and in. My arm ached for forty-five seconds but, as I had suspected, the door jamb splintered beautifully when I put my weight into the door.

This was not the finest apartment I'd stepped inside. There was a living room, diner, kitchen area, and two doors. My guess was that one was a bathroom and the other was a bedroom. I opened both in case Valdez was playing games then returned to the living quarters.

There were two easy chairs and a portable TV on a small table, a dining table with a set of four plastic chairs, and the usual stuff you'd expect to see in a kitchen diner including a fridge. I opened the fridge and found a couple of unopened TV dinners and some cheese turning blue. This matched the milk carton whose contents were heading the same color. I nearly retched and turned my head away but I held my breath and opened the freezer box in case it had any secrets to reveal. Ice cubes and a half empty bottle of vodka.

I opened all the cupboards in the kitchenette and found bupkis. So I turned my attention to the living room area.

# 14

THERE WAS NOTHING on the dining table except an empty fruit bowl. I checked under the chairs in case the parcel had been taped under them, but nothing. There were no shelves in a bookcase to go through and so I made my way into the bathroom.

Pulling open the shower curtain, I was hoping to find a lovely brown paper parcel tied up with string, but instead, there was a once-white shower unit with a deeply unpleasant brown stain running from the place where the hose came out of the wall down to the drain. I pretended to myself this was rust.

The bathroom cabinet contained an opened bottle of Tylenol and a couple of sticking plasters, but nothing parcel shaped or even anything to give me an idea where the parcel might be – or where Valdez had got to either.

Then to the bedroom where there was a bed, of course, but also a wardrobe and a wooden chest of drawers, as well as a bedside cabinet with a snazzy Formica top. I opened every door and drawer and all I found were some women's underwear and a couple of hangars. The bird had flown the coop, but I needed to figure out where the avian had gone.

I slumped down in one of the easy chairs for a moment's contemplation because unless I came up with something all bets would be off and there'd be a seriously displeased Don to deal with.

Leaning forward, I covered my eyes with my hands, elbows resting on my lap. What to do? What to do?

And then it struck me. Or rather, then it poked me in the thigh. Down the side of the chair, between the armrest and the cushion, were a couple of pieces of paper, which had fallen between the cracks on some previous occasion. Both were information leaflets, one for the Wisconsin State Fair and the other for the Disneyland Resort. Neither were exactly a short walk away and they were in quite different directions. So I needed to figure out which one was Valdez' destination.

I yanked off the cushions from both chairs just in case there were other hidden gems to be found, but all I got was a large number of crumbs and balls of hair. Sleuthing is such a glamorous life, I don't know why I ever stopped.

AFTER I LEFT the apartment, I tried to close the door as best I could but the shards of wood on the floor prevented a real tight fit. Instead, I hammered on a couple of neighboring doors, but no one was home or answering.

I figured the best thing to do would be to check into a hotel and then come back to this block and do some old-fashioned house-to-house. Also, I reckoned I'd need to splash some cash to get some of these critters to spill, so I made a mental note to go to an ATM before I returned.

Half a dozen blocks away was a Vacation Villa, which I'd spotted on the way in from the airport, so I walked over and paid for a room's bed and breakfast. Then I grabbed a cab back to the airport to pick up my bag from a locker there and returned to the hotel. By the time I got back, it was near six and I had a hunger on me.

Unpacked, I went down to the restaurant and ordered a chicken salad and fries, with a side of onion rings. And a cup of coffee. Munching through the pile of food placed in front of me, I pondered how Valdez had heard I was coming and why he had decided to go to one of two tourist destinations to hide.

Someone must have told him the don had sent out the goon squad, which meant there was an inside man – or woman. As for the tourist destination? Well, a great way to not be seen is to hide in plain sight among thousands of other people; makes you hard to spot.

But he could have just gone downtown and hidden in a casino. No windows, no clocks. A man could spend a week or a month in one of those caves and never be noticed by another human soul, even one you've sat next to for twelve straight hours with a poker hand in your mitts.

There was more to the location than just fleeing and hiding. I reckoned there was a purpose to the place too, but I couldn't think what that purpose could be. And did Valdez have a clue as to what was in the parcel? If he did, he might just be trying to sell it on to a third party before the don's tentacles reached him, in which case what better place for a transaction than surrounded by a bunch of tourists not giving no never mind.

With no substantive conclusions drawn, but a whole load more thoughts whirling around my brain, I headed back to the apartment block because it was eight o'clock and anyone at work would be back by now.

The elevator was still out of action and the same acrid stench permeated the lobby. The good news was the lights in the stairwell still worked and there was no one shooting up on them. Must have been a public vacation in heroin city.

I STARTED WITH 4D and 4H as they were right next to Valdez but neither answered – and I couldn't hear any noise coming out of them so the occupants were likely out. As luck would have it, I got a response from 4E opposite. A tired-looking woman with a cigarette hanging out the corner of her mouth slouched against the doorpost as we talked. I'd flashed my PI badge and told her Valdez had come into some money. An old story that works with most people, because it feeds their greed and desire for easy cash.

Her eyes lit up slightly when I mentioned a lottery win and she asked if I'd be able to help her out remembering information about Valdez. She wasn't that green.

I smiled and said I'd be happy to help her make a donation to her favorite charity if she was able to help me get the winnings to Valdez. Now it was her turn to smile slightly because she knew I had no lottery winnings to offer Valdez either.

She was wearing house casual clothes – a pair of shorts and a loose-fitting tee shirt. I could see the curves of her breasts popping out the top of the low-hung neckline and could most definitely see her nipples poking through the material of the tee shirt. Vanessa watched me eyeing her up and reminded me that the information was inside her head, not her tits. I blushed and proceeded to keep my mind on the job at hand.

I pulled out a Jackson and asked her when she'd last seen Valdez.

"Baby, I ain't seen him in a week."

"A week? Do you have any idea when he split this place?"

"Nah, but it must have been the Monday or Tuesday, 'cause I saw's him on the Sunday when I got back from church."

"You don't say, Vanessa."

"Yes 'n' I do.

"And did he say where he was planning to go? Or mention anything like that?"

"No, sir. I don't think so. We talked a while and he asked about my girl," at which point Vanessa opened the door to show me the inside of her apartment and there on the far side of the living area was a cot with a child in it, "and that was about all. Didn't mention no traveling that I recall."

Her eyes were focused on the Jackson which I was holding, folded longwise, between my first and second fingers.

"But it is so hard to remember details from a week or so ago, wouldn't you say?"

She was hustling me but she was my best witness, for the moment, so I put the twenty-dollar bill between her breasts. We both knew what kind of church-going girl she was.

"Well, now that I think about it," and Vanessa took the bill out from her tee shirt and popped it into her shorts pocket, "Dakila did say something about a vacation."

"And what did he say?" I took out another Jackson from the roll in my pocket. This was going to be a long and expensive conversation.

"Give me a moment to reflect, darling."

"Sure thing, babe."

I placed the second note in between those round breasts and her eyes lit up a bit more.

"I got it! He said he was thinking of heading north to the Great Lakes."

"The Great Lakes, are you sure?"

"Yeah, he said something about the cheese state, but I didn't pay no never mind to that dairy talk."

"Wisconsin?"

"Yeah, that was it, babe."

"Vanessa, you have been a very helpful young lady."

"Babe, you're only as young as you feel and you can come inside and feel this young lady's body if you'd like."

There was something about that black woman's manner from the first moment she opened the door that made me think she might have been a hooker. And I wasn't wrong.

Despite myself, I nodded and went into her apartment. I hadn't had any black ass in my life and I hadn't had a woman for more years than I could remember. Why the hell not, I thought.

An hour and a further fifty bucks later, I was back in my Vacation Villa room with a smile on my face. I was going to take a trip to Wisconsin; Disneyland was not for me.

15

AFTER A GOOD night's sleep, I was ready for Wisconsin and I grabbed a taxi to the airport. When we got there, I went straight to the sales desk and asked for the first flight to Mitchell Airport. Trouble was there was no direct route and I decided to go to Chicago and drive from there. Even so, I had a three-hour wait before takeoff.

I went to a bar, sat down in a booth, and ordered a beer. Just the one – to kill the boredom and no more. I stared at the napkin, which the waitress had put down on the table in anticipation of the impending arrival of the Budweiser. And saw nothing but the paper serviette that the napkin was made of because my thoughts extended no further than that.

My plan when I arrived in Milwaukee was to head to the fair and make it up from there. It wasn't the greatest scheme of all time, but it was literally all I had. With no photo, I'd need some way to find the Valdez needle in the tens of thousands of people haystack.

I carried on staring at the napkin until the round beer bottle appeared and took up most of the space on the square napkin. I stared at the bottle instead, hoping some better idea would pop into my head because the current one was pretty rubbish.

Briefly, I looked up, as much to give my neck a rest and give myself a different distance to focus on as anything else. On the far side of the bar, in a booth by himself, was a face I thought I recognized. There were more wrinkles than when we'd first met, but

I was sure it was the same man. I tried to catch his eye, but he too was staring into a napkin. Must be a bored traveler thing.

I took a chance and, carrying my drink in my hand wrapped in its napkin, I walked over to get a better look and see if I was right. I was.

Mumford only spotted me when I was right by his side, catching me in his peripheral vision.

"Colonel Mumford, I presume," I said and smiled.

"Major General nowadays. Hi, Jake." Mumford returned my smile, briefly, but the sadness I'd left him with all those years ago had not departed his shores.

We shook hands and he invited me to sit down. I dropped my beer onto his table and went back for my bag. When I returned, he looked up at me as though he was pleased to see me – more than he'd looked a couple of minutes earlier when I first appeared back in his life.

"Long time no see."

"Yeah, how're you keepin'?" I replied.

"Fine, just fine."

"Yeah? Still in the same game?"

"Retired. Retired quite a while ago."

"Oh, me too. Are you visiting family or friends? Or have you been playing the tables out here?" He smiled because we both knew he was not a gambler. He had spent way too many years working in a high-risk environment, where he'd want to twist the odds in his favor, that there was no way he'd let himself submit to the randomness of the roulette wheel or the turn of a card.

"No, not the tables. What are you up to nowadays?"

"Me?" Now it was my turn to smile.

"I'm retired like I said, but I still dabble here and there and I have a golf handicap I'm trying to get in check."

"Really. Golf? You?"

"And why not? It's a pleasant walk in the park following a ball that's too small to see from far away. It's a great game."

"Can't see the fuss myself."

"Me neither. I played once and it did nothing for me whatsoever."

"So no golf then?"

"Nah, I was just messing with you. Yes, I'm retired but I don't get up to much anymore."

"So what're you been doing in Atlantic City's airport. Have you been playing the tables, then?"

"Oh no. That's a mug's game. The house always wins. Once you understand that, there's no point playing as far as I'm concerned."

"You got any family out here?"

"No, no family. Never married, never divorced."

"Married once, divorced once. About a year after Sophia…"

His voice trailed off and I nodded because I completely understood and didn't feel the need to force him to open that painful wound just so we could make small talk.

"Let me save you further obfuscation, Jake."

I scrunched up my face because I had precisely zero idea what he had just said to me.

"The don sent me."

"Ah! Got it."

Made sense. The chance meeting had to be more than a coincidence and, if that was the case, then the only mutual connection we had was Lambretti.

"He contacted me after he spoke with you and suggested that two heads would be better than one."

"Understood. And how the hell did you find me?"

"I had the same address as you and I waited until you showed up and followed you. Followed you to Vanessa's last night and then from the hotel today."

I blushed at the mention of Vanessa, but Mumford had the decency not to labor it or mention the incident again. What a gentleman.

WE GRABBED OUR flight to O'Hare and settled in for a long journey; just short of three hours stuck in the plane and another two hours in a car, depending on traffic. We wouldn't get there before dusk unless we were lucky, but we talked and laughed and tried not to remember the image of his daughter spewing with blood in that Boston warehouse.

The plane landed and we went straight to the car rental and chose a mid-sized saloon, so at least we'd have some space between us on the haul up to Wisconsin.

I drove because Mumford's British driving license might have aroused suspicion and, if not, then it might have been something noteworthy to be remembered if anyone was trying to follow our trail. I hadn't thought about it, but Mumford had and vocalized the thought. Me? I just wanted the package and to go home, so he got no argument from me.

The car journey was as uneventful as you can imagine. We stopped once, not because of the length of the journey, but because Mumford wanted the restroom and I wanted a coffee. Apart from that, it was plain sailing all the way.

The only downside was the journey took ages and, by the time we reached West Allis, the fair was over and our chances of finding Valdez that night were slim to zilch. So instead, we found the nearest motel a couple of blocks away to rest our heads overnight.

We checked into separate but adjacent rooms and headed there straight away. Adjacent? Even though the fare was on, this particular flea pit was none too busy so we were able to get next to each other. Not that it mattered, but I'd thought I'd ask, anyway. It was like old times at the Hilton. Kinda.

THE FOLLOWING MORNING, we spoke with Hugh, the day receptionist, who also happened to be the owner and manager of the joint. Hugh kept himself upright on the reception desk by leaning both hands heavily with straight arms. Either he suffered from a leg disorder or he was still hammered from the night before. Or both. When we checked out, I found he had polio. Bad break.

I asked him about any Philippine visitors he might have had the last few days and Hugh told me he couldn't remember there being any, and he would know because he checked everyone into the Allis Motel.

"Sure you do – apart from the people who arrive late at night like my friend and I did."

He was silent for a spell and swallowed hard, his cheeks reddening.

"Yes'm. Apart from the late arrivals."

"And have there been any of them in the last week?" I enquired calmly and without any need for the sarcasm that was welling within me.

"Um… Just the one."

"Who was that?" I asked quietly, not wishing to make a big deal out of it.

"Well, state law prevents me from sharing that information with you, I'm afraid."

"I'm sure we can come to some arrangement…" and I showed him yet another Jackson. Before I'd retired, I was finding that ten dollars doesn't buy you shit, so I'd upped the allowance to tremendously positive effect.

Hugh took the note from my hand and shoved it into his pants pocket. Then he rotated the guestbook one hundred and eighty so I could read it easily and tapped on one entry three times. Dakila Valdez, room three. He hadn't even tried to use a false name.

We were in rooms four and five, which meant he had been sleeping no more than a couple of feet away from us all last night.

RUNNING BACK TO our rooms, I saw Mumford just leaving his hovel. I clicked my fingers at him to get his attention and then held my finger to my mouth to keep him quiet.

I pointed at room three and we both hugged the wall in case Valdez looked out just when we wanted to burst in. Mumford was nearest to the door, so he mimed a countdown with his fingers. Three, two, one.

He put his shoulder against the door and it swung open with little effort. Mumford pounced into the room and I followed. By the time I'd entered the bedroom area, Mumford was already in the bathroom. He walked out shaking his head.

"Nothing. No one."

"Do you think he's flown the coop?" I asked, turning my head one way then the other to try to get some kind of scope on the room.

The wardrobe door was closed so I looked inside. A couple of shirts and a pair of pants were hanging up.

"Unlikely," replied Mumford, looking at the clothes too, "unless he is in the habit of leaving his clothes across several states."

I nodded – this would constitute quite strange behavior – and proceeded to the inevitable desk and chair. There was a single drawer but it had nothing but envelopes and writing paper in it. Mumford checked the bedside table and the only thing inside was the predictable Gideon's. No hotel room should be without one.

"Reckon we've missed him," I intoned.

"For now," added Mumford, who was proving himself to be a man of few words when he was working. Not that there's anything wrong with that, just he was a lot more fun to be around when we were hanging out at airports and on planes.

The good news was that we'd tracked down Valdez and he was close. Real close.

So we put everything back in the room exactly as we'd found it and shut the door behind us. As my room was next to his, we staked the place out using my digs. One of us kept an ear on the shared wall at all times.

BY NIGHTFALL, HE hadn't shown so we figured the best thing to do was to go to the fair. Whatever he was planning on doing, or whoever he was planning on doing it with, they were going to be there otherwise it all could have happened in AC.

Mumford and I walked down the road, bought tickets, and entered the Wisconsin State Fair. It had all the charm of a ninety-year-old hooker and smelled as pleasant too.

The cultural highlights included a guy dressed as Abe Lincoln on a unicycle and George Washington on a high wire all of four feet off the ground. The audience laughed. Mumford and I looked at each other and moved on.

We walked past the livestock and the food kiosks until we came upon a noodle bar. An unusual offering for Wisconsin; Asians were still not popular in '79.

Curious, I thought, and Mumford must have had a similar set of thoughts running through his head because we both stopped a few feet away to see what we could see.

Two guys were talking in a huddle, one behind the counter and the other apparently a customer. Only thing was he wasn't ordering noodles or eating anything. The guy was shooting the breeze. Strange.

The customer shook hands with the owner and walked away, ambling down one row of kiosks, ambling up another. He never turned his head around, but he sure wasn't acting like someone who had come to check out the sights, sounds, and smells of the state fair.

We kept following him until he popped round the corner, near the fence, to have a piss. Mumford grabbed one arm and I grabbed the other.

"Valdez!" I spat at him and his eyes widened for a second and then the initial surprise wore off and he regained control of his expression.

"Not me. Not me. You wan' somebody else."

"No dice. Grab his wallet," I instructed Mumford, who silently shoved his hand into the guy's pants pocket, took out the wallet deftly with one hand, and somehow managed to extract the driving license while hanging on to the guy's arm. Nice.

"Dakila Valdez, it says here."

"Okay, Valdez. No more bullshit. The don has sent us to collect a parcel you are holding for him. We want it and we want it now."

"Don' know what you mean. Parcel? What parcel?"

I twisted his arm round towards his back so that the shoulder socket squeaked. Valdez let out a yelp, but nothing more.

"My friend can beat the living shit out of you right here and no one will hear you scream. So get us the package and we can be on our way and no one needs to get hurt."

"I know nothing," repeated Valdez.

Mumford got to work on him immediately and without prompting. Teeth, blood, and mucus fell to the floor until Valdez was nearly unconscious. Then between the gaps in his teeth and pained wheezes, he admitted that he did know something about the parcel.

Turns out that before he flew over to Milwaukee, he hit the west coast and left the parcel in a safe deposit box in San Francisco. Not only that, but he took off his right shoe, opened a compartment in the heel, and, hey presto, there was the very key we'd need to open it. We double-checked the location of the deposit box and left Valdez for dead.

Back at the motel, we paid up for the room before we went to bed because we knew we'd be getting up very early to leave town and we didn't want anyone to know exactly what time that was. Also, we knew we could get more info from Valdez if he came back to the motel, but he never did. Not that night, anyway.

# BALTIMORE 1956

# 16

THERE WE WERE chasing our tails out of the state of Wisconsin, heading west to put a key in a lock.

I experienced quieter times when I was based in Baltimore for a while after I came back from Korea. As ever, a different town and yet another serviced office in a no-name building on the edge of the right side of the tracks. I've found these locations got me the easiest money; people with enough cash to burn on missing people, but generally nothing too unpleasant to deal with along the way. If you go all upmarket, unpleasantness can ensue.

It was another Thursday morning with my feet up on my battered desk and a cigarette hanging out my mouth as I read the funnies in the paper. At this point in my career, I'd managed to be doing sufficiently well that I had a secretary to keep the worst of the riffraff at bay. Sheila only let the monied bums into my field of vision.

So it was that Mary O'Donald walked into my room and sat down on the chair I had conveniently located opposite mine, the other side of my battered desk.

There were tears in her eyes as she explained to me that her husband, Peter had been missing for two days now.

"Has he ever gone off and vanished for this long before?"

"No, no. Not for this long." There was a sadness in her expression that went deeper than a missing husband.

"And can you think of anywhere he might have gone?"

"Well, no. He doesn't go off like other men. Pete's the kind to stay at home. He don't have roamin' eyes."

"So there's no one he might have gone off with then?"

"Pete? No, sir. He stays at home; he don't really have many friends, you might say."

Indeed I might. Here we had a man with no reason to leave the family home except to go to work – he was a local plumber – but there was one simple fact, the guy wasn't at home.

"And what did the police say?"

"They told me to wait another day or two before I started to ruffle their feathers. They think he's got drunk somewhere and will come back when he's sober."

"Is that likely?"

"The man's teetotal. He took the pledge the year before we got married. He ain't the drinkin' kind."

"And the police still think he's hit the bottle hard somewhere?"

"Reckon so. But I know he hasn't. You gotta help me. No one else seems to care what's happened to ole Pete."

To be honest, I didn't care what happened to ole Pete either, but as Mrs. O'Donald was prepared to give me a daily allowance to try to find the man, I started to care ever so slightly. Just enough to take the cash she proffered in her quivering, hands and put it in the drawer of my battered old desk.

"I'll see what I can do."

"That's all I can ask of anyone," she said. Then added, "I just feel like something bad has happened to him. Very bad, you know."

"Do you think he might have been… killed?"

"Oh my. I hadn't thought of that. He might be dead – hit by a truck or something – but I can't imagine anyone actually going to murder my Pete."

"I'll spend a day or two having a real good look for your Pete, Mrs. O'Donald. In the meantime, if you think of anything that might help, just call my secretary. And don't be surprised if you see me in the neighborhood. The best place to look for a man who stays close to his home, is probably near his home, wouldn't you say?"

Mary O'Donald nodded, thanked me, and left the room, sniffing back the tears from her unhappy eyes.

Putting my feet back on my desk, I leaned back and finished reading the funnies. There was nothing like an amusing cartoon about an anthropomorphized animal attempting to slaughter a different animal to raise my spirits, back then.

Once I'd soaked all the humor out of the picture jokes in the paper, I took a fresh batch of business cards from my drawer, popped my hat on my head, and told Sheila to hold all my calls as I wouldn't be back for a while, and left. I told her the same joke every time I left the office on a case and she had the decency to smile every time. She understood I might not be funny, but I did pay her wages every week and never got fresh with her, despite how pointy her breasts were under those roll-neck jumpers of hers.

HAWTHORNE LANE WAS all white picket fences and large backyards that litter America from east to west, north to south. Folks were cutting the grass, kids were playing in the streets. There was a real wholesome atmosphere as soon as I turned the corner and strolled down the road.

I'd got the cab to park a block away so I could get a real sense of what this corner of town was like. I'd never found the need to walk through the suburbs of Baltimore; my time was spent in the city, not surrounded by families and loving couples. Nature of the job I suppose.

I tipped my hat at Mrs. Mary O'Donald when I stood in front of her house and she smiled back – her eyes flitting left then right as though embarrassed to acknowledge me. Never mind. Goes with the territory.

The best place to start finding out about people is to go to their neighbors first and then slowly fan out until you find yourself speaking to people who don't even recognize the name or a face in a photo.

The O'Donalds lived at number 748 Hawthorne Lane, so I went to 750 to see what would happen.

I knocked on the red-painted door and a girl answered, thirteen maybe fourteen years old.

"Yeah?"

The insolence with which that single syllable was uttered made quite an impression on me. She was what we had all started to call a real teenager.

"Your mom or dad home, hon'?"

"Yeah."

"Can you get one of them for me then?"

"Yeah." She walked away to get a parent, leaving the front door wide open and no more communication than that one word repeated three times. She was probably nearer fourteen than thirteen, thinking about it.

A woman appeared, mid to late thirties, wearing an apron, pants, and a blouse, wiping her hands on a tea towel.

"Can I help you?"

"Why I surely hope so, ma'am."

"How so?"

"Mr. O'Donald next door. I'm trying to find him. He's not been seen for a day or two, did you know?"

"Why no. I haven't spoken to Mary for a week."

"And you are…?"

"Betty Grant. My husband's Cecil and you've met Norma?"

"Oh yes, I met Norma," I smiled that adult to adult smile, which means *Gee, kids. What can you do, eh?* "And are your two families close would you say?"

"Well, I wouldn't say close."

"What would you say, then, Mrs. Grant?"

"We're just neighbors. That's all. Yes, we talk to one another if we're passing but that's all. We are not friends with the O'Donalds."

And with that, she closed the door on me. I didn't think I was stepping on anyone's toes just yet, but Betty Grant wasn't happy with someone in the O'Donald house. Whether it was Peter or Mary, I couldn't rightly say, but something was definitely not smelling right in the state of Maryland.

◆ ◆ ◆

I CARRIED ON attempting to speak with the other neighbors, but they were either out, not answering, or not particularly helpful. Not that anyone slammed the door on me after Betty Grant, they just had nothing interesting or useful to tell me.

He spent most of his time at home when he wasn't fixing people's faucets. He'd hang around the street, play with the kids. The usual dad about town. No one had any complaints. No one could think of anyone who might wish him harm. No one could tell me much about good old Pete. Seems he was seen from afar rather than the type to pop over for a chat and chug a beer.

So it was that I met Phil McNamara, an FBI agent who was assigned to the case even though the cops had told Mary not to worry. Apparently, he was in the city working a different case when he heard about this one and he pricked up his ears. He liked his chances with a missing husband who no one had a bad word to say against.

Phil had Irish ancestry, judging by the red tinge to his brown hair, cropped with tight curls. He had that slow drawl that comes from only one side of the Boston tracks, but it didn't bother me. Even so, I tried not to think ill of people because of where they'd come from. It's where you're going that mostly concerns me.

"And what brings you to this part of Baltimore?"

"Like I said, someone has hired me on a case and, as part of that, I'm looking for the whereabouts of Peter O'Donald. His wife visited this precinct to report him missing and was told to come back when she was sure he wasn't out on a bender.

"The police are taking things a little more seriously now you are in town."

McNamara looked at me, really looked at me with his blue piercing eyes, and inhaled. And laughed.

"You're all right, kid." I chose not to remind him that he looked only a spit away from my own age because he obviously needed to play a power trip on me.

"Are you working any angles, Agent?"

"Call me Phil. Everyone does. I like it that way."

"Okay, Phil. Are you working any angles at the minute?"

"Nah. Chances are the locals are right and the gent will roll back from whatever bar he's been getting soaked in over the next couple of days.

"As I'm here, I'd thought I'd take a poke, but he hasn't been AWOL long enough for me to be too concerned. It's not like there's been a ransom note or anything like that. Has there?"

"Geez, no. Nothing as exciting or specific as that. I'll keep sniffing around for a day or two and if nothing happens, I'll call it quits."

"You mean when her money runs out."

"Well, yes, I'll stay until I find something or the money runs out. After that, I'll leave the mystery to you fine folks with the badges and the early retirement and fat pension."

I smiled and, before McNamara could respond, walked out of the precinct house, and made my way back to Hawthorne Lane.

THIS TIME I figured I'd wait until the evening and speak to the men as I'd got zilch from most of the female figures on the road and a question mark hanging over one. Until then, with permission, I sat on the O'Donalds' porch and watched the world go by – and even got a lemonade for my troubles from Mary.

Dusk slowly lowered its veil on the burbs of Baltimore and I waited a while longer to make sure that everyone was fed, so I wouldn't be interrupting anyone's meals. Then I stood up and picked out the nearby houses with lights on; no point knocking on a door when nobody's home.

As it turned out, the men were as helpful as the women. Good ole Pete was a man who kept himself to himself. Everyone had a good word to say about him, but no one really could be said to know him. It was more like hearing a series of testimonials for his plumbing capabilities.

Finally, I knocked on the Grants' front door. This time Betty opened it up instead of little insolent Norma.

"Yes?" There was an edge to Betty's voice this time.

"Sorry to bother you again, but could I speak with Mr. Grant, please?"

"What?"

"Mr. Grant. May I speak with him, please?"

"Cecil? He's not in."

"Oh. Does he usually skip his dinner?"

"Huh? No. Not usually, but he's… out right now."

"I see. Where's he gone?"

"To visit a friend."

"And miss his dinner. Is his friend ill?"

"Um… no?"

Her answers were strange, uttered as though she didn't believe them herself, although they weren't lies. More that Cecil had told her one thing and she was thinking something else.

"Okay. Are you expecting him back later or do you think he'll be staying at his friend's house tonight?"

"Oh, I'm sure he'll be back, but he did say he'd be late though."

"Right. I don't want to disturb your evening again, so maybe I could catch Cecil daytime instead. Where does he work exactly?"

"At the hardware store round the corner. We own the hardware store on Lipton Street."

"Nice. I'll catch him there then, eh?"

"Sure."

With a tip of my hat, I spun round to leave her porch and I could tell she was just standing, watching me as I left because I could sense the glow of the light from their home still bathing me in its yellow feel as I walked away. Something was up with Cecil for sure. Whether it had anything to do with Peter O'Donald was another thing entirely: Cecil could have a mistress or just be out boozing. I had no idea at all.

# 17

I WENT BACK to my apartment in the city after that to dwell on what had happened. There was something going on with the Grants but Betty and Cecil could just be going through a rough patch. Families do things like that. The O'Donalds, on the other hand, were a couple. No children, which was unusual – at least on Hawthorne Lane.

After a good night's sleep, I decided to go to the one group you can rely on to know everything – the kids. They get ignored most of the time, but they are in the room when the most enormous shit goes down and they have the added advantage that they remember everything too; their young brains haven't been addled by hooch or distractions like having to pay the rent. So off to high school I went, guessing I might catch Norma there too.

Even back then, if you weren't a parent of one of the little lovelies, you were not welcome inside a school. So instead, I waited until lunchtime and hung around the corner from the side entrance.

As I figured, a few of these well-heeled members of the community snuck off campus for a well-earned cigarette break. I'd turned up casual, as nothing says inquisitive adult as much as a suit and hat, and I asked for a light to spark my own Marlboro alive.

"Thanks," I replied to the greasy-haired lummox who had lent me a match. "How's it going?"

"Just fine, mister. What's it to you?"

"Oh, nothing. Just paying no never mind is all."

"Cool."

The girl sat next to him, on the little wall they were perching on, shared his Camel with him, and stared at me every time she inhaled. They were bold, I'd say, because they were young for high school, around Norma's age.

"I know this sounds crazy, but you don't happen to know Norma Grant, do you?"

"Huh?" monotoned the boy.

"Norma, do you know her?"

"Yeah," said the girl, morphing the word into a two-syllable piece of cheek.

"What's she like?"

"Who wants to know, cop?" said the girl.

"I ain't no cop." I pulled a fin out of my pocket. "Just interested to hear about Norma. If you know anything that is."

Her eyes slipped from my face to the five-spot and stayed there.

"Maybe I do," she said.

"Well, is she popular at school?"

"Wouldn't say so. Keeps herself mainly to herself, you know?"

"Sure thing."

"But… there is a rumor going round." She licked her lips and continued to stare at the fin.

"And what are people saying?"

"Well, that she has a boyfriend."

"Is that so unusual? That a girl has a boyfriend?" I motioned to put the note back in my pocket because this conversation was going nowhere.

"No, but it is unusual to have a guy that's not from school. I mean, not from any school."

"What?" The fin came back front and center so the girl could get a better look.

"Yeah, word is that she's got an older boyfriend."

"Older?"

"Yeah, much older."

"Older than high school. That much older?"

"Yeah, older than high school." She snorted out a derisive laugh and I realized that our Norma sure was something special.

"College old?"

"Nah. Older than that." She smiled a brief smile and licked her lips again. Jeez, a million thoughts ran through my head.

I handed the five-spot over to the girl who snatched it and put it straight down the neck of her blouse and into her bra. Kids.

"You got anything to say for yourself?" I asked the greasy-haired boy, who'd remained silent this whole time.

"Nope. I'm just here for the smoke."

"Figures."

I turned my attention back to the girl.

"My name's Jake. Do you guys smoke here most lunchtimes – if I need to talk to you again?"

"Well…"

"I'm not the smoke police. I don't care what you guys get up to, but I might need to lay some more dough on ya, is all."

Her eyes lit up again.

"Yeah, most times we're here or a little further down if the deputy is prowling."

I smiled. The perils of being a teenager.

"What's your name, by the way?"

"Sally. And he's Steve." She pointed her cigarette butt at the greasy excuse for a human sat next to her.

"See you around, Sally."

I was beginning to see why Betty Grant was so uptight with a daughter like Norma appeared to be. And with good ole Pete missing, you had to wonder just a little…

SO I WALKED back to Mary O'Donald and invited myself in for another lemonade. We sat in the kitchen, chatting, talking about this and that. Sometimes the trick is not to ask about anything you care about because that can put people more at their ease and then they tell you anyway. I might only be a PI, but sometimes it feels like I'm a priest in a confession box.

"There are lots of kids in this street, I've noticed."

"Yes, there are. I like the sound of laughing children, don't you?"

"Sure," I lied, to keep the conversation flowing.

"But Pete and I haven't been blessed with them."

Mary looked down at her lap and was silent for a spell, caught in thoughts of regret and, potentially, loss.

"Sometimes it doesn't quite happen, does it?" I offered.

"No." Mary's back stiffened and she sat upright again, even though the lack of sons and daughters weighed down on her.

"Still, Pete has been good about it. He doesn't blame me or nothing. It's one of those things. We haven't been blessed, is all.

"And Pete has been like a second father to Norma next door, you know. Playing and helping with her schoolwork as Cecil spends so much time at his store, earning to put bread on the table."

My eyes wandered out to their backyard, thinking about Pete helping out next door, and Betty Grant not wanting to talk to me about Pete. Perhaps there was an affair taking place right under poor Mary's nose. Cecil found out and now Pete had vanished. Maybe.

At the left of the backyard, the garage stuck out a long, long way. Long enough for there to be more than enough space for a room beyond the cars if you were so minded. My attention went back to Mary.

"And the other kids too. Pete so loves playing their games, especially the younger ones. This might be a quiet road, but it never hurts to have an adult out front keeping an eye for traffic."

"Sorry, I know this is left field but is there a room at the back of the garage?"

"Yes. Yes, there is. Why?"

"No reason really. Does Pete use it much? Could I take a look?'

"Yes, it's his little nook. Of course. Is there anything you're looking for?"

"Not really. Just'll help me get a better picture of the man."

Mary walked me out the kitchen, into the garage, and there at the back of the garage was a door. Mary tried the handle but it was locked.

"I'm sure it's not normally locked and I don't know where the key's got to."

"Don't worry about it. You go back into the kitchen and I'll see what I can do."

After Mary had left the scene, I put my shoulder to the door and, with one push, I was in. A husband who locks a room from his wife in their own home has something to hide. I closed the door behind me as I entered.

# 18

EVEN THOUGH THERE was a small window, the room was dark. What little light came from the moon did nothing to show me what the place was like. I spotted a table lamp and switched it on.

There was a desk, a chair, a trunk, and a wall full of plumbers equipment. I checked the drawers of the desk but nothing, unless you count paid invoices, bills, and the sundry shit of life as something worth mentioning. I know I don't. That left the trunk.

No lock on it, so I just flipped it open and hit the mother lode. There were bundles of photos on the left-hand side of the trunk and on the other side of a partition were clothes. And all the clothes had one theme – they were girl's underwear. Some white, some blue, some black. But a lot. All scrunched up, not ironed neat and tidy. Oh no. These had just been thrown in there as though they had just been in a ball in someone's hand and dropped in.

As for the photos, they were all of one person and one person alone: Norma Grant. Perhaps the most disturbing thing was that I reckoned I could match up the panties on the right-hand side of the trunk with the photos from the left because there wasn't a single photo I could see where Norma was wearing anything apart from her undies.

Sick fucking bastard.

And there were so many pictures. This must have been going on for weeks, months, even longer. Years? At the bottom of the trunk were photos of a much younger Norma. They were all close-ups of her so it was impossible to work out where they were taken. Then I glanced beneath the shelves with all the equipment and saw some blankets and cushions. I'd missed them when I first came in.

I looked round at the opposite wall and noticed a couple of big lights mounted on the wall near the ceiling. Good ole Pete had got himself a photo studio in the back of his garage.

I thought I was going to throw up, but instead, I put everything away – just as I found it – and went back into the kitchen.

"Don't go into the room. The police will need to check it out later." Mary looked at me quizzically.

"You really don't want to know right now… I can't explain anything at this point, but I need to know if you have a place nearby or anywhere that Pete might have holed up. Think. Think, f'chrissake."

Mary was silent, stood leaning against the kitchen sink, looking down at her shoes.

"We don't have anywhere. We can barely make the payments on this place. We're not like the Grants with their vacation cabin in Swan Creek."

"Swan Creek?"

"Yes, it's outside Aberdeen, off the I-95."

Mary gave me more detailed directions and I returned to the city and grabbed my car, then I hightailed it out to Swan Creek.

THE CASE WAS coming together. There was good ole Pete and his photos of Norma. He'd probably done much worse than take photos of that curvy young girl, but I'd leave that for the cops to figure out. Cecil Grant wasn't around, which meant both men were effectively missing and there was a log cabin a couple of hours drive away. Doesn't take a genius to add up to four.

I arrived just after midnight. The moon was full and casting a whitish glow on the trees, reflected in the ripples in the water in the creek. This gave me enough light to go from my vehicle to the cabin.

The place was isolated; the nearest cabin was a quarter of a mile away and this wasn't vacation time. In these woods, no one would hear you scream.

Except me. My thoughts were intercepted by a blood-curdling yell, followed by a series of whimpers. I scampered to the cabin and ducked under one of the side windows.

Popping my head above the sill, I could see two men, one tied to a chair with blood pouring out of his head and the other towering over him holding some hardware tool or hunting knife or something. I slumped back down under the window because I really didn't fancy seeing any more right now. You don't need to pass the sergeants' exam to figure out I'd found Cecil and Pete and that Cecil was mutilating Pete. And for good reason.

I had a couple of options. Option one, burst in there and save Pete from torture and attack a man wielding a large knife or hammer or who knows what. Option two, go get help.

The second sounded better, so I crept away, back into my car and off to Aberdeen where I went to the local cops, told them all about what I'd seen, and got them to put out a call to Phil McNamara. I reckoned he'd want to claim this for his own.

Sure enough, about an hour later, the posse had surrounded the cabin. Me, Phil, and a local cop, Duane. Duane wasn't the brightest to leave the academy but he had a gun and he knew how to use it, so he assured Phil.

There were two doors into the cabin, one front, one back, and at least one window on each side. I couldn't see how many rooms there were, but based on Phil's binoculars, there was a living room with a kitchenette, one or two bedrooms, and a bathroom.

Right now, Pete and Cecil were in the middle of the living space. Pete was still tied to a chair with his hands bound behind his back, screaming and crying aplenty. Cecil was stood over him, poking at him with a knife, and generally creating mayhem on Pete's body. Perhaps I shouldn't have left him to get help.

DUANE AND PHIL stood at each door, guns ready, and I stood near one of the side windows. When I gave the signal, they'd both dive in at the same time.

Cecil had turned his back on Pete and held a hunting knife, all serrated edge and big brown handle. Pete had blood pouring from an eye socket.

I whistled. Phil and Duane burst through each door. I watched as Phil shouted, "FBI! Put the weapon down and put your hands on your head!" Duane, on the other hand, fired a shot off at Cecil, who had spun round in surprise at Phil's statement and was no more a threat at that moment than I was. But Duane knew how to use a gun.

Cecil carried on spinning round and lurched towards Phil due to the force of the bullet hitting his side. Seeing this, and misunderstanding basic physics, Duane let off another round and Cecil plunged to the ground, spitting blood and bile.

Both law officers holstered their firearms and by the time they had done that, Cecil had breathed his last.

Phil went over to Pete, untied his hands, and ripped off the bindings that held him to the chair. Then he arrested him and got Duane to call for an ambulance after slapping Duane in the face. "Fucking hick! Why d'you shoot him? He wasn't going to hurt anyone other than O'Donald. The guy was raping his daughter for fuck's sake!"

Duane slunk off and I stood there, looking through the window, staring at bits of eyeball I could see lying on the floor by the legs of the chair.

Phil came round the cabin to see how I was doing and to shake my hand.

"Good job, fella."

"Hey?"

"Yep. Our sources told us that O'Donald was a pederast but we had no hard evidence. We couldn't get a warrant to check out his home so we had nothing to arrest him with."

"You knew?"

"Yeah, but I couldn't tell you because he might easily have been drunk in some bar."

"How long…"

"Couple of weeks. That's why I was in the neighborhood. Hey, come back!"

I couldn't take it anymore. McNamara had let good ole Pete fuck that girl for two weeks and had done nothing. She might have been a sullen, rude teenager, but she didn't deserve that.

Back in my car, I lit a cigarette and rolled down the window to get some air. Then I drove back to Baltimore and my apartment, but I couldn't sit still. Couldn't deal with what had happened out in Hawthorne Lane. So I walked the streets most of the day until I stopped at a hotel. Truly, I have no memory of which one. I brown-bagged a couple of bottles of vodka and took a room for the night.

After a shower to clear my head, I dried myself down and put my shorts back on. I set myself up with three shots and the next thing I knew both bottles were empty and I was lying face up on the hotel carpet.

Now, you're not going to believe this, but there was a glow in the room and a guy like Charlton Heston hovered wearing a long white smock and I knew that he was Jesus Christ himself come to visit.

"At least you solved the case," came a deep voice from somewhere in the room. "She paid you to find her husband and you did." Clearly this Jesus wasn't the spiritual type, only a mouthpiece for my thoughts and unexpressed self-loathing.

I ran to the bathroom and threw up into the toilet. Twice. Three times if you count the dry-gulching. By the time I returned to the room Charlton Christ had vanished. While not all that surprising, I didn't touch another drop of vodka for five years straight, and nowadays I only have it in martinis, never straight. I don't need Charlton Heston visiting me again. No way.

# CHICAGO 1963

# 19

HOLDING MY BAGS at the top of the airplane steps and seeing Simone down there, made me think about her old man. The second time I came across him was still in New York, but a couple of years later. This time I didn't know I was dealing with Don Michael until I was almost face-to-face with him.

Bernie Levin was a good man, well-intentioned with a high moral code. We were opposites, but I liked him. He reminded me of my old partner, Ed – and not because they were both Jewish. Well, maybe.

Anyway, Bernie worked for the Teamsters, a union man through and through. He believed in that shit, really did, but as ever when matters got complicated, he didn't call Groucho Marx. He called me instead.

"Thanks for taking the time out of your day to see me, Jake." Bernie always saw things from the other dude's perspective.

"It's cool, Bernie. What's up?"

Bernie frowned at me, then pointed to his throat. I shrugged and asked, "Fancy a cup of java?"

"Well, don't mind if I do as you've been so kind as to ask," he replied and smiled a warm smile at me. Bernie was always the same.

With a hot cup of weak java in his hand, I asked, "What's up, Bernie? You don't write, you don't call and suddenly out of the blue, poof, here you are." Now it was my turn to smile warmly at Bernie.

"As you know, we live in difficult times."

"Tell me about it." I shrugged and cast an arm across my empire; a serviced office and a receptionist shared by the entire floor. Sleuthing wasn't what it was cracked up to be.

"But you didn't come over to hear my problems."

"No, I didn't. I've got enough of my own."

"Then why don't you start at the beginning."

I settled back in my chair because I knew what Bernie was like. If he could tell a tale in five sentences, he'd take fifty. It would be a great story but it would not be a short one.

"We are a union that works for our members, who come together to represent themselves as more than mere units of labor. They come together for compassion, for community, for humanity."

At this point, I put my hand up to stop him for a second.

"I don't need the sermon, rabbi. I'm no truck driver so I'm not going to join your merry band. Spare me the eulogizing over the hearts and souls of the all-American man."

"They come together," Bernie hissed slowly, "in the name of strength because as individuals they cannot fight the oppression of the slave owners."

"Slavery was abolished a long time ago, Bernie."

"Modern Capital is the new slave owner, my friend, and make no mistake, it'll come for you too." I shook my head and waited for Bernie to take some sips from his coffee. As he wound himself up again, I drummed my fingertips on my desk, because this was getting tedious, despite how much I liked Bernie.

"I'LL CUT TO the chase if you'd like, as I know you are a busy man." I raised my eyebrows as if to utter the words, 'You don't say', sarcastically.

"There is a chain of delicatessens owned by a man called Harry Pilkerton. They are called Harry's Deli for all the obvious reasons. They sell the finest cakes, cookies, Danish, and smoked salmon as you are likely to find in Chicago, if not the entire United States."

"I'll buy shares or go there for lunch tomorrow. Why should I care about Pilkerton and his food shops?"

"For Harry to have such a successful set of delis, he must source the finest ingredients and, ashamed as the Windy City would be to admit it, they don't all come from this fair city but from Los Angeles and New York, cheeses from Wisconsin, chili peppers from Texas…"

"I get it. He buys in stock from all over the place. Big whoop."

"Big whoop, you say? How dare you!"

"Huh?"

"My friend, the ingredients arrive at Harry's Delis because of the blood, sweat, and tears of my members. The goods are driven across country. No freight trains here. Truckers."

"And…?"

"Mr. P believes in making a large profit."

"Now, Bernie. We've had this conversation once too many times in the past. He's entitled to make some money for himself. He owns the company and takes the risks. Let's not rehash this again."

"Jake, I'm not trying to. I accept that under the current economic conditions, Harry will make money out of the toil of my members. Understood, but in order for him to make as much money as he does, Mr. P is refusing to pay a proper wage or follow basic safety precautions.

"He pays a fixed amount per shipment, but it's a long way to the east or the west coast. So the only way drivers can earn enough to feed their families is to drive for twenty hours straight or longer. Their hourly rate is below the poverty line and they are putting their lives at risk as well. They literally can't afford to stop and sleep. They drive on empty."

"Tough break," I said, but I had little sympathy with a bunch of truckers who should only pick the short runs if they wanted to get some shut-eye more often.

"Tough break indeed, Jake. But we at the Teamsters National Union are not prepared to let this situation persist. We have given Pilkerton notice that, unless our demands for better pay and safer working conditions are met, we will withdraw our labor and strike."

"Well good luck to you – and your members with that – but I'm still at a loss as to why you've come to my office."

"I'm getting there, Jake. I'm getting there. If there was only a strike then I wouldn't be here. But there's a little problem around the edges I do need your assistance with."

"Do tell."

"Harry has friends, who are making their presence known."

"Huh?"

"They are trying to break us before we've even stopped working. There have been threats against me. Bricks thrown through the locals' windows. Anonymous letters sent, threatening all manner of unpleasantness if we strike."

"Nasty. How do you think I can help?"

"I'd like you to find these guys and convince them to get off our backs and allow us the right to lawfully strike for our rights."

"Have you any idea who these guys are?"

"Let me put it this way, they have Italian last names."

Finally, I got what was being asked of me. Bernie wanted me to go to the local organized crime syndicate and plead his case to let the strike go ahead. Fifty sentences versus five. Bernie won again.

THIS WOULD BE a dangerous thing to attempt so I asked for two hundred a day plus expenses. I figured the Teamsters could afford it so I asked for a week up front before I'd start. You have to hand it to Bernie; the man had the cash in his pocket and just handed it over. No receipt, no invoice requested. A stand-up guy from a stand-up union.

I went over to the north-west corner of Amigo Park at West Lexington and South Loomis, the heart of Little Italy because the best way to get to Italians of influence was to hang out near Italians and listen hard and talk little.

And it didn't take me long to find a guy, who knew a fella I could speak with. I swigged my espresso and followed the guy down a dark alley, one of my least favorite locations in the whole of Chicago.

The guy introduced me to the dude he knew, and we stood and talked at the rear of the alley for a minute and then he knocked a particular rat-a-tat on the door behind him, which opened and I was invited in.

Down a corridor and into a comfortably furnished room, after the usual check of my inside leg measurements. If these dudes ever left organized crime behind them, they'd make brilliant tailors.

In the corner of the room was a figure sat with one arm resting on a table, legs crossed foot pointing downwards, and a cigarette in the other hand. And a beautiful gray suit.

"I believe you wanted to see me."

"I believe so too. My name is Jack Adkins, but my friends call me Jake."

"Well Mr. Adkins, you are here."

"Yes, I am. I'll keep this short."

"We are both busy men, I am sure."

"Indeed. I've been asked to speak to someone about the situation between Harry's Deli and the Teamsters."

Fancy Suit held his cigarette hand up to halt my words.

"You appear to misunderstand. We have no relationship with the Teamsters National Union nor do we have a relationship with Harry's Deli – apart from buying the occasional loaf of bread."

My shoulders sagged. Waste of time. Shit.

"But we do move in interesting circles. If we were to have a conversation on this matter with other individuals more closely associated with the situation you describe…" His voice trailed off and his hand waved a continuing motion to me. I got the drift and picked up the conversation.

"Well, I don't care about the rights and wrongs of the grievances the truckers have. I really don't, but I'm a moderate man who doesn't like to hear of violence being done to others.

"So I'd like to understand what the Teamsters could do for your… friends, were you to bump into them some time… to avoid any unpleasantness like bricks in windows or baseball bats on brains."

Fancy Suit smiled.

"Nicely put. I appreciate your consideration in this matter. Wait outside a few minutes and we can continue our conversation then."

# 20

I WALKED OUT the room, just as Fancy Suit picked up a phone from his table and placed a call. By the time I was outside, I couldn't hear a word he was saying. Sure enough, shortly after I was ushered back inside.

"Jake. The answer to your question is simple. A cash donation to a charity of our choice to the tune of fifty racks would solve the matter." He let the number 'fifty thousand' sink into my head.

"And Mr. Lambretti sends his regards."

Of course, why did I think the don didn't have his hand in this affair all the way from New York? He was one powerful man.

"Thank you for taking the time to listen to me. As you can imagine, I will relay your request to the relevant parties."

"You are most welcome. Tell the Jew to pay up or he'll have more than a broken window to worry about."

"I'll let Bernie know, don't worry."

"I'm not worried, Jake, but Bernie Levin should be."

He motioned me out, and I left the building the same way I'd come in and headed back to Bernie to give him the good news, not that he saw it that way.

"It's extortion is what it is. Pay them off so we can strike in peace. Such chutzpah, I've never heard."

"Nonetheless, Bernie. It sounds a sensible plan. That or end the strike. No strike, none of your blood will land on the floor, my friend."

"I cannot allow the strike to stop before it has even started. We gave Pilkerton warning before we downed tools to give him a chance to do the right thing by us. Not to employ goons to try to break us."

"These guys are way more than goons," I interrupted because I didn't want Bernie to consider them as mere hired thugs. They sure weren't. They had the might of Don Michael behind them.

"I know, I know, but the other way to get this to end nice and peaceable is if Pilkerton agrees to our demands. Go and see him and find out if he's prepared to compromise."

"Are you serious?" I was surprised he wanted me to do union business, but at two hundred a day I couldn't complain about being asked to have a chat with a baker.

The headquarters of Harry's Deli was a warehouse that supplied all seven establishments with stock. At the back were a series of shutters to which trucks could back up to disgorge their contents. The front of the building had a reception and offices, inside one of which sat Harry Pilkerton smoking a Camel.

"I understand you are about to have some union problems, Mr. Pilkerton."

"You are remarkably well-informed Mr. Adkins."

"Call me Jake, all my friends do."

"I'll be your friend if you can get those communists to keep on making their deliveries."

"Their politics may be flakey, but you need them as much as they need you."

"And how do you reckon on that?"

"You need to have items in your delis to sell and you need trucks to deliver the goods to this warehouse cheaply, otherwise you can't make your profit and wear your nice suit and that nice watch of yours.

"But the truckers need you too. Without your money, they don't get wages and feed their families and do the stuff that truckers do in their spare time. Drink and gamble, I would guess."

Pilkerton nodded. He shared the same general disinterest in the welfare of the Teamsters members as I did.

"And that means that both sides need to come to some sort of arrangement over this disagreement so that everything can run smoothly again."

Pilkerton stopped nodding and opened his mouth to speak, causing a parabola of spittle to fly through the air and land on his desk, next to a snow globe paperweight.

"Who do you think you are, coming into my building and telling me what I should do with these communist drivers?"

"No, wait. All I'm suggesting is that you find a small bone to throw their way so they can be okay with stopping the strike. Any inconsequential offer will enable them to save face and for you to win."

"Save face? Why should I let that Jew, Levin save face?"

"But…"

"No ifs or buts. Tell Levin he can go fuck himself and the rest of his commie union. I've got muscle to help me and drivers who'll do the work without complaining. Why do I need to throw a bone to Levin? Fuck him and fuck you!"

Like all good negotiators, I left at this point because Harry Pilkerton was definitely not interested in hearing the others' point of view. Someone had made him angry, and I didn't think it was me.

We were heading towards the end of Thursday and the strike was set to start nine Saturday morning. Back at Bernie's, I told him what had gone down.

"At least you tried with Pilkerton. Thank you for that."

"*De nada*. Trouble is that it's got us no further than we were before. You seriously need to think about finding fifty big ones and fast."

"That won't be necessary."

"How so, Bernie? Are you planning on just striking and be damned? Possibly from a hospital bed or the morgue?"

He laughed.

"You see, Jake, Pilkerton isn't the only one who has friends in… special… places."

"What?"

"We've got us some good old-fashioned protection. I phoned a guy, who knew a guy, while you were out seeing Harry P."

"Protection? Protection from Pilkerton's goons. These are connected people, Bernie. You can't go up against connected people."

"You can if you have your own protected people to counter them with."

"You've hired mobsters to protect you from the mob? Crazy, dumb son of a bitch."

I just sat there in silence, upper limbs dangling on the armrests of my chair in Bernie's office in the Teamster building.

"This isn't going to be some kind of Mexican standoff, you know, just because you've got muscle, Bernie."

"I know, Jake. I'm no fool. I believe in the cause but I also believe in staying alive to fight another day. Really."

"So how is this going to work?"

"I'm expecting my muscle to speak to his muscle and for the whole thing to get called off."

"And if it doesn't?"

"My men will fight for the right to have better pay and conditions like we wanted to do in the first place."

"You're playing a mighty queer game, Bernie, and I'm not sure you will be on the winning side."

"If Pilkerton loses then we win – even if we don't get all our demands met. We win if he loses. And every day he pays money to his New York muscle, he makes less profit and he loses. My Chicago muscle can fight his New York muscle if it makes them feel any better to earn their respective fees. That's fine. But Pilkerton must lose."

He fixed me with a steely stare and, despite his leftie rants and moaning, I knew he was serious about this matter. He wanted to stick it to the man.

SATURDAY MORNING ARRIVED and there I was, manning the barricades, in the name of the workers' rights. Or, more accurately, there I was leaning on a wall with a cigarette hanging out my mouth near some other men who were manning the barricades in the name of their rights.

I was stood on the opposite side of the street to the warehouse, whose gates were unsurprisingly locked as Pilkerton didn't want to let any of the strikers onto his property. Outside the gates, there were ten, twenty men with placards in their hands and hate in their eyes, shouting and chanting appropriate slogans. I tried not to take it in too deeply as I knew I would hear the same words repeated for many hours and I didn't want them to get under my skin.

This position also gave me good visibility as to what or – more importantly – who was coming down the road. The chances were something would happen today, although I reckoned Pilkerton's men would wait until this afternoon. If I were him, I'd let the truckers get tired out, from chanting and waving signs to the occasional passing vehicle before I waded in to bust their heads.

Sure enough, around three, a truck careered round the corner and screeched to a stop about thirty feet from the crowd outside the gate. I'd found a makeshift seat by this time on a couple of boxes, but I stood up, knowing that some bad shit was going to go down.

But nothing for five, ten, fifteen minutes. Every one of the strikers stood still too. They could sense something was about to happen.

Then the back of the van opened up and a horde of guys in balaclavas, brandishing baseball bats, leaped out and attacked any damn thing that moved near the gate.

Of course, I stood there and watched. This was not my fight. Not even close, not even in the same neighborhood. My job was to help Bernie and he wasn't here. My job was not to fight with a bunch of goons, all of whom were probably being paid far more than I was.

Five minutes later and the men bundled themselves back in the truck and sped off down the street, leaving a melee of bashed, bruised, and assaulted strikers in their wake.

I put out my latest cigarette with the tip of my shoe and walked over to the gates, just to make sure no one needed hospital treatment, but the goons had done a good job. Every last one of them had been hurt real bad, but no one would go squealing to the cops or have their injuries reported to the cops by some doing-the-right-thing ER nurse.

The question was whether they'd done enough damage to get Bernie to either call off the strike or pay up the fifty large. The other thing I wondered was what the hell happened to Bernie's muscle because their camouflage was so good, you could be forgiven for thinking they weren't there at all.

# 21

I'D PARKED MY car two blocks away in an open-air parking lot as I didn't want to lose my vehicle in the name of communism or workers' rights or whatever. Walking away from that whole mess I wondered why Bernie hadn't been there with his people, showing support for his guys.

"They're all mensches. They didn't need me to be stood beside them, but at least they weren't too badly hurt. It was inevitable really. As soon as Pilkerton hired outside muscle, things were going to turn sour pretty fast."

"That's as may be, but there's a simple way for you to stop your men getting hurt: pay up the money and you'll be left alone. Easy."

"Easy for you but not for me and the Teamsters. If we gave up every time some capitalist lapdog kicked us in the teeth, we'd have got nowhere by now."

"But, Bernie."

"No ifs and buts. We stand tall or not at all."

"And what happened to your hired hounds? Where did they get to?"

"They said they'd be available to deal with my problem on Monday."

"You're kidding me. Why give them the weekend off?"

"Not my choice. They said they weren't free until then."

"Sounds to me like you've been set up. How much do your guys cost you then?"

"Twenty-five large for the first week, but we shouldn't need the whole week."

"You really are crazy. If you've got that much spare cash, you could have paid off the hit squad that beat your men into a pulp only a few hours ago."

"Jake, Jake. It's not about the money. The union has money. It's about what's right. And bribing someone to stop hitting you is not right. They should stop because they want to stop."

"That's an easy thing to say when you're not the one cowering on the ground with a baseball bat beating your brains onto the street."

"Don't exaggerate, Jake. No brains were spilled today. These were professional men. They drew blood and knocked out a couple of teeth, but nothing more. They understand how this game is played."

I was lost for words. Bernie was playing to his own set of rules and they sounded screwy. It was almost as if he wanted the violence to rain down on his men so they could look beautifully oppressed by the capitalist beast. Screwy.

I shook my head, walked out the door, and went back to my apartment. Cooked me up a real nice steak and potatoes, had a shower, and went to bed. The union game was not all it was cracked up to be.

There was a knock on my door shortly after nine thirty. I was already up but hadn't finished my breakfast yet. I still had half a slice of toast and a second cup of coffee to complete. But I answered the door anyway because you never know what opportunity lies on the other side of a piece of wood.

On this occasion, there were two thickset dudes, neither with a noticeable neck, who encouraged me to take a trip with them. A short time later, their Cadillac took us to the self-same alley I'd had the luck to visit a day or two before.

Back in the same room, my host sat in the same chair and the same cross-legged position.

"Well, Mr. Adkins. Do you have our money?"

"I hope you believe me because I truly say this with all due respect. I have spoken with the third party and he is choosing not to take up your kind and generous offer.

"In this, I am only the messenger and I hope you remember this if there are any consequences for Mr. Levin's decision."

"Do not fret, Mr. Adkins. We are very aware of your circumstances. If Levin doesn't want our help then he must deal with what happens to his men, not you."

I relaxed slightly because I really didn't want to get a beating, just because Bernie was too stubborn to submit to an old-fashioned piece of extortion.

"But as a self-confessed messenger, you must pass on my words and know I mean every one of them." I nodded.

"If Bernie Levin doesn't call off the strike by Monday then Bernie Levin's family will be burying him on Tuesday. Understood."

I nodded again, this time with greater urgency. I was dropped back at my apartment. At least the hoods operate an efficient shuttle service too.

Calling Bernie on the phone, I figured I'd lay it out straight to him. The money was off the table and his life very much was on the same piece of furniture.

"Jake, they are bluffing. No matter how powerful they may be, no gangland mobster will off a union official. These things just don't happen."

"I gotta tell you, Bernie. They are not bluffing. They really will do it. I don't know why this strike is so important to them, but it is now. Maybe the fact you refused to pay them off, just made them pissed. Perhaps someone else is paying them more. I don't know.

"But you've got to decide how you are going to end this strike before Monday because there'll be Kaddish said shortly after if you don't."

"Nah. Bluff I say." And Bernie put the phone down on me.

There was nothing else I could do at that point. The only decision made was by me: I'd stay with Bernie on Monday to try to help him survive the day, but the man was not for turning.

❖ ◆ ❖

MONDAY ARRIVED AS predicted the day before. I was awake before six, having spent the previous night thinking about Bernie and the trouble he was in and the trouble he was just not recognizing himself to be in.

I scooted over to his house so I could be with him from the start of the day. At the very least, I could watch out for him. I was good at judging early signs of threats as my natural reaction was always to head the other way.

Today I would stand firm with Bernie – at least for a while. I hadn't decided what I would do when the heat in the kitchen rose. But I knew I'd figure it out later, one way or another.

After he'd had breakfast with Mrs. Levin, I drove Bernie round to the union building so he could pick up some papers, and then we went over to the Harry's Deli warehouse. Today Bernie had decided to stand by his men. This also meant he would be surrounded by witnesses should anything go down, I thought. Less noble. A more practical side of Bernie was shining forth this morning.

By ten, there was a sizeable gathering outside the gates and no one had been let in. Then a van appeared across the road, near where I'd stood on Saturday, and a bunch of hooded thugs stepped out. This time, their baseball bats had nails sticking out of them and some had long, clanking chains. They had upgraded from wooden to metal objects and it wasn't going to be pretty.

"There's still a chance to stop this bloodshed, Bernie."

"No there isn't. These men are striking for better pay and conditions. They deserve it and no hired hands can stop the purity of their actions."

"No, but they can stop the solidity of their bodies, Bernie. You gotta stop this now. If this is what the mob has in mind for your men, you can bet your bottom dollar, they'll plug you full of lead. They'll keep their promise and kill you dead."

Just as I said those words, the hooded dudes started their attack, running forwards with weapons raised, flailing their bats and chains around, knowing they didn't need to get too close and could still do some serious damage. In fact, they were doing some significant damage to the strikers, who were falling left, right, and center.

That said, at one point, three drivers had somehow surrounded one of the hoods and had grabbed the end of his bat. Pulling him to the ground, they kicked him and pounded at him and generally made a mess of him all over.

Our attention was diverted away for a minute, I happened to spot a flash, a glint of light from the top of the opposite building. I immediately knew exactly what was happening and pulled Bernie to the ground by grabbing his sleeve and throwing myself to the floor, forcing him to follow me down.

A shot sounded out and caught Bernie in the left arm. If I hadn't shifted his position, it would've been his heart, so the doctors said later.

I lay there, cowering next to Bernie for a minute or two, happy that all the men around us were still standing and providing the perfect cover. I pulled out my handgun and aimlessly pointed it toward the sniper, but there was nothing to see and nothing to do. It just made me feel better.

Later that day, when I was allowed into Bernie's room in the hospital, he looked in a much better way than I'd anticipated. Given the man had survived an assassination attempt, I'd have expected him to be in good spirits, but I sensed there was something more.

"The strike's over, Jake."

"Is it? How?"

"Pilkerton has let the drivers have longer paid breaks."

"Is that it? Is that all you got? What about the amount he was paying you guys?"

"You can't have everything, Jake."

"Who got to you, Bernie? This morning you were prepared to die for your men and now you've sold them down the river for a few minutes extra shut-eye. What gives?"

Bernie smiled at me and shook his head.

"You know, Jake, sometimes it's not about the money."

"No?"

"No, sometimes it's about other things."

"What about your friends with the muscle? They weren't here today either and you told me that Monday was their starting day."

"Yeah, well, our hired hands didn't work out so well. Some other… friends… appeared and convinced me to change strategy. For the good of my health."

"Did the don get to you?"

Bernie smiled and nodded and let his head fall back on the pillow. He was a tired man.

But not tired enough to stop himself from taking a union job in Washington later that year. I'm sure the two events weren't unconnected.

You still get the best bagels in Chicago at Harry's Deli; you should try them if you're ever in town.

# BOSTON 1977

# 22

I THOUGHT I'D come to the end of my sleuthing only a few years ago. There was yet another dame and yet another room with another camera. This time I'd bought myself a tripod and a telephoto lens.

On this occasion, Lenny Almaguer had been a New York walk-in with the usual yadda yadda yadda and I'd followed his wife on a girls' weekend over to Boston. Mrs. Christina Almaguer was in the apartment block opposite me, but there were no girls or women with her. Just one man. Lenny should be thankful for that one small mercy, I suppose.

Anyway, the job sounded simple. I wait for something worth photographing for Lenny and then I return to New York and get my fee. To be honest, even though I knew this was going to be a dull job, it still drove me over the edge with boredom. So afterward I stopped being in the game. Kept my licensed gun, just in case, but hung up my sleuthing hat for good. More or less.

So this was the set-up. I'd figured out which room they were in by watching which floor they'd got off in the elevator and then sweet-talking the concierge for the room number with a ten spot. The dive was swanky enough for a concierge but it was Boston, not New York. I'd have needed a twenty in New York.

Then off I trotted to the hotel opposite and took a room overlooking the apartment block. In my case, I'd brought a camera and a tripod, like I said. I didn't mention the binoculars, but that was what I was using to stare into their room and wait for the money shot.

Of course, that was the easy bit. The kitchen blinds were open, and the living room curtains were open, but the lovebirds were in the bedroom and those curtains were stubbornly shut. So I had to wait to earn my fee.

I rotated the easy chair that every decent hotel comes supplied with and dragged the footstool so I could put my feet up and watch in comfort. This was completed by adding a side table next to my armchair to place a drink from the minibar. I closed my own curtains, so that there was only a gap left, out of which I could peer into the darkness and catch me two Hispanic humpers.

Glancing down at my watch, I saw that it was past eleven. I stood up and found a light jazz FM station to listen to – otherwise the silence would do me in.

By eleven thirty, I was bored. Plain bored and all I could do, to stop myself falling into a pit of tedious despair, was to check out other windows with more interesting things to see.

All the apartments were laid out exactly the same; a small hallway, living room, separate kitchen, a bathroom, and a bedroom. Apart from the bathroom, each room had floor to ceiling windows, so I had total visibility inside. The only differences between the apartments were the paint or wallpaper on the walls, the carpets, and the furniture. Other than that, all the rabbit hutches were identical.

Above the trysting apartment was a black and white one. The walls were white, the easy chairs in the living room were black and they had gray photos on the walls in black frames. All the lights were on but the inhabitants were in the bedroom.

A man and a woman were sat up in bed, reading. She had a magazine and he had a book. Nothing strange about that, but I could sense they were both naked. I mean, I could see that she was naked, at least her top half, for the simple reason her magazine was resting on her lap and I could see her tits resting under her arms. And the man's chest was visible too.

That then begged the question, what the hell were they up to? They couldn't be finished for the night because all the lights were on.

Trouble is, I've never heard of people going to bed to read late in the evening only to hop out and do something else or then get the place ready for sleeping. Made no sense to me.

Perhaps they were night owls and instead of witnessing the end of their day, I was seeing their beginning. They'd read a bit, get up and dressed, put on their party clothes, and go out to some club in downtown Boston where the night people met.

Their nocturnal meanderings around the city would culminate in some debauched sadomasochistic orgy around six or seven and they would return, replete, for a few hours before they hit the hay in the mid-afternoon, in readiness for the next day's fun.

Weekdays, he was a financial adviser by trade, who made his own investments on the side, otherwise how else could they afford that apartment? She would spend her days in the local markets, finding interesting *object d'art* and other bric-à-brac. Then she'd come home and cook something up a storm. If it was steak, it would be red raw.

Wait. I was wrong. Next, the man rolled over, pecked the woman on the cheek, got out of bed to close the bedroom door, leaving the other lights on, and returned to bed. By this time, she'd put her magazine down and thrown the covers off herself to reveal her total nakedness beneath. He got back into bed, switched the bedside light off, and, in the murky, inky gray darkness, I could just about make out the movement of their bodies as they fucked. People behave in the strangest ways.

I left them to it because I couldn't honestly tell anything anymore and there's nothing more annoying than not quite being able to see people making out.

So I shifted my binoculars one apartment to the right and found a guy standing in front of the mirror in his living room. Full-length and attached to the wall opposite the window. He had his back to me but, because of the angle, I caught everything going on with him through his reflection in the mirror.

Now, that wasn't what drew my attention to him, because a man looking at himself in a mirror is not what I'd call interesting. Oh no, this guy wore a one-piece Elvis Presley outfit, straight out of a Vegas show. His legs wobbled like he had Elvis's thighs and he held a hairbrush.

Again, people hold hairbrushes. There's nothing odd about that. But if you are holding it so the bristles are pointing downwards and the handle is up in the air and your lips are moving, the only conclusion must be that the dude was treating it like a microphone. He sang along to his very own King show at the International. Only it was inside his head in an apartment in Boston.

His pelvic thrusts took a turn for the worse. Well, they got more aggressive anyway. Who knows what song this was associated with – I guessed not *Love Me Tender*. So the gyrations became more intense and the guy's arms were wobbling around, presumably to help him keep his balance given the flailing of the rest of his body.

Weird but under control. Until it moved to weird but not under control. Abruptly, the dude vanished from view. I mean, one minute he was there and the next minute, he lost his balance and fell on the floor, what with all his contortions 'n' all. As there was a sofa between him and me, when he fell, he plain vanished from sight.

I was almost worried and thought about calling the cops, but then I'd have some mighty fine explaining to do all of my own. So I sat in my easy chair and waited to see if he would get up. A minute later, I spotted a hand hanging onto the back of the chair so I knew he must be conscious.

Eventually, he crawled on all fours round the chair and leaned on its seat to haul himself up and into it. He sat there for five, ten minutes, clearly deep breathing and presumably in agony because, after a while, he somehow got himself upright and trundled to the bathroom and came back with something in his hand. Shuffling to the kitchen, he poured himself a glass of water and popped the aspirin down his neck.

Still chortling at his misfortune, I decided to give up on him because there's only so much stupidity I can stomach.

The binoculars headed downward, to the right of Christina Almaguer, and on to an apartment painted in a variety of bright colors. One wall red in the living room, another green, blue in the kitchen, and so on. I wouldn't have chosen it myself, but it wasn't my apartment.

# The Case

I noticed the bedroom was filled with wooden artifacts: carved heads, elephants, that sort of thing. All the lights were on, but I had real problems spotting any occupants.

A girl appeared from the bathroom. She was wrapped in a yellow towel, tied just under her armpits. In her early twenties at the most. She walked towards a low table in the living room and to a basket on it. She picked up the woven basket using the handles on both sides and took it into the bathroom.

The door closed behind her and she vanished but the door swung back on itself to reveal the space inside. Beth – I decided – pulled out a string from one side of the bathroom to another to hang up her washing. Now, I will admit I almost moved onto the next apartment until I realized quite what she was hanging up.

First, there was a string of panties. Plain red, white and blue stripe, pink spots on blue. The red ones looked particularly skimpy and I imagined what she might look like wearing them.

She moved onto her bras. The colors of each bra matched the panties, one-for-one. After each was hung up, I paired them up in my head and I placed the image of Beth wearing top and bottom, walking in front of me and sitting down next to me.

Finally, she hung up her pantyhose. And then Beth had the most wonderful private moment. She took off the towel that was covering her and hung it up somewhere in the bathroom, a radiator, or just a hook behind the door. I couldn't say because I couldn't see.

So there she was, having turned around to leave the bathroom, standing there with her tits and her bush for me to see. She stretched her arms up as high as they would go and then bent down to touch her toes with straight legs, her long hair trailing onto the floor. Straightened up, she placed a hand on each of her tits and had a good feel. Casually, she let one hand drop down to her crotch and she fingered herself briefly. Then she flipped a switch outside the bathroom to take its light out, still naked, giving me a great sight of side boob and bush hair. And what a cute ass. Then she padded slowly into her bedroom, switched the light on and I could clearly see the roundness of her breasts and the nipples sticking out. Was she cold?

She hopped into bed and I imagined her and all the contours of her body beneath the sheets. I spent a minute or two doing just that and noticed that I'd stopped looking through the binoculars and had begun daydreaming over the thoughts of her nubile, young body.

I shook my head twice and shifted the binoculars down and onto another apartment. Different decor and different circumstances. This time it was a couple but not in the same room as each other. A woman stood by the sink in the kitchen and a man faced out of the head-to-toe window in the living room.

He had his hands in his pants pockets, legs apart, standing, staring. In contrast, she was busy, scrubbing, frothing, rinsing, drying. Women's lib hadn't reached their relationship just yet.

And so she carried on, plate after plate, pots, knives, forks. All cleaned by her fair hands. When it was all over, she switched off the faucets and picked up a towel and began the task of drying each item she'd left on the draining board, and putting them on the kitchen table. Once all the crockery and cutlery was dried, she took each item and put them away in the cupboards and drawers.

She dropped down on one of the kitchen chairs and slumped her head into her hands. All the while, the man stood there in the living room, facing out into the night's darkness. I might not have seen her face, but I got the sense she was crying; her shoulders were shaking up and down and, thirty seconds into this behavior, she took a tissue to blew her nose and then put her head back in her hands.

Meanwhile, he stood there, hands still in his pockets, rocking forwards and back. There was something going on in that apartment, but it was hard for me to figure out quite what. He had much power over her, that was for sure. But why did she take it? And why be so sad about washing up? Surely, it was the kind of task you'd do every day. What straw broke the camel's back this evening? I could only imagine.

Perhaps, over their evening meal, he had told his wife he'd met someone else and that he'd be leaving her. They had spent hours talking it over, about what they would do, when it was going to happen. And that was why it took so long for the washing up to get done. And that would explain why he was doing nothing but staring and why she found the dinner plates so miserable.

Or perhaps this was the first evening they'd spent after they left the hospital as they witnessed their son die in front of their eyes. And neither was able to talk anymore. It had all been too much.

I focused left to the next apartment on my travels, making me immediately below the one I was meant to be surveying.

# 23

FLORAL WALLPAPER IN the living room showed I was looking at a totally different kind of place and a different situation. On this occasion, there was a single person, sat down, watching the TV. Although the TV was facing the wrong way for me – hardly surprising as that would have meant it was facing out of the apartment – I knew it was switched on because there was a constant flickering of projected images onto the woman's face.

With one blink, I spotted the fact, which I hadn't noticed until this point. She was sitting in a wheelchair with a rug flopped onto her lap. Although the light wasn't great, in between the penumbra of the shadows, I saw she was in her late thirties or early forties.

That begged the question, why she was in the wheelchair in the first place. Was it a childhood disease that crippled her? An innocent casualty in a shootout outside a bank? A spinal injury caused by a drunk driving accident. All were possible and anything might be possible. I had no idea.

But that didn't stop me from wondering whether it was self-inflicted or otherwise. Perhaps she'd thrown herself off the top of a building, high enough to cause herself permanent damage but not sufficient to kill herself.

She'd recently been to her mother's funeral and had visited her sister in hospital, in a coma with less than a five percent chance of ever gaining consciousness again.

That was the least of her problems because while she was in the hospital, she was mistaken for a witness to a mob hit. Her hitman bungled the job and the bullet from his silencer embedded itself in her spine and not her heart – for reasons that are irrelevant right now.

After that, things got tough for her. In the ICU next to her sister, once she regained consciousness, she turned her head sufficiently to watch her sister escape from the coma, only to heave a massive exhalation, have a single drop of blood trickle out her nose, and hear the sister's last breath exit her lungs.

Now she was able to speak, she told the doctors how she was shot at for no reason and they figured that the best thing to do was to move her to another room, especially as her vitals were surprisingly strong.

Her spinal cord shot to hell, quite literally, she discovered over the next few days the exact meaning of those words. She worked on her upper body strength so she was able to push herself around in her wheelchair, but from that day she was haunted by the memories of being shot and watching her sister die. And the grief from her mother's loss never left her.

Or she might have been like that from birth and was in the apartment because it was the only one in the area to have an elevator for the money.

THEN I MOVED left again so I was diagonally below and to the left of Christina's sex pad. All the lights were out apart from a single bulb hanging over a table in the living room. There was a green baize cloth covering the round table and, as you might have guessed, there were playing cards littering the table.

Four guys sat there, each holding a set of cards tightly to their chests or firmly face down on the table.

The first thing I wanted to figure out was what game they were playing: poker, rummy, gin, blackjack. Endless possibilities. The only game I was certain they were not playing was bridge because none of the guys looked like noses-in-the-air bridge types. This was a dollar ante game and nothing more, although it was hard to tell because they used chips and not cash for their bets.

Admittedly that made it more upmarket than I'd first imagined, but hey even chimps can have a tea party.

Took me a while, but I reckoned it was poker. Five cards dealt a hand, three rounds of betting, made sense. Also, let's face it, how many times do a bunch of young guys get together for a weekly game of gin. Nah, it was poker.

Unfortunately for me, I could only see one hand – the guy who had his back to me. The two on his side were at right angles to him so I had no chance with them and the dude sat opposite was completely the wrong way round because he faced me and the first dude. My guy seemed a cunning player. He liked to bluff.

The first hand I properly watched he had a pair of threes and won the pot beating two-pair by having a good poker face, not that I could see it, mind you. There was at least one hundred dollars in that pot. So maybe this game was for more than chump change after all.

The next hand he quit early and the following one too. Then he started betting up a storm. I saw he had an ace and king of hearts but there didn't appear to be anything else interesting in his hand. And I was right. What became obvious was that there was a mirror facing my man and the window, which meant he had a clear line of sight on the cards of the guy opposite him.

So once I'd noticed this discrepancy, I too understood much better what he was up to. He had the smarts to only play his advantage every so often, otherwise, he would have cleaned up far too quickly and far too obviously.

Instead, he took his time and slowly squeezed their money out of them. He wasn't so much a bluffer as a card cheat. One day, he'd be thrown out of the window, but tonight continued to be his lucky night.

Upwards went my binoculars so I was to the left of Christina's special place. One guy on his own in the living room, sitting at a desk facing a wall to the right. There were all sorts of bits of paper stuck to the wall and a typewriter on the desk.

The man had salt and pepper shortish hair and looked around his late forties or early fifties. His fingers jabbed at the keys in short, sharp bursts. Each paragraph hammered out of the ends of his fingertips.

I couldn't quite see what he was writing but there was a big pile of paper neatly forming several inches of written words, so it was something way longer than a letter to the *New York Times*.

He sat there and typed, fingers a-blur as the ideas left his head, and emerged on the paper. What was he writing about though? Maybe he recalled his adventures in Western Africa, where he'd gone to help his friend and lover discover her ancestry. Perhaps he'd come back from Saigon and captured his thoughts about this war that never seemed to end and Nixon promised to stop.

They'd gone up some river or other and found a tribe, almost unchanged since the slave ships last set sail and met a family that shared her original family name – before her slave name took over and created the lie at the foundation of her identity.

Or he's writing a recipe book and what he's really interested in is cookies and cakes. It's a baking book for people allergic to eggs. Or mustard. I had no fucking clue what he was writing and, no matter how much I twisted the zoom wheel, I could not see the letters that appeared on the paper. He was typing too fast for me to focus on that small space. The letters flew across the page and then the page would shift up one line and I'd need to reset my focus again. By the time I'd done that, the damn thing shifted up and I was back at the beginning again. Infuriating.

He stood up and walked into the kitchen to make himself a cup of coffee. Now was my chance. I stared at the sheet in the typewriter, all stationary and readable, and zoomed in closely, hoping to discover what it was:

*The real problem is*

And then he came back and started up again. God damn it!

SO I MOVED up to the last apartment surrounding the target one with Christina inside and found another guy on his own. Again, he was in his living room but that was where the similarity ended.

This guy was in his seventies and had a golfing putter in his hand. I couldn't see it because of the furniture, but I guessed there was a ball. He practiced his swing several times then he'd stop, walk along the length of the apartment, and bend down, presumably to collect the ball, and then walk back to the living room. And so on.

The repetitions were impressive and his concentration was focused, but I couldn't believe he spent so much time doing the one same thing, over and over again. Mindless. Dull. You had to hope he learned a lot about his putting.

I was hardly a regular player, but even I knew he wasn't following through enough, which would mean he missed the pin left or right – or fell short much of the time. He tried out different length putts and got the same result, one way or another, but I couldn't see him altering his stance or stroke or anything. Swing, hit, stroll, collect. And repeat and repeat…

SOMEHOW I FELL asleep in the middle of the night and I woke with a start around seven. Everything was still, everything was quiet. There was a hotel letter pushed under my door, notifying me that a complimentary newspaper was awaiting me the other side of the door.

I settled back into my chair and looked across to the apartment block. All the people I'd watched were there apart from the poker game which had given up the ghost. Even the writer was continuing to hammer away at his prose.

Then the curtains in the bedroom, where Christina Almaguer had slept, were pulled open by the man. I decided to call him Juan, for no obvious reason at all.

He stood there, bare-ass naked, and stretched, facing me, arms and legs making a starfish shape. His dick dangled between his legs. He went back and lay on the bed, facing away from me but towards Christina, still under the covers.

Then they kissed and cuddled and I aimed my camera and took a photo. Click, whir, snap as the shutter let in enough light onto the film to capture the moment forever.

Click, whir, snap again in case the first one didn't come out so good. She stroked his ass and kissed his belly, so he rolled over and lay on his back. Her kissing carried on until she was much lower than his stomach but much higher than his knees. Click, whir, snap. Click, whir, snap.

She stopped all that slobbering and sat astride him, moving upwards until her crotch approached his mouth. Click, whir, snap.

She let her head flop back so her spine arched, leaning her hands on the bed. She sure enjoyed his tongue. Click, whir, snap.

Christina pushed Juan's head away from her and sidled back down his body, rubbing herself against his torso along the way. For a second, she lifted herself up and positioned herself so his dick could get inside her. Click, whir, snap. Pelvic thrusts ensued and no doubt some deep breathing. I kept my finger on the shutter, capturing every movement of their two bodies. I must admit the scene intrigued me and turned me on. They humped away like two tanned beetles and I watched them, my spare hand down my pants, until the film roll was spent – like them.

Juan and Christina both lay on the bed doing nothing, but recovering from their sex and I did the same with a helpful squeeze of my own hand.

To be honest, I had more than enough of what I needed. The first shot with Juan outstretched and Christina's tits in the background was all I had required to get full payment from Lenny. The rest, you might say, was fun.

That was when I realized I needed to get out of this game. The tedium of the night was not something I especially wanted to experience again too often and the morning's photoshoot showed I was more interested in imagining myself fucking the client's wife than in getting the paid job done. That is the moment to hang up your hat and do something else instead. And that is what I did.

When I got back to town, I met up with Lenny and showed him one or two of the photos, explaining to him I had a bucket load more if he, or his lawyer, wanted or needed them. There were the usual tears, but nothing I wasn't used to. Once all that was over and he'd handed over my money, I went back to my office and served notice on the lease and never looked back – until the call came from the

Don, which got me chasing round the country to get to Dakila Valdez.

I played chess in Central Park with a guy I met there in the afternoons and I carried on hanging out in the cop bars just to enjoy their conversation and company. There'd be the odd fling with a woman I'd meet in a bar or whatever, but nothing lasted more than a few weeks or a couple of dates. That suited me fine because I had no interest in being tied down by the responsibility of having to keep a relationship going for years and having to put up with someone else's bullshit. I wanted to be myself and do my thing. No strings attached.

# HOUSTON 1965

# 24

SOMETIMES YOU DO good, of sorts. A few years earlier, Edgar and Irene Phelps got in touch with me because their son, Brad was missing.

When I heard this news on the phone, I sighed, because my gut feel was that he'd gone off whoring with his college friends and would be back when his money or his dick ran out.

The more they spoke, the more I listened; this had more to it than most missing person cases and I invited them to my office to discuss the matter in more detail. The other reason the case intrigued me was that I could see the number of days this would take me to get sorted and that spelled moolah with a capital M.

"When was the last time you saw Brad, then?" I enquired once everyone had settled down and I'd made coffee for all those who wanted it.

"Three or four weeks," said Mr. Phelps. These were classic New York upstate Democrat liberals, who believed all people should have a fair shake and Brad had caught that fever big time. Big enough to want to change the world. My New York office looked like something at that point; times got a lot tougher after Bobby Kennedy was assassinated, but not then.

"And why, now, do you think he's missing?"

"Well," explained Mrs. Phelps, "he always phones us collect once a week. But last weekend, he didn't. So we know something must have happened to him. He wouldn't miss our weekly call."

"And what was he doing?"

"He had gone south to help with the Negro situation." Too many or too few, I wondered.

"How was he doing that?"

"Brad went to Texas to help protect the rights of the Negros there. They are being attacked and no one is doing anything about it."

"Apart from Brad, that is."

"Yes, and his friends… and the League for Equal Rights for All."

"Haven't come across them before. How do they operate? Was Brad a member?"

"LERA provides legal advice and financial support for black families. Brad went to Houston to give free legal advice – he is in his third year at Harvard after all – and to help in any other way he could."

"Free legal advice doesn't make you missing, does it?"

"No," said Mr. Phelps, hesitating. "Over the last week or so, Brad has become more deeply involved. He wouldn't tell us all the details, but you are right, there was more to his activities than legal opinion to poor Negros."

We were all silent for a spell, knowing the chances were Brad was embroiled in something very dangerous. So dangerous violent men might have applied some force. The best I could hope for was that Brad was in hiding somewhere and that I had to follow his trail until I got him and dragged his sorry liberal ass back home. Worst case was a lot worse and none of us wanted to imagine what that looked like right now.

The next day I flew down to Houston, checked into my motel, and went to the local precinct house. Amazing to say, if someone is missing, ask a policeman and they often have the answer which can save a gumshoe a lot of leather.

The wonderful thing about this job is how small the world is. About half an hour after I left the precinct, I'd returned to my motel and a knock on the door erupted from the silence. Nothing hurried, but firm and insistent. I opened it and a face from my past appeared; I hadn't seen him for over fifteen years. More gray on top and many more wrinkles on the side, especially near the eyes. But there stood FBI Agent Phil McNamara.

"Hey, Jake."

"Well I never…"

"I hear you're looking for the Phelps boy."

"Sure am. What're you doing in the south? I thought you were an East Seaboard kinda guy."

"Left Baltimore over ten years ago. Been covering Texas since then. Better weather, bigger guns. Better pay."

"That helps. Come on in."

Phil sat in the room's easy chair and I sat on the bed.

"So, do you have any news about the boy?" I asked, hoping Phil had done all the work for me and I could have two days paid R 'n' R before returning home triumphant. But this was not the case.

"We've been monitoring LERA for four or five months now. They are well-intentioned, but we think they might be funded by the Communist Party, hence our initial interest.

"But recently they've moved on from offering free legal advice to the local Blacks to getting directly involved with fighting the local nativists."

I nodded and realized that Brad was in deep. Phil's euphemism for the Klan was a peculiar one, although the new breed of Klansman was miles away from the pro-Catholic bunch of white hoods from my great grandfather's day. The constant, though, was their tactics – intimidation of the poor and disenfranchised, looting, burning, lynching.

"So, do you have any track on young Brad?"

"Bradley? Not quite. LERA has been encouraging the younger, northern members to work in the ghettos to fulminate against despondency and to get the blacks to strike and make a nuisance of themselves. About a month now."

"And…?"

"After the first week, LERA members started disappearing, mainly at night when they were on their own. Surprise, surprise."

"Any leads?"

"Pick a white guy with a Confederate flag on his vehicle and that's your suspect list."

Silence. This was not looking good at all and I reckoned I'd be taking bad news back to Edgar and Irene.

"Still, if you hear anything, let me know."

"Sure will, Phil. And can you do the same for me?"

"Yeah, for old times' sake, sure."

We caught up more on what had been happening in our lives and, at the point when we got to reminisce about Norma O'Donald and trigger happy Duane, Phil stood up and called it quits – both of us knowing there was nothing more to be said after that.

Phil had pointed out most LERA activity was centered around Independence Heights, a ragtag of a suburb, trying to hide just west of the interstate, dripping with poverty and economic injustice.

Armed only with a black-and-white photo of Brad, I wandered my way around the neighborhood, hoping to bump into someone who would acknowledge recognition. My problem was reversed. Almost everyone I met admitted to having spoken to Brad in the last week or two and I was regaled with stories of how he was helping them make better lives for themselves.

My guess was all white guys looked the same to them because there was no way Brad could have helped all these people in only seven days. He had already vanished at this point and was unlikely to be dragging his heels all over town without a care in the world. A simple test of the veracity of the witness.

This also meant it would be harder to find any concrete news on Brad because everybody was lying.

What this did give me was a reasonable picture of the community that Brad was trying to help. With his East Coast liberal concern, Brad was right to be appalled at the fate of these people. Although I was never a civil rights campaigner, I still believed every sucker deserved an even break, so black or white they could pay me. Now as a white middle-aged man I'm even less interested in the plight of those less fortunate than myself, but I still think we are born equal saps and that is how it should remain.

I have helped the rich and powerful and I've helped people who can barely rub two coins together, but I've never thought one person was better than another because of the color of their skin. They are all part of my gravy train and that's the way it should be."

Anyhow, this community had spent decades living in the dirt, cleaning white folks' houses, shining their shoes, tidying their gardens. You get the picture. And there was a point in their lives, especially for the younger blacks, when they decided for themselves this was no longer good enough – that they should have higher career aspirations than eating shit all their lives. Quite right too.

And Brad and the band from LERA had turned up at just the perfect time to harness those thoughts into direct action. They were talking about marching on the state capital to demand change.

There was also talk, in more hushed tones, of a more personal direct action – of torching the houses of the whites who had raped their daughters or had attacked their churches. This aggressive group were outliers from the church community itself and were comprised of the young male population. What wasn't clear was whether Brad was working with them to attack the Klansmen or to encourage them to stay within the law. No one was that holy, but Brad always received a good write up.

With nothing concrete to hang my hat on, I made my way to the other side of the tracks to talk to some Klansmen. I wandered down the street, east, away from Independence Heights, and over the interstate. Like most residential areas right next to major transport, this was not the glamorous end of town, but it differed from the Heights in one particular way – not a single black face on the streets. It was as if God had thrown the population down like cards and split the red suits from the black.

I figured the best approach would be to go to the nearest bar with a Confederate flag visible and see what I could see. Not a great plan, but you must tread real careful when you are mixing with guys who'll string you up just for coughing.

A bottle of local beer in my hand, I sipped its cold contents. And waited, because it's not just in the Westerns that the piano stops playing when a stranger walks into the bar.

Sure enough, after a minute, two rednecks asked me what I was doing in these parts.

"Just having myself a drink before I get on my way."

"Well, why don't you get on your ways now, city boy?" Clearly Chuck, or whatever his name was, had noticed my northern accent and wasn't happy about it. No one likes a stranger in hick bars down south.

"Just having a cold one and looking for a guy."

"What're you looking for him for, you streak of pussy-curse blood?"

"He's gone missing and his parents are worried about him, a nice white boy in the depths of the Lone Star State."

"No white boy need be worried about being in my country," added Chuck's friend.

"Well, this one's gone and got himself missing and I'm trying to find him." I took a sip of my beer. "His name's Brad Phelps. Come across him?"

Now the chances of them saying yes stood at a million to one, and they didn't nod their heads and give me a set of directions to him. But they looked at each other shiftily, as though they knew more than they said. And that was enough for me.

"Why don't you drink your beer and get out of here, you with all your questions." Chuck's tone had grown darker and I made certain my free hand rested in my pants pocket, along with my gun.

"No problem. Just passing by," I said, low key, and I swigged the last dregs of booze from the bottle, turned, and walked out the bar. I could feel all eyes on me as I did this and I made sure I didn't turn my head to check that I was right. I got the sense some of the patrons would have used any excuse to deal with this inquisitive stranger.

As I walked away from the bar, I reminded myself how Phil had had to be coaxed into giving me information about my case, so I headed back to visit him and see if I could prise anything out of him.

He smiled when he saw me enter his makeshift office at the back of the precinct. You could tell he was not what you'd call welcomed by the local cops because his desk was parked right by the john.

# 25

HIS OFFICE CONSTITUTED a desk, two chairs, and a phone, about ten feet away from the john door. His back, at least, was toward the door and there was a partition between himself and the next desk, occupied by a cop not old enough to shave, let alone discharge a weapon in the line of duty.

"How goes it?"

"Just fine, thanks, Phil. Been enjoying the hospitality of the local communities."

"Made any new friends?"

"Well, let's say east of the tracks everyone was my friend, but not so west of the interstate. Nice people though. Good and patriotic, which isn't a bad thing in these dark days of Asian conflict."

"Yeah, you could say that, Jake."

"So, what have you heard about Brad then? They wouldn't have put you onto me if your investigations and my case didn't match closely."

Smile. "Brad was last seen eight days ago coming out of a redneck bar near the corner of Berry Road and Airline Drive."

"That's close to where I was this afternoon. Could have been the same place for all I know."

"Did you get to talkin'?"

"The patrons were more eager to see me leave than buy me a drink."

"You don't say."

"Well, they weren't happy I was there and then, when I mentioned Brad, they were less happy still."

"You don't say."

"Got any names of any suspects?"

"For the Phelps disappearance? Not specifically, no. But if you really want to know what's going on with the Klansmen, you can rub your nose in the business of Gordon Dickinson."

"Thanks."

"Don't thank me until you've come back safely. We reckon he's the local Grand Wizard, so watch your step with him otherwise we'll be digging your body out of the desert some time soon. And neither of us wants that, now, do we?"

"We sure as hell don't," I said as I winked at Phil and walked out to face the Grand Wizard of old Houston town.

I HEADED BACK to the bar, *The True American*. This time I headed straight to the bar and didn't bother asking for a drink because it was not what I wanted. Chuck and his pal were still there, I saw, which meant they'd been drinking for many, many hours, and were to be avoided at all costs.

Chuck nudged his neighbor, and they were about to stand up and give me hassle when I sauntered up to the bar and asked for Mr. Gordon Dickinson's whereabouts. The barman, who predictably was drying a glass with a cloth, nodded at me and stared directly into my eyes, all the while cleaning the glass.

Finally, the glass gleamed and he put the thing down on the bar, still staring.

"Who wants him?"

"I'm looking for a missing boy, Brad Phelps. Do you know where I can find Gordon Dickinson?"

"Yep, reckon I do.".

"So where is he?"

The barman pointed into a corner with his head and, in the shadows, sat a man wearing a Stetson and a white suit with an open-neck shirt.

I nodded back to the barman and sauntered over to Dickinson. He sat at a table with two others, both of whom stood up to prevent me from reaching him.

"Now then, let's be civil to our guest. Sit yourself down, boy."

"Thank you, sir," I responded and sat myself down opposite him.

"I hear you're seeking the nigger lover, Bradley Phelps."

"I'm looking for Brad, yes."

"You know he was helping the blacks, don't you?"

"So I hear, but I don't care about that. I'm just trying to help his parents, who are worried about him."

"Well, you should care. If we dilute our racial purity then we will be left with nothing but browns and that sure as hell ain't good."

"Some say he came to no good. Have you heard anything about that?"

"Me, sir? No, sir. I do not get involved in any kind of criminal activity, sir."

"I notice the bulge in your jacket, though. Are you packing?"

"Well, I may not perform criminal acts, but that doesn't stop others from trying to perpetrate criminal acts on my person."

I nodded.

"So you only have a gun to protect yourself?"

"Oh yes, sir. Protect myself from vermin criminal elements, sir. Anyone who wants to stop me from living my life the way I choose. Anyone who wants to stop the white race from propagating this fine land. Anyone who wants to stop the American way of life in its tracks. I'll use my gun on those cocksuckers any day of the week."

I nodded again because there's not much you can say to a man like that when all you want to know is if he's lynched a boy for helping some poor Negroes.

Dickinson carried on ruminating on the plight of the white man facing the rising tide of black blood and miscegenated progeny for several minutes, but he bored me and wasn't answering any of my questions.

His evasion counted as implicit proof that Dickinson, or more likely some of his men, had done away with Brad or held him somewhere. Something like that. My throat felt dry, so I wished Gordon a fond farewell and left *The True American* for the night.

At about three in the morning, I awoke from my sleep with a start due to an incredible crackling sound and bright light. I couldn't figure it out.

Then I looked out of my motel window and understood. There, dug into the ground, stood a ten-foot-high cross, made of two pieces of very solid timber. And it was on fire, flickering yellows and oranges bursting out of its arms and heading into the night sky.

By the time I had registered this event, it became obvious I was the last, as what seemed to be all the other guests were huddled on the road, nightclothes covered by coats. Most of them had the good sense to cover their mouths with either their hands or kerchiefs because the taste of soot is noxious.

# 26

I THREW ON my jacket, put on shoes and socks, and left my room. As the fire was on the outside and not inside the building, I felt no need to rush. There was no imminent danger and there would be a long day ahead.

To punctuate this belief, as soon as I joined the throng, staring at that cross, the cops turned up with lights flashing, quickly followed by Phil in his own car.

"What happened?"

"Dunno, Phil. When I woke up, this was the view from my window."

"Well, you came to Texas to see what you could see."

"Sure did."

"And now you've seen it."

"Sure have."

"Seen enough?"

"Not yet. I need to see Brad Phelps before I can go back."

"Who did you speak with this afternoon after our chat?"

"Gordon Dickinson."

"So do you think this is related to that meeting?"

"What do you think, Phil?"

"I don't believe in coincidences, for sure."

"The motel looks full. Could someone else be the target?"

"Of course, someone else could have interviewed the Grand Wizard and a few hours later, there's a burning cross in their front yard. Of course."

He looked at me like I was a fool and I searched inside myself and agreed. This was a message for me. The good news; they didn't want to kill me because I'd be dead by now if they did.

No, this message was too big to fit on a greetings card. I guessed they wanted me out of town. Trouble was I couldn't think of an easy way to do that without getting to Brad first.

And this was the problem. I had no better idea of his whereabouts now than I had when I first came to town. The sinking feeling in the pit of my stomach told me he was dead, but I knew I had to find the body or find the boy – I hadn't mentioned it, but I'd receive a double bonus from the Phelps to bring him back, dead or alive. An extra week's pay.

"You'll have to come in for questioning, okay, Jake?"

"Yeah. Anything to help, officer."

A fire crew had just about extinguished the flames and the motel residents were preparing to go back inside to catch some more shut-eye.

"Can it wait until the morning though? I could do with more sleep… and a change of clothes."

"Sure, Jake. Sure."

"Thanks."

"You know where to find me. Just make sure you come over in the morning. Twelve and no later."

"Right. No problems."

Despite myself, I had trouble getting back to sleep. Partly, this was just because my night had been interrupted, but the bigger part was because it had also started to get a bit too real for me. It's one thing to be talking to a local crime lord and nigger hater about shooting anyone who fails to meet his exacting Aryan standards. It's another to know they'd worked out where I was staying – in only a handful of hours – and were very serious about wanting me out of the way.

This was their polite notice for my departure; the next time would be more assertive and would involve a lot more pain, I guessed. But the fact they'd erect a cross and ignite it – just for a message – showed me I was on the right track which meant I was close to Brad and close to my money.

I CAUGHT TWO- or three-hours catnap but couldn't sleep afterward, so I got up, ate breakfast, and made my way over to Phil's luxurious police accommodation.

When he said he wanted to question me, I was okay about that. If the Klan had made me a target, the FBI was the organization I'd want batting for me. Only, Phil was not doing the questioning. Detective Wayne Dickinson was the man in charge of the interview.

"Where were you yesterday afternoon?"

"Why, officer, I was working a case. As Mr. McNamara would have told you, I am a private investigator. You have spoken to Phil McNamara of the FBI, right?"

"Don't get fresh with me, boy. And I'm the one asking the questions."

"Sure thing. And I've just answered. Working a case."

"What case was that?"

"You know that's privileged information."

"Who were you looking for?"

"That would again be privileged information if I was looking for somebody or not. You will need to get a judge to see just cause to get anything more out of me about my client's case. We both know that."

"Someone burned a cross outside your motel and you don't appear to want to help us catch who did it."

"As I told FBI Agent McNamara, I was inside asleep when the thing was combusted so you will need to find an actual eyewitness if you want to catch the perps. What's your name again?"

"Detective Dickinson, boy."

"Detective, it was the middle of the night and we were asleep. Maybe the town drunk saw something but it certainly wasn't me. The first I knew anything was when I woke to see the damn thing alight outside my window. You're not related to Gordon Dickinson, are you?"

"We're cousins. What's it to you?"

"Nothing, nothing."

"The trouble with you East Coast liberal types is you come down here expecting everything to be handed to you on a velvety cushion. But we don't like people snooping round our neighborhoods, especially when they refuse to help officers following criminal investigations. So crawl back under whatever shit-stickin' rock you came from in your fancy New York suit and tie."

That was the second time, someone from the Dickinson family had encouraged me to leave town in under twenty-four hours. I had received the message loud and clear, but I had to stay until I found Brad and my money.

I THOUGHT ABOUT moving rooms to a different motel but realized there was no point. If they'd found me once, they'd find me again.

Instead, I needed to heed their words but keep my end of the bargain with the Phelps family. So I went back to the *True American* as that was where Brad was last seen and the first place I'd felt anxious since I arrived in the state.

Armed with a pistol in my pants and a picture of Brad in my hand, I went round each shop and building near the bar, hoping someone might talk. Within five minutes I was being followed by two well-built dudes. They were young enough to be in the army but the chances were their last name was Dickinson and I'd put money down the local army recruitment office also contained someone with the same name. Nepotism is a wonderful thing.

The longer the guys were near me, the less anyone would even give me the time of day. And it wasn't like in a city where I could ditch them in the subway. This was a sleepy set of streets in a sleepy suburb where cruelty to your fellow man was the norm – at least if the man was black.

I walked down an alleyway that cut through two streets. There was no way I'd have let myself be followed into a dead end with the two goons on my tail; the usual mix of refuse trolleys, cardboard boxes for the winos to sleep in, and the odd rat or two. Nothing much to speak for this tract of land that ran from Berry Road to Wellford Street.

When I got to the other end, there was a welcoming committee. I swiftly looked back and saw only one of the goons behind me. Not good. Two men were standing, smoking. Others were chewing matchsticks. One had a cycle chain in his hand and was slowly moving his wrist back and forth to get the metal weapon to snake by his leg. It was not a mob exactly, but there was more than an ordinary number of men standing at the end of an alleyway for me to feel easy.

Then out of the huddle appeared a face I recognized – Gordon Dickinson, Grand Wizard of the Houston chapter of the Ku Klux Klan.

"Hey, boy. I see you're still snooping round our town."

"Yes, still here. Someone woke me up in the middle of the night, which plain annoyed me."

"Oh yes? That was mighty inconsiderate of them, wouldn't you say?"

"Sure would. Whoever organized for it to happen must be one prize motherfucker." The tension in the muscles in the upper arms of those surrounding Dickinson physically increased. I was just making a point. I figured if the Klan had taken Brad, the best way to find out was to do the one thing I had singularly failed to do. The obvious thing, really. Ask the guy in charge of the Klan if they'd done it.

"But that was last night and this is today," I added, changing my tone to a more airy aspect.

"All I need to know before I leave town is this. Where's Brad Phelps? Any ideas?"

Dickinson thought for a spell, classically rubbing his chin with his thumb.

"I see you've been looking in our alleyways. Did you turn up anything of interest, boy?"

"Not yet. Most of the people round here have been right unfriendly."

"Like I told you before, we don't like nigger lovers here."

"And as I said to you before, I don't care about that. I'll be gone when I find Brad. Until then, I'm staying put.

"I understand your concerns are not our concerns and that you are a hired hand, a paid worker who must earn his money to put bread on your family's table." I chose not to correct his misdiagnosis of my marital status.

"You should check those alleyways a little more carefully, boy." And with that, he walked away along with his whole entourage. I stood watching them leave until they had all vanished round the corner. Turning about face, I stared into the dark to see if a goon stood behind me, but he had left too.

Dickinson's words rattled in my head for a minute and I headed back down the alleyway. The man had given me a clear message. He wanted me gone, but he knew I'd stick around until I either found Brad or they had to kill me because I'd found other stuff instead.

When I reached the cardboard boxes, I saw a foot sticking out from under them. That was the bad news. The good news was that the rest of a body was attached to it. Despite the dried blood and dirt over the face, I could tell it was Brad.

The body was still warm. They'd had him all this time, alive. God knows what they'd thought they could achieve with him. Torture information out of him about LERA maybe. Who knows? Didn't matter because he was dead now.

I called Phil and the cops showed up to put Brad into a body bag. Their idea of a house-to-house search involved tipping a hat to Gordon Dickinson as he stood, leaning on the door jamb of the *True American*.

Back near the precinct, I wired the Phelps family with the only news I could give them, but I'm sure they expected no more. Deep down they knew their son was dead even before they hired a private investigator to find him.

I stayed in town until the postmortem and I helped the Phelps make arrangements to ship the body north. Then I popped round to Phil to say my goodbyes. There'd been no usable prints on any of Brad's belongings – he'd had his neck broken with a single twist – presumably unconscious at the time because he'd been beaten severely more than once.

The day after I left, a riot in Independence Heights broke out. The locals marched in solidarity with their fallen hero and matters got out of hand. I read about it in the New York Times, buried on page seventeen. One paragraph, three inches of news.

The next day I visited the Phelps to pick up my money and offer my condolences, but mainly to get my money.

# New York 1969

# 27

LOOKING DOWN THOSE airplane steps, with Simone's young curvaceous body at the bottom, I couldn't help feel that life had dragged me, trudging, to this point. Me holding someone else's bag, filled with papers I guessed, and she, waiting to receive it, unaware of the blood shed in its name.

Brad's face, beaten and dried red around his bulged-out eyes, flashed in my mind. And that then sparked another thought. He had been a missing person, but once I had to find a missing thing, an object.

Towards the end of the sixties, I was still based in New York and had lived there almost a decade. I was young, and the city was alive, but there was an underbelly of tension throughout Manhattan. Nowadays, everything has been Disneyfied, but back then Times Square was not the place to take your family sightseeing. Other entertainment was available for the fee-paying customer.

So it was that by '69 when the hippies were proclaiming free love on the other side of the country, I had me an office with my name etched on the glass front door and a secretary, Madeleine. She stayed with me until after the Christina Almaguer photoshoot when I left the game, for what I thought would be for good.

Dorothea Schroder was walked into my office by Maddy, looking like she was about to fall apart. To be honest, this was how most of my clients first appeared. They never visited when all was great.

There was always something they needed to get off their chest. This time, Dorothea had a significantly large enough chest, both literally and metaphorically, to have a lot to confide in me.

She had come over from Holland a year or so before to make a new life for herself with Uncle Sam. Like so many immigrants, the lure of the pavements filled with gold had morphed into something which just about glistered yellow but was ultimately very tarnished. Welcome to America.

Bottom line – Dorothea had a boyfriend. I settled back in my leather-bound seat and let the sob story wash over me. This would be a tale of heartbreak and sorrow and it was all I could do to not spend my whole time staring at that chest as it rose up and down as the sobs left her eyes and moved her torso in sympathy.

My best plan was to lean my elbows on the arms of my chair, rest the fingertips of one hand on the fingertips of the other and close my eyes like I was some kind of Bond villain. While it stopped my staring, this did nothing for my imagination and I dreamed about those breasts in slightly more detail than is appropriate for a man to think about his client.

SO DOROTHEA HAD a boyfriend called Alex Steinmann she'd met in a bar in the Village. Nothing wrong so far, I thought. They'd been seeing each other about six months and had a healthy, normal relationship. She might have been young, free, and a little single but Dorothea was still reticent to state out loud that she and Alex had sex together. That coyness sounded like it was her undoing.

Long story short, Alex had set up an Arriflex in the corner of his room, behind an air grille, and had filmed them as they fucked. Needless to say, not only had he failed to mention this to Dorothea, but he intended to edit and sell the footage unless she gave him a thousand dollars. Naturally, she didn't have that kind of dough because she came over here to make her fortune and she hadn't quite got there yet. One year is not enough time for a toots like Dorothea to make a fortune unless she wanted to sell her titties. And she wasn't that kind of girl, otherwise, she'd be suggesting they shoot more footage and do the job properly.

This meant she had a problem. Alex was no longer her boyfriend, but he had film negatives and a threat hanging over her and Dorothea wanted both to go away, which was why Maddy had brought her into my office. Unfortunately for me, the size of the sob story was a strong indicator I could not charge my top rate and I'd have to lowball my fee.

One reason for my success in the 60s was that I altered my rates so that even the poorer members of our community could hire me to snoop on their spouses. That way, I could get paid for doing something on occasions when my diary for rich people was empty. The other reason was that Maddy kept on top of chasing invoices and paying bills. I lost count of the number of times in Chicago I had to run from bailiffs or change my home address so's they couldn't catch up with me. Not my favorite time.

So I said goodbye to Dorothea's chest and led her breasts and the rest of her body to the door. She told me Alex was no longer living in his apartment; he'd flown the coop but she gave me directions to his nighttime haunt in the Village, where she was sure I'd find him.

The clock showed only four in the afternoon and there was no point going downtown until much later, so I did the next best thing. I hopped in a cab to Times Square.

As I said before, back then the place was a shit hole, populated by a fascinating mix of winos, druggies, and prostitutes. The porn industry was also thriving with a plethora of cinemas peddling XXX movies for their discerning clientele.

There were many movie theaters in the area, but they were owned by very few people, so I thought if I went to one or two of the flea pits, I'd be able to find out whether Alex had started to peddle his wares.

The cab driver was not happy with my destination, so I negotiated his stop on 46th and 8th and walked east to Times Square. On the opposite side of the square, on Seventh Avenue, was a large skin-show theater, which was as good a place to start as any.

The *Orion* had stood on Times Square ever since I'd lived in the city, but I had never been inside until then. The carpet was sticky underfoot, and I pretended to myself this was because they'd got the soap mix out of whack when the carpets were last cleaned. At best, spilled alcohol was to blame. For sure.

The girl at the box office was filing her nails, legs crossed, sat on a high stool behind the glass.

"Is the boss about?"

"You wanna buy a ticket?"

"No, I'd like to see your manager, if he's about," I spoke more insistently because she wasn't listening. She had cuticles to deal with.

"Dunno. I'm here to sell tickets, that's all. You wanna buy one, buddy, or what?"

I had three options: continue arguing with her until I lost the will to live – only minutes away – buy a ticket just to get past the dullest sentry in the world or barge through the door and hope she didn't have a phone to call the National Guard.

The easiest option was to hand over a buck to gain entry to the *Orion's* cinematic fare. I pushed open the door and found myself in a corridor with a small concession run by another girl – this time blonde – who had two shelves stocked with cigarettes, chocolate bars, and soda drinks.

"Hi there."

"What you want, Mac? We got Camels, we got Marlboro. We got 100 Grand, we got Scooter Pie. We got Coke."

"Do you know a guy called Alex Steinmann, peddles films?"

"Listen, Mac, I'm here to sell shit. What do you need?"

"No bother, no worries. Where could I go to speak to the manager, please?"

"Mac, I'm just not going to answer your questions. No need to call the manager on me."

"No, no, no. I came in here to talk to the guy. Nothing against you, for sure. Do you know where the dude is?" Betsy, or whatever her name was, relaxed. I offered her a cigarette which she took, and I lit it for her.

"Thanks, Mac."

"My pleasure. I'm Jake by the way."

"Thanks, Jake. Why d'you want to talk to Frank?"

"I'm trying to find a guy I reckon might have visited him."

"What's he look like?"

"Alex is five eight, a hundred and forty pounds, light brown hair, blue eyes. Young."

"Young for you or young for me?" Betsy smiled as she puckered up her lips and took another drag on her Camel. I thought for a second about what she'd said as I was only in my late thirties.

"Young for me. He's early twenties. Very early."

She sucked again on the filter tip of her cigarette and shook her head.

"Doesn't chime with any john I've seen round here."

"Shame, so do you think you could point me in Frank's direction?"

"Sure, Jake. You can find him that-away." Betsy pointed to a door near her concession stand, which had a sign stating *Staff Only*. I thanked her and put a couple of greenbacks in her tip cup. She was a cute kid and if she ever got out from this flea pit, she'd go far, but the chances were she'd live and die in the place. Shame.

I pushed the door through to another corridor with a series of office entrances along the left-hand side. I ambled over to the first office and, leaning on the door jamb, I popped my head round to see if Frank was there.

"Is Frank around?" I asked a middle-aged guy, who was counting a pile of notes.

"Forty-nine, fifty… What? No, not here. Try next door… Fifty-one…"

So I moved a few feet further on and tried again. This time there was a younger dude sitting behind a desk, reading a newspaper. There was filing all over the place. Looked like a real mess.

"You Frank?"

"Me Frank, you Jane?"

I smiled at the fact that the guy had a sense of humor and picked me up on my curtness.

"Yes, but most people call me Jake."

"Hi, Jake, what can I do for you apart from Johnny Weissmuller impersonations?"

"Glad you asked. I'm looking for a boy." And with that Frank's eyebrows raised, implying much more than I'd said. I smiled again though.

"We're not in that kind of business, Jake. This is strictly a movie house."

"And I'm not looking for that kind of boy either, Frank. This boy's peddling homemade movies… of the kind you'd show in this theater."

"Adult entertainment is a wonderful thing, Jake. Great product, great product."

"I'm sure. The boy's name is Alex Steinmann and he's going round trying to sell a little candid camera number. Ring a bell?"

Frank thought for a second, head pointing to the ceiling.

"Maybe it does, Jake. Maybe it does. Is there anything in it for me apart from helping a guy find another guy."

"I'm sure I can make a donation to your favorite charity." Now it was Frank's turn to smile and I took out my wallet and flashed some notes – and gave Alex's physical description.

"There was a dude came round yesterday offering some domestic product. Not really our market. We prefer higher production values. But he left his number in case I changed my mind. You want the number?"

"That'd be mighty upright of you."

Frank scrabbled through his piles of paper until he reached a spiral-bound notebook, flipped the pages, and tore one out.

"Have it. It's of no use to me. Get this, he tried to sell a sixteen-millimeter film to a professional theater. Asshole amateur."

I handed over two twenties and took the page with the scribbled down phone number.

"Thanks, Frank."

"No problemo, Jake," he said as he grabbed the Jacksons and pushed them into his pants pocket. I nodded and left the room, walked past Betsy, who still looked cute but, on a second look, was no older than fifteen or sixteen, and left the *Orion*.

Now I had a contact number but no location for the guy, so I went to a payphone and realized the last thing you should do in Times Square is go to a payphone. There was a crumpled-up excuse for a human being, with a needle sticking out of his arm, leaning on the post, and a strong stench of piss around him. I walked east a block until I found Sixth and then I found a phone booth more to my liking; devoid of drugged-out heroin fiends.

The phone number worked but after twenty rings I gave up because no one was answering then looked at my watch. It was still too early to hit the Village, but at least I now had two possible ways of getting to Alex, and the rest would take care of itself.

I swung back to my office and checked for any messages with Maddy and then tried the phone number again. Still zip. Eight is either too early or too late to do anything really useful, so I popped round the corner to my local diner, *Joe's Diner*, run by a guy called Joe, and grabbed a burger, fries, and a cup of java. That took me thirty minutes and still it was too early to go to the Village.

Out of a mix of absolute boredom and relative tedium, I went back to the office and caught up on my paperwork. Maddy would be pleased with me in the morning. Two yawningly dull hours later, I was ready to hit the Village and took a cab downtown.

The front of *The Greenwich Bar* looked like any other building in the row; the only thing that differentiated it from its neighbors was the large number of people stood inside, visible through its larger-than-average windows. The other difference, of course, was the sign saying *The Greenwich Bar*.

Opening the door, I realized this was one of those places where the hep-cats hung out, which meant I stood out like a nipple on a cold, dark night. I scanned the room for Alex and, sure enough, he was propping up the far left of the bar. He was sat on his own with a bottle of imported beer in front of him, his body facing the bar itself. Alex was chilling, hugging a drink, waiting for the world to happen around him.

I sashayed over and sat down beside him, as a patron had just stood up and vacated a stool. While waiting my turn, I ordered the same beer as Alex.

"Snap!" I said as I turned my head towards him and raised my bottle in his general direction.

He looked at me like I was a plate of cold sick, so I averted my gaze and carried on drinking in silence. This would be harder than

I'd thought and I'd been waiting hours for the game to even start. Damn the sonofabitch.

"Did ya hear about the Yankees?"

Steely silence still.

"Don't talk much, do ya?"

Alex half turned his head in my direction and shifted his eyes towards me, then reversed the action without changing his expression or uttering a single word. Nice job.

"Will you talk to me if I say that I'm here on behalf of Dorothea?"

A half-smile ripped across his lips and he turned to face me.

# 28

"FIGURED IT WAS that or you were hitting on me. Didn't mind either, just wanted to know which."

"Yeah, right. You're not my type – far too much dick for my taste. No offense, mind."

"None taken, buddy."

"Call me Jake."

"Whatever. So what have you got to say for yourself – on behalf of Dorothea?"

"She's asked me to help you and her iron things out between yous two."

"Fine. She gives me the money and we are free and clear."

"There are two problems. First, you shouldn't have filmed her and, second, she's not paying for the film. Instead, you will give me the negatives and any processed film, and then you will be free and clear."

"No dice, daddy o. That film is worth a damn sight more than a thousand and I'm doing her a favor."

"I think it only fair to let you know, at this point, I know some people who can ensure you eat hospital food for several months to come and they would be happy to visit you to make sure you comfortably remain sucking through a straw all that time."

"It'd be cheaper to pay me my money though, wouldn't it?"

Alex had a point. Anyone I hired to lean on him would end up costing me a grand at least – if they were any good, which they would need to be. There is a gulf of difference between leaning on someone to break a few bones and killing them by crushing their windpipe. And not all operatives can do the former with sufficient professionalism and not end up doing the latter by mistake.

"Let's split the difference. We'll pay you five hundred and I won't send you to Mount Sinai."

"One thousand spondulix and not a penny less."

Haggling in a bar when I had no money on me, well not that much, and he didn't have the materials on him seemed pointless so I took the conversation to the next stage – and dealt with the details of the negotiation once we both had some skin in the game.

"Look, we can talk about this for days, so let's just do a deal and move on in our lives. If I bring the money, will you bring the original negative and all prints you've made?"

"Sure thing, buddy. A deal's a deal with me."

"Good. It'll take Dorothea a few days to get the cash together. Where's your place so we can do the deal in private? I'm not taking a thousand dollars out my pocket in some dive bar in the Village, y'know?"

"Sure thing, let's keep this all pleasant, right?"

"Damn straight."

Alex gave me his address, schmuck, and we agreed I'd go over in three days' time at four in the afternoon. That way, he'd know he'd be awake. Must be a hard life being an extortionist and pornographer. I sank my beer and left, throwing a dollar tip onto the counter for the bartender.

THE NEXT DAY, I visited Dorothea to tell her I had a plan to get the film back without her having to lay out the dough. Although she was skeptical, she was calm and avoided the need to spend most of her time bawling her eyes out. This also gave me another chance to be near that chest of hers. On this occasion, I noticed she wasn't wearing a bra beneath her roll-top jumper – I detected the shape of a nipple or two through the material. I didn't think it was my imagination, anyway.

For two long days, I did nothing for the case because that is precisely what needed to be done. All that mattered was what happened when Alex and I met up again. My plan was simple and deliberate and I didn't need any practice before it began. The good thing was I could charge Dorothea for each day I was reading the newspaper and placing the odd bet on the horses. A guy has to earn a living somehow.

Then the moment came for me to leave the office and get to work. Alex lived on the lower east side, Avenue B to be precise, which back then was far from the throbbing metropolis. Not even the cockroaches lived there because even they had standards. But it created housing opportunities for the less choosy of New York's population. And Alex was definitely one of those. From what Dorothea told me, she made me think that the apartment where the dirty filming had occurred was a long way from here, but the truth was that it was on Avenue A, so by alphabet city's hierarchy, Alex was slumming it.

He buzzed me into his building and I made my way up the stairs, strewn with needles, and winos sheltering from the rain and the rest of the world.

On the third floor, I came upon his apartment. I knocked and waited. And waited. About thirty seconds later, there was Alex, stood in a tee shirt and pants with nothing on his feet.

"You got the money?"

"I'm here, aren't I? You lettin' me in or what?"

He shrugged and walked away from the door, leaving me to push it open fully and close it behind myself. As soon as I entered the room, the sweet smell of reefer engulfed me and I could taste the smoke it was so thick, even though there was nothing lit that I could see. Chances were Alex had taken so long to come to the door because he was finishing a spliff. No matter.

"SO WHERE'S THE money, man?" he enquired, with a directness I could have predicted, but which displayed his youth and impatience. An older man would have schmoozed a little before we got down to business.

A black cat slunk across the room and hopped onto a windowsill above a radiator. It owned this apartment and Alex was just the latest to rent it out. The cat licked itself and then settled down to sleep.

"You got any cameras set up here, Alex?"

"What? Hee hee. No, man, we're cool."

"Good. I wouldn't want to end up in no skin-flick like Dorothea," I said with a note of whimsy in my voice because I needed Alex to feel at ease with me. We hadn't got on too well the last time and I wanted today's conversation to be a lot more pleasant.

Alex gave another one of his empty half-smiles and I realized this was the most positive emotion he showed. His brain was dulled by the number of marijuana cigarettes he smoked. He flopped onto his couch, slumped almost horizontal with his legs apart.

"Okay. You got my money?"

"Well, do you have the negative and prints? Otherwise, there's no cash coming your way."

"Be cool. I've got it all in the apartment. Let's see the money and I'll get the stuff."

I placed my attaché case on the table in front of the couch and sat in a chair opposite, so the table stood between Alex and myself, pulled out a little key and unlocked the case, and flipped the lid open. I could see the brown envelope and the handgun, but Alex could only see the lid of the case.

With the envelope placed on the table, I thought now was the time to see the goods. Alex nodded and went to another room – the bedroom I assumed – and returned with a shoebox. He sat back on the couch and put it on the table near him.

I pushed the envelope over to Alex and he reciprocated with the shoebox. I took off the lid and saw a set of 16mm reel cans. While Alex just sat there, I opened the reels and held each up to the light to make sure I wasn't getting stiffed. Then I found the negative reel. This was much harder to check, but with a bit of imagination, you could tell all was kosher.

Alex took the envelope, ripped it open and looked inside, then scrunched up his face.

"What's this, man?"

He pulled out a handful of rectangular pieces of paper the size of dollar bills but made from cut-up magazines. I grabbed the gun from my still-open case and stood up, pointing the barrel directly at him.

"Alex. I offered you five hundred dollars for the materials but you refused. That offer has closed. The price has now reduced."

"Hey, man. Just spread some bread, you know. No need to get heavy."

"You created this shitty situation for yourself when you filmed Dorothea and tried to blackmail her, scumbag."

"Take the film. Jesus, man. Just take the film. I don't need this shit."

I picked up the shoebox and poured the contents into my case, while still aiming square at Alex, only diverting my gaze for the shortest amount of time possible to make sure the reels fell into the case and not onto the floor.

Sat in the chair again and still looking at Alex, I cast my hand down on the case to close the lid. Then I felt along the edge until I was able flip both locks shut. I didn't make the mistake of messing about with the miniature key, because that would be far too fiddly while training a gun on the guy.

Holding the handle, I stood up.

"Stay sat down and everything will be cool. Otherwise, a world of shit will descend on you. A world. Of. Shit."

Alex put his hands up in surrender. Didn't look like I was getting any trouble from the pothead. I shuffled back to the door, turned to leave, and put my hand on the door latch. Then I remembered the other part of my contract and let go of the door and strolled back to Alex.

"Dorothea asked me to do two things," I snarled.

"Get this filth back to her."

"You got that, man, you got that!"

"And to teach you a lesson."

"A lesson. What the hell does that mean, man?"

I raised an eyebrow and, still leaning over him, I wondered myself what exactly I meant, because until I'd got to the door, I'd clean forgot about the punishment. And, to be honest, I wasn't too sure how serious Dorothea was on this, because she had spent quite some time sobbing her eyes out about how much she still really liked him, even though he was a dirtbag. Then it dawned on me.

"Are you left or right handed?"

"Huh?"

"You heard me, don't mess me about."

"Right handed?"

I grabbed his right hand and slammed it palm down onto the table. Then I took the butt of my gun and smashed it onto his fingers. He just plain screamed and I hit him on the side of the head with the gun butt to shut him up – certainly didn't want any company showing up – and he slumped back in the chair, unconscious. I smashed down on his fingers again to make sure they were well and truly broken. Then I checked out the apartment to make sure there wasn't any trouble hiding in any of the other rooms. All clear.

Finally, I picked up the envelope and scooped up all the bits of paper and put them in my case then wiped my prints off the table and any other surface and, using my handkerchief, I left the apartment and closed the door behind me.

It was late, so I scooted home and snoozed until the morning, having cleaned Alex's blood from my gun.

The following day, I visited Dorothea to give her the good news and all the reels I'd taken from Alex. She thanked me and came in for a hug and I let her breasts rest against my chest for slightly longer than was appropriate between a private investigator and his client.

She paid me for the last three days' work and we said goodbye. Six months later, I was at a stag night and a projector was brought out and pointed at a white wall. The lights were taken down and the film kicked off.

It started with a long shot of a girl, fully clothed mind, walking into her bathroom, and slowly taking her clothes off. First her roll-neck top, then she pulled down her miniskirt. Next she took off her bra and panties and then she turned to camera and beckoned someone to join her.

I nearly dropped my beer because there was Dorothea's chest in all its full glory. I had had those nipples nestling against my chest only a few months before.

Nobody came to join her so she stepped into the bath by herself and lathered up the water and rubbed the soap all over her body. You could see that her hand was underwater between her legs for quite a while and her head was back like she was experiencing sheer delight. It was hard to see because of the distance from the camera to the bathroom, but what your eye couldn't see, your imagination took care of.

Then a jump cut and Dorothea was lying on a bed – must have been the other camera position that Alex had used. There was a guy humping her in a number of cuts. Each time they had different sheets, different clothes being taken off, so this was clearly the best showreel Alex had put together from his time with Dorothea. And, inter-cut with these mid-shots, were a series of close-ups of hardcore dick-and-pussy action, which were obviously not of the same bodies and distracted me from the reality of what I was watching.

We watched her being fucked from behind, we saw her jiggle up and down, riding her man like a bronco – that was my favorite bit because we got to see those breasts bounce up and down, over and over. Man, what a chest that girl had.

The final section got all kinky as Alex tied Dorothea to the bed with four scarves, two for her wrists and two for her ankles, and then proceeded to go down on her and come all over her torso. He undid her arms and she rubbed and wiped his spunk all over those tits of hers.

And nowadays, there's all these discussions about how women are exploited in porn, but man, the one thing I knew for certain was that Dorothea was up for everything that I was watching.

How Alex had hidden extra copies from me, I don't know, but that was the only time I ever saw that film on a stag night. I never saw Dorothea again, except in my dreams.

# SEATTLE 1975

# 29

WITH THE MYSTERIOUS contents of the bag in my hand and staring at Simone at the bottom of the stairs, as I prepared to walk down the steps, I remembered the only time we had met before when she was an adult. This was a meeting that, as far as her father was concerned, never happened. I mean it just did not occur, got it?

I was in Seattle on yet another missing person case – more of a runaway than an actual missing person. The kid – Darryl Pierson – had left a note before he flew to say he was off to Seattle because it was all not fair. Yadda, yadda. We've all heard it a thousand times before.

Good ol' Jake was dispatched to get the boy back, which meant I had a free flight and some paid time to find a boy who wanted to be found. Big whoop. And because he was a teenager, and it was the high days of disco, I figured the best place to go to find him was a club. So it was, I found myself holding a Polaroid and showing it to every bartender in every bar in town – or at least that's how it felt.

The kid was very early twenties, which meant he would have no problem hiding in clubs every night, hanging out with the cool kids of Seattle. Besides, he had no family in the area, so there must have been a pretty good reason for choosing this city and I guessed the pretty good reason was a pretty piece of ass. Darryl wouldn't have been the first guy to travel thousands of miles for a babe – and he wouldn't be the last.

His parents were unaware of this possibility. Their only thought had been that he wouldn't complete his degree and that he would tailspin into oblivion, eventually crashing and burning into some hippy commune in San Francisco. As soon as they voiced these concerns, I had my doubts. If you intend to not be found and want to start a fresh life somewhere, you tend not to leave breadcrumbs to your first port of call on your journey. Darryl just wanted attention and to have fun for a short while.

But his parents were willing to give me money to follow him and bring him home and I rarely argue with President Jackson, especially when he appears in an envelope with several of his friends.

So it was that I stood at the threshold of the *Swinging Cabriolet*, one of the hippest venues in Seattle, hoping to spot Darryl somewhere in the crowd. I'd hit five or six venues every night for a lifetime and was tired of being stared at by bunches of college kids with beers in their hands.

I made my way to the main dance floor, keeping a lookout for any male Caucasian who might have fitted Darryl's description and also, inevitably, keeping an eye on the female talent, bobbing up and down around me, wearing those tight-fitting hot pants that were all the rage then. They left nothing to the imagination, so I concentrated on Darryl while drooling at the sexy young dames.

The bartender there was no help either. They never were, but I got him to pass the photos round to the others behind the bar just in case. But *nada*.

I decided to make one sweep round the room because there were several booths to the back and the side of the dance space, where kids were hanging out and chatting.

Darryl was nowhere to be seen, but as I mentally traveled from one booth to the next, something – or rather someone – caught my eye.

THERE WAS A group of young girls, all dressed in quality schmatte, huddled at the last booth in the row. Two guys were leaning into the booth, trying to catch a fish, but they were having no luck at all. The double act had been a good plan for them, although they had not factored into consideration who they were hitting on. Sat at that table was none other than Simone Lambretti, the don's oldest daughter. The apple of his eye, the pride of his loins. You get the picture.

A whole pile of thoughts landed in my frontal lobe all at the same time. Before I'd recognized her, I thought how incredibly hot she looked, with her hair tied back and her breasts pointing out. Then I laughed at the boys – not men – hoping to score by pretending they wanted to buy the ladies a drink. Finally, my jaw dropped because I could not imagine the circumstances that would have allowed Simone to be this far away from the don unless he was dead or deranged. Neither of these states would lead to positive outcomes when I returned to New York City in a few days.

I sauntered up to the table and Simone, for some unknown reason, nodded an acknowledgment. I stood there until the boys walked away with nothing but unfulfilled longing in their hearts.

"Sit down," said Simone and I smiled and did exactly what she said.

"Thank you, Simone. I'm sure you don't remember me. We haven't met for many years."

"Oh, I'm sure you are right, but I can tell a man who knows my father. They all look at me the same way. The way you just did."

"Oh?"

"Yeah. Want a drink?"

A waiter had arrived at Simone's side almost as soon as she looked for one. The girl warranted top quality service. I sat down, as I had been stood there all this time, and ordered a vodka martini, straight up with a twist.

"So, what's a nice girl like you doing in a place like this?" I asked, in a mock tone. Simone laughed out loud, knocking her head back to accentuate the extent to which she'd found me funny.

"You are funny," she said, holding a pause between each word, her Brooklyn drawl inescapable even with the music pounding in my ears. The dimples near the corners of her mouth reminded me of the last time I'd seen her in the flesh, in her father's library holding her dress up to show me her stomach. Now, without lifting anything up, she had a lot more flesh on show and I can confirm that her four-year-old's outward belly button had become an inward belly button in the intervening fifteen years. And those curves, my oh my, she sure had grown into a complete woman.

"Thanks," I replied, "but seriously, I'm surprised to see you so far from home with no one with you."

To be heard, I'd leaned forward and put my lips almost touching her ear. Of course, I pulled back as soon as I'd finished speaking; she might have been an extraordinarily beautiful young woman, but she was the don's extraordinarily beautiful daughter and I knew to keep a respectful distance.

Simone leaned forward, draping an arm around my neck to draw me in so she could reply.

"You're not as stupid as you look."

"I'll take that as a compliment. Call me Jake."

"Sure thing, Jacko. Can you keep a secret?"

"Sure can. And it's Jake."

"Heard you the first time, Jacko."

I shrugged, knowing I had lost the battle over my name.

"I've run away from home."

"Really? Run away."

She held a finger up to her lips in a tipsy way and said "Sh" and giggled. I took the bait.

"Why have you run away?"

"Just to get away from my old man. Jeez, you have no idea what it's like to be the great Don Michael's daughter."

"No, I don't. Tough?"

"You betcha," she slurred and carried on. "Officially, I'm visiting family friends out here, but I slipped my leash a coupla days ago. I'm surprised my father hasn't called in the hounds yet."

"I'm sure he has, It's only a matter of time before his people find you. Sorry, but it's true."

"Don't sweat it, Jacko. I know. I'm just enjoying my only shot at freedom and figure if I stay in the clubs, those goons will find it harder to find me."

"You're probably right. I'm a PI and have done work for your father. But don't worry, I'm on a different job altogether, looking for a boy who's gone missing in this town. I'm also trawling through clubs trying to find him like those goons will soon be finding you."

"Are you going to tell my father you've seen me?"

"Nah, you carry on with your vacation."

Simone placed her spare hand on my cheek and a perfectly formed light kiss on the other cheek.

"Thanks, Jake."

"We're cool, Simone."

"Sure are, Jacko. Have another drink."

"Thanks, but no thanks. I'd love to stay and chat, but I've got work to do, like I said, and the boys will flutter around you once I leave. I appear to have scared them off."

Simone giggled and removed her arm from my neck. I took her hand and kissed the back of it. She blushed to only a light red and waved me goodbye. I dropped a business card on the table and wrote my hotel and room number on it, in case she needed a real friend in this town. Then I stood up.

As I walked away across the dance floor, I glanced back and saw I'd been right, the boys were circling again. A wry smile ripped across my mouth and I left the thumping sounds of the club behind me and headed back to my hotel.

WHEN I GOT to my room, I sat on my bed and threw my shoes onto the floor. I intended to flop back and have a rest before I clambered into bed, but instead, I closed my eyes and let sleep envelop me until the morning.

I awoke around six feeling cold and crumpled and stumbled around the room, trying to remove my clothes from the day before while simultaneously putting on today's threads. After tripping over myself twice, I decided the best thing was to remove everything I had on and start from scratch. Wise choice.

Having splashed water on my face to wake myself up in lieu of a shower, I wandered downstairs for breakfast, as I needed to eat. I'd freshen up afterward, for sure.

Toast, coffee, and half a grapefruit later, I returned to my room and kept the pledge to myself to shower, shave, and brush those teeth. At reception, I'd grabbed a paper, so I sat down in my room's easy chair to catch up on the world before I went out and resumed my search for Darryl.

I had just turned page three and was gazing at page four's headlines when the phone rang. I dropped the paper on the floor and walked to the bedside table.

"Hello."

"Is that Jacko?"

I smiled.

"Sure is, Simone. How's it going?"

"I need your help."

"Why? What's happened? Are you in trouble?"

"Stay cool, man. It's not me, it's a friend."

"A friend?"

"Yes, a friend. And it's not what you think."

"What do I think, Simone?"

"That the friend is me but I'm too embarrassed to admit it."

"No, that's not what I was thinking. I reckoned this friend was some dude who's got himself in trouble and you think I'm going to spend my day keeping him out of jail."

"Way off, Jacko. Way off."

"I met Sally in one of the bars here and that was cool. She's all the things I'm not. Blonde, pretty, but not very street smart, you dig?" I let the self-delusion about her beauty go as now was not the time.

"It's nice that you made a friend so quick, but where's the help needed?"

"She's vanished."

"Missing, you mean? Do me a favor. How d'you know she's just not hooked up with some guy or stayed in last night instead of meeting with you?"

"Simple. The last couple of times we've met, she's brought along this Arab guy and he's seemed pretty cool, but last night Sammy, another friend I've met here, said she saw Sally being dragged into a taxi by Badri. And we've tried calling her, and Sammy even visited her folks, but she's not there. She's vanished."

"How do you know they aren't holed up at this Badri's place, making whoopee?"

"Because Sally's not that kind of girl. She told us she wouldn't spread her legs for the first guy she met and we believed her. Also, every club we went to with Sally and Badri, he'd always work the club and try to sell drugs. Sammy and I pretended not to notice, but he was quite shady, you know?"

"I know. And you watched him sell drugs but took none yourselves, right?"

"Jacko, you're not my father, so play nice."

"Okay. I'll see what I can do."

Simone gave me her contact details and we hung up. I figured Badri and Sally were shacked up somewhere. Simple. A girl's allowed to change her mind if the guy is hunky enough, I reckoned. But, to play it safe, I left chasing the enigmatic Darryl for a day to find a different kid in town.

By the evening, I'd figured out where an Arab guy and porcelain white girl were holed up. Seattle wasn't the most multicultural city in the country and I knocked on a door in the quaintly named Arab Quarter around the time dusk was settling itself in for a long night ahead.

The door opened and I found myself in a reception area with rugs on the walls and thick piled rugs on the floors. The swirly patterns made me assume the proprietor had bought a job lot by accident and had decorated the place to get them all out of his warehouse.

In the space of about five seconds, I realized Simone was right to be concerned about Sally. I'd thought this another of those private sex clubs springing up all around the city, but I was wrong.

I was greeted by an old Chinese woman, who grabbed me by the arm and led me into the next room. There was a wide dude with no neck stood at the entrance and he, literally, stepped aside to let us through. No one would get past him without his express permission.

Then the old crone shuffled me along until she stopped and pulled down on my arm and forced me onto the ground. I figured that a bunch of underage girls was about to be paraded in front of me so's I could pick one to fuck. But, again, I was wrong.

The woman prepped a long pipe and passed it over. What the hell, I thought, and took a drag of the warm smoke. Two deep tokes later and I was lying on the ground, my head turning somersaults in my cranium as a million warm thoughts dribbled around my brain. I was in an opium den and Sally was in here too.

Truth was, at that point, I didn't care about Sally or Badri or anything. I wanted another hit off that pipe.

# 30

WHEN I CRAWLED out the following day sometime, as I reached the reception, I noticed a corridor leading off away from the opium room and in the distance, I thought I saw a blonde girl with broadly the same face as the one in the photo in my pocket. Sally was here and I'd have to get her out somehow.

The chances were the men holding her were keeping her subdued with the opium, which was freely available in the rest of the building. However, that was the good news, because they were unlikely to be holding her for fun and to get her hooked on the pipe.

Young, white blondes kidnapped by Africans were more prone to leave the country via the backdoor and end up married to some Moroccan merchant before you could whistle dixie. And that was the best she could hope for. More likely, is that her ass would be sold to the highest bidder at some flesh auction in Marrakesh. I'd read about this trade in a Sunday supplement last year in the New York Times but this was the first time I had come across it for real.

The problem I was facing now was to figure out how I could get close to her when most of the johns were chasing the dragon rather than chasing pussy. This would be much harder than I'd first thought. An overbearing boyfriend was one thing, a gang collecting underage hookers was another story entirely and that was what Simone had lined up for me.

I needed to get back in there and to figure out some way to grab Sally safely. There was no point in holding the cold dead body of the don's daughter's friend in my arms.

A plan hatched in my mind, but I'd need dough – and more than I carried on a normal missing person case. I could go to my bank and see if they'd give me a loan, but I was far from home and even if I'd been next door, I knew the answer would be nada. So I did the next best thing; I put a call through to Simone and met up with her for lunch.

TO KEEP THINGS simple, we used a restaurant round the corner from Simone's apartment. She was staying in a serviced condo and had the smarts to pay cash so no one could trace her whereabouts. The don's brains had been passed through the genes, for sure.

The place was swankier than I was used to, but that was fine because I knew Simone would pick up the check. She needed to keep me sweet to keep her father off her back and to get Sally's safe return. The price of a decent meal was the least she would owe me and the most I would get.

So I made sure we took a lingering three courses and a decent slug of red vino. Simone was eager to get to business, but I was more determined to guarantee three courses in this square meal. I zigzagged around the conversation until I had ordered cheesecake and coffee.

"You were right," I admitted, "Badri is far from all that he appears."

"What… what does that mean?"

"He's taken Sally to a place in the Arab Quarter."

"Well, let's go there and get her out. What are we waiting for?"

"It's more complicated than that. He didn't take her back to his house."

"No?" She hesitated, knowing bad news was around the corner – it showed in the corners of her eyes.

"No. It's a house of various kinds of ill repute."

"Huh?"

I was hoping not to have to say out loud what was going on, that a vague idea would keep Simone happy. But the Lambrettis were smarter than that.

"It's a whorehouse and opium den. And possibly worse. I haven't had a chance to find out."

"What could be worse?"

"Well, white girls can get sold to rich Arabs and Sally might be one of them. I don't know yet."

"Sally?"

"Yes," I said firmly and looked square into Simone's eyes so she knew I was being straight with her and also to suggest this level of information was probably the most she wanted to know.

I got silence from Simone and I knew my gaze had worked.

"So, the next step is for me to go back and extricate Sally. I will need cash – quite a bit of cash – so's I can appear to be a high roller and that will hopefully get me to the inner reaches of the place."

"How much do you need?"

I gave her the figure and she nodded and walked over to the payphone. When she came back, she told me she'd sorted out the money to be delivered in about an hour, so we returned to her apartment to wait the sixty minutes for the cash to appear.

The apartment itself redefined the meaning of swanky. White leather chairs and tiger skin rugs on the floor of the living room and the centerpiece was a dramatic fireplace.

Simone coiled herself on one of the rugs next to the fire and patted a space next to her to encourage me to sit beside her. She'd already thrown off her shoes and was sitting there with her skirt shifted up past her knees so she could sit as though she was riding side-saddle. Her olive skin was visible around her neck and I needed to remind myself that she was the daughter of the don and that she and I were not the same generation and if I made a move, it would be plain wrong. But she sure looked hot on that tiger rug.

I sat next to her to keep her happy, but I made sure there was sufficient distance between us so that my loins wouldn't take over my brains. It'd happened in the past and would no doubt happen again. Just not with this babe, I reminded myself again.

We talked the hour away – about Simone's friends on the West Coast and what she'd been up to since she ran away from home. But we were both careful not to mention Don Michael because that would break the spell. That would remind Simone of the outside world and the impending normality of living within the confines of Don Michael's world.

Eventually, the cash arrived, and the courier drove away. I took the money from Simone and headed back to the Arab Quarter.

A rat-a-tat on the door got it opened faster this time, now I was known by the minder. Again, I sat in the waiting room, but before I could say or do anything about Sally, the old woman scurried across the floor, grabbed me by the elbow, hustled me into the next-door room, thrust me onto the floor, and put lit a pipe into my hand. I could do nothing but inhale deeply and let the smoke envelop me and I did this with all the love in the world for the opium in the pipe. The warm smoke filled my lungs and the opiate populated my head with thoughts.

WITH NO IDEA how long I had been unconscious, once I realized I had been totally out of it, I checked in my pants pocket; I still had Simone's cash. Would have been terrible to have been stiffed while in an opium den. The don would not have been happy.

After a refreshing cup of green tea, I got myself fully upright and returned to the anteroom. I stood there for a second with the minder already holding the handle of the door to let me out and, for a second, I forgot what I was there for. Then a rush of memory slapped me in the face and I knew I needed to get down that other corridor and reach Sally.

"Do you have anything else here to entertain a man then?" I asked the doorman because the old woman had scurried back into whatever dark hole she'd come from.

He nodded in the affirmative but chose not to offer me any additional information.

"Who should I speak to about that?"

He pointed his head towards the corridor and, in an almost whisper said, "Go down there, my friend, and someone will look after you."

I thanked him and gingerly walked down the passageway until I came to the first door on the right, which was wide open, and contained a middle-aged woman sitting by a desk and a string of girls sat in near silence, semi-naked, on chairs and a sofa by the far wall. I quickly checked each of them out to see if I recognized Sally, but no joy. All titties and bare belly buttons. No Sally.

The madam listened carefully as I explained how I was looking for a particular kind of girl. And I described Sally in all but name. The woman nodded and told me she understood how some of her patrons were more particular in their needs than others. She suggested I sat down with the girls and she'd see if they had anything special I'd be interested in.

So there I was, still recovering from the excesses of the pipe, with several semi-naked girls stroking, touching, and generally meandering their hands all over my body. And I mean all over; there was no part of me left untouched by their desire to get me to splash cash in their direction.

I popped five-spots in the G-strings of the girls who had actually groped me and left the rest of them alone. If any were over sixteen, I'd have been amazed. With some of them, you could see the track marks lining their arms and those whose track marks weren't visible were probably mainlining in between their toes or somewhere worse.

The madam returned and beckoned me over to the door. We walked further down the corridor, away from the main entrance until we reached the third doorway on the right. She opened the door just wide enough for me to walk in and closed it behind me.

The room was dark: just a single bulb on a bedside light, so I took a minute to adjust my eyes to the darkness. First of all, there was a blonde girl on the bed and then, as I became used to the light, I could see more details. Next, I realized her arms and legs were naked and the only reason I could sense darkness in her middle was that she was covering her groin with a black silk cushion. She was lying on her side, but you could see her body was riven with tension.

As my eyes moved from the cushion up past her pointy young breasts towards her face, I could see this was Sally, friend of Simone, and a woman totally out of her depth.

"Time for us to take you home. Simone sent me," I explained because I knew there would be little time between this brief greeting and our need to get the hell out of there.

Sally didn't move; didn't say a thing.

"Are your clothes in here? Do you have any clothes to put on?"

She shook her head, not wanting to believe her time in this place might soon be over. I grabbed a blanket lying on the floor near the bed. It was the best I could do on short notice with nothing to work with.

"Sit up and let me help you."

She did as I instructed almost immediately. I bent down to wrap her in the blanket and I saw the needle marks in her arms and the circular burns caused by tips of cigarettes. She'd been in the wars this one.

"Stand up," I whispered, so she'd know not to stomp about and that we'd be exiting this room shortly. I held her hand firmly and took us both to the door. I leaned in to hear what was happening on the other side of the wood, but I couldn't discern a single thing.

Gingerly, I opened the door; slowly, slowly until I was certain there was no one immediately near us. Still squeezing Sally's hand, I bolted out of the room, dragging the girl in my wake.

Somehow, as soon as we were in the corridor with nowhere to hide, an Arab guy appeared at the end where I had come from.

"Badri!" screamed Sally and that was all she needed to say. We scrambled away from him down the corridor and tore left at the end. There were two closed doors, both identical. I had no idea which to go for.

"Which one's the way out?"

Sally pushed the left one and we piled down a fire escape. There were voices behind us and it didn't take an Einstein to figure they'd worked out where we were going.

Sure enough, round the corner came two heavies with Badri only a couple of paces behind them. The dude sure could run.

Badri's henchmen blocked our progress down the alley we found ourselves in, but I had a secret up my sleeve. I always kept a small lady's gun in a hidden holster, so I drew it and pointed the dainty thing at the heavies in my way.

"Might look like a pea shooter, but the bullets'll rip through you all the same," I warned. One of the no-necks turned to Badri to see what to do.

"What are you waiting for? Kill him, just don't harm the merchandise."

Hearing the news, I squeezed two shots out at each of them. A pair at their hearts; much better to aim at the torso rather than the head. Much easier kill.

As the two bodies toppled over onto one another, Badri leaped forward to grab Sally and reached her other arm. He yanked her towards him and as I held my ground, he revealed that in his hand was a small plastic bottle. He squeezed it and a rippling arc of clear, acrid liquid shot out of the bottle and onto Sally's face.

She screamed and fell to the floor. Acid.

I aimed at Badri's head and plugged him first in the eye and then, as he took his turn to scream, into his groin. I put my arm under Sally and we scurried away from the scene of destruction, down the alley, and along a side street. Then we bundled into a taxi and headed straight for the ER. Once I knew Sally was being looked after, I called Simone to tell her where we were.

When she arrived at the hospital, Simone gave me a peck on the cheek.

"Thanks, Jacko. You're a decent man."

Sally's face was all bandaged up, but the doctor had told us the damage was not too bad under the circumstances. Several skin grafts and she might not be as good as new, but she'd get along fine for the rest of her life.

I left them to be alone. Besides, I'd done all that Simone had asked of me and there was nothing more to be said.

I walked down the road, sauntering along with my hands in my pants pocket. My right hand came upon the roll of money I'd got from Simone. My original plan had been to buy her off Badri, but that wouldn't have worked. I clenched the cash in my pocket and realized this had been quite a profitable day.

Twenty-four hours later, I got a call from Darryl's parents. The weaselly little kid had appeared at their doorstep that morning. The hunt was over, but I made certain they agreed to pay me until my return to New York.

I spent the rest of the day in a different opium den before I flew back to receive my payment. Sure loved that warm smoke.

# SAN FRANCISCO 1979

31

THE MOMENT I received the final installment for Daryl, I forgot his existence, but I can't say the same for the image that echoed round my head of Simone, bending over Sally's acid-scarred face in that hospital room. Simone's skirt was tight on her body and I could sense the roundness of her butt cheeks. Took me weeks to get that out of my mind. The next time I saw her was getting out of that airplane and walking down the steps.

But, if you remember, last time I mentioned all of this, Colonel Mumford and I were beating the crap out of Dakila Valdez at the Wisconsin State Fair and heading off to San Francisco with a key in our hands on a wing and a prayer.

We landed at San Francisco International by around ten in the morning and grabbed our baggage off the conveyor belt. The key had remained in my pocket the entire journey. So far it had cost one man his teeth and an eye socket – and I didn't want to be added to that list.

We followed signs around the building until we realized we needed to get to Terminal 2 instead. The transit bus took us over there while we kept a watch out for imagined people following us. If I had been on my own, I reckon my head would have twisted off my neck. As it was, Mumford covered half the panorama for me, but the truth was we were alone in the sea of passengers. The only guys who could have followed us were on the plane we took and there was no one from that flight anywhere near us.

We got to the left luggage lockers and only then did I take the key out of the safe haven of my right pocket. We walked along the rows until we found the right one and I pushed the metal into the hole and, once I'd found that it fit just right, I twisted the key until the door popped open and I heard the mechanism reset itself, waiting for another quarter to drop into the coin slot.

I pulled the small door wide and Mumford and I peered inside at what we figured was so important contained within the depths of that space. Then we looked at each other quizzically and looked back into the locker. I grabbed the contents and shoved them into my jacket pockets; a newspaper – the *Boston Globe* from March 27, 1976 – into my inside right pocket and a white envelope which I popped into the inside left to balance things out.

We both checked up and down the locker aisle to ensure there was no one trying to crowd us out and then we headed straight to the taxi rank to go somewhere private to study the contents because there was no way on God's green earth that Don Michael was paying us to hunt down a copy of an East Coast paper he could have read in the New York Public Library.

A Vacation Villa seemed the best option as there was one near the airport – surprise, surprise – and there was bound to be a room for hire at zero notice. We took two adjacent rooms, just like in the good old days, and after three minutes in the room, there was a knock on the door and the best of the British Secret Service appeared.

I let Mumford in and he sat down on the easy chair and I sat on the edge of the bed. We peered at the occasional table where I had put the paper and the envelope placed one next to the other.

"Well open it, goddamn it," said Mumford after a spell.

"Yeah, yeah, I was just getting to it."

I turned the envelope over twice, trying to get a handle on its weight, what might be in it, and how to open it up without ripping the contents too.

It felt like a sheet or two of paper but almost all the gum had been licked and stuck down. I held the thing up to the light to see how much the paper occupied the envelope. There was a clear inch on one side after I'd tapped it down one edge to shift the paper contents to that same end. So I tore the envelope along one of the shorter edges until I could reach in and pull out the sheet. Just the one sheet, folded in half.

I opened the paper, placed it next to the newspaper on top of the envelope and we both stared at its contents for several seconds.

"What the hell does that mean?" I asked after about half a minute of utter bemused silence.

"Beats the hell out of me," was Mumford's honest reply. In front of us was a page filled with about fifteen letter and number pairs, neatly spaced out.

"One hell of a code," I intoned.

"You don't say?" sneered Mumford and I gave him a look that would kill.

We turned our heads back to the page and carried on staring, hoping that some sense would materialize through the act of looking. But no joy.

I shrugged and picked up the newspaper. The fact it was in the locker meant it had some kind of significance and I hoped we could use it to crack the code.

The Globe felt pristine, like no one had ever opened it before, but then there was a knock on the door. Mumford looked at me, looking at him. We both placed our hands on our firearms and I padded to the door, hoping not to make a sound with my footsteps. Looking through the eyeglass, I saw a stretched-out face through the fish-eye lens. Despite the distortion, it had a familiarity I was not expecting.

"Be cool," I intoned to Mumford and I undid the chain and opened the door to let Phil McNamara, FBI Agent, into the room. We shook hands and I made the introductions. When I looked down, I saw the page was missing from the table: Mumford had hidden it just as I had put the newspaper back into my jacket pocket. Before you think my jacket was gigantic, there were only a few of the outer pages of the Globe actually in the newspaper, so it wasn't that hard to do.

"How d'you trace me to this hotel, Phil? I paid cash."

"You did but I've had your name on alert as soon as I thought you might head into town. We've been following you ever since you landed."

"I'm glad the FBI is so concerned over my whereabouts."

"Not really, I was kidding with you. It was the locker we had under surveillance, so once you guys had cracked it open, we realized we had a live one."

The three of us were silent for fifteen seconds as those words sank in. The FBI already knew about the locker and were waiting to catch whoever opened it. Once Phil recognized me, he'd come over for a visit rather than send in the goon squad. Kind of him. But that still meant the FBI knew about the locker.

"And what was your interest in the locker, anyway?" asked Mumford, who had just reached the same conclusion.

McNamara looked at Mumford and then eyed me and back to Mumford.

"We were interested in the contents – and also whoever picked it up."

"Do you know what was inside?"

"No. We left everything alone to sit and wait to catch a fish."

"And here we both are, Phil."

"Yes, here you both are, Jake… and where are the contents by the way?"

"Safe," said Mumford, who didn't trust this Hoover man enough to disclose any information unless he had to. British Secret Service versus US federal government. Good luck with that.

I took a chance because I might not trust the FBI, but I trusted Phil; a shared past goes a long way in this life.

"There was a code and an old newspaper. We only just got to look at them when you came a-knockin'."

Mumford was not happy with my big reveal, but I ignored the cold stare bearing down on me from his direction. He knew to trust me too and I knew I had to wait for him to remember that and he'd be okay.

Mumford nodded and pointed out we'd be much better off figuring out the code if we went to the local FBI office so we could use their resources, instead of sitting in a hotel room by San Francisco International.

The local office was in the middle of an industrial estate in the exact middle of nowhere. Good news was it was an unassuming building, completely anonymous. Bad news was it was a bleak building in the middle of absolutely nowhere.

Anyway, real-estate considerations to one side for a minute, we huddled round McNamara's desk with the code page and the newspaper staring back at us. We were as defeated as when we'd been in the hotel room, only now we had free coffee on tap. McNamara took a copy of the page and faxed it over to the cipher department back in Washington. He said he'd let the eggheads take a look. They'd do no worse than us.

At one point, I tried flipping through the pages of the Globe hoping to see the connection between the code letters and numbers and the newspaper, but nothing spoke to me.

The rest of the day was spent staring at those pieces of paper and writing all sorts of rubbish down as we tried to decode the indecipherable.

By five, we'd all had enough and called it quits. McNamara took us to a local bar for a bite to eat and, maybe, the odd slug of beer. We shot the breeze for an hour or two over a burger although Mumford ordered a steak because he said he didn't want to eat a sandwich for his dinner.

We agreed we knew no more about the code than we had that morning and not one of us had any real idea why we were chasing the package. Don Michael was the connecting factor, but he'd not explained why he wanted it nor what we were chasing – other than some kind of parcel.

Three beers later and we were all set for sleep, so off we went.

Next morning we met up back at the FBI building, but as soon as we arrived in the reception space, I knew something was amiss. The hustle and bustle had an air of tension. Not only were there a lot of suits walking around, but they kept their eyes down on the floor. No one acknowledged anyone else's existence, like they didn't know each other or didn't care about keeping connected to their fellow workers. Even in a place like the FBI, you work your network to succeed. So something was up.

WHEN MCNAMARA CAME out of the back to bring us in, he looked like someone had died. I mean *really* died, no joke.

"Follow me, there've been some, ahem, developments."

Mumford and I looked at each other and followed him. He took us into the same meeting room as before and we sat down. There were still people walking up and down the corridor outside, traveling at full pace. Something had surely happened.

"Spill," I said to McNamara as soon as we were in our chairs. He sighed.

"This is it. There was a break-in last night."

"You gotta be kiddin'," I replied under my breath. McNamara faltered for a second and carried on.

"The whole place is a mess but one thing I know is they took the code. No idea about anything else; this is the only case I'm working on. But my colleagues said other paperwork has been taken too."

"So you have no idea who are the perpetrators?"

"No, Colonel. Not right now."

"The only people we can rule out are the three of us and our respective agencies," I proffered.

"That leaves a lot of others. Could be a foreign power..." Mumford then trailed off into his thoughts, trying to work out which country could be interested in the don's code.

I knew Mumford's first thought would be to blame the Soviets. From memory, he always blamed the Soviets and with some cause. Back then, the Cold War was still raging and we blamed the Ruskies for just about everything that went wrong in our country. Easier than blaming the people running the damn country.

Besides, in this instance the Russians might not be such a bad place to start, I thought. If the FBI, British Secret Service, and the Mafia were interested in the package, why wouldn't the Russians want to take a peek inside the envelope too? But then I thought some more and reckoned if it was the Russians, they'd have done more than steal a code for Don Michael's parcel. They'd have had overnight access to a bunch of FBI files far juicier than whatever it was Don Michael had us chasing our tails all over the country for.

Conclusion – not the Soviets and, therefore, not likely to be any other country either. Despite what McNamara said as the day wore on there was less evidence that anything else had been stolen, just a lot of mess. The precise nature of the steal meant we were dealing with an enemy of the don's and I had no desire to be messing with anyone like that. Uncle Sam paid McNamara a mighty fine wage to fight the good fight against the nation's enemies. I was on a daily retainer and chump change.

# 32

AS THE HOURS progressed, the one thing we could be certain of became painfully apparent; whoever took the papers might decode the cipher and then they'd be able to get to the package before us. And that would be as far from good as we could go and still be breathing. Trouble was, once the don heard what had happened, the chances were we wouldn't be breathing much after that.

Mumford pointed out that the burglary of an FBI office had an eerie echo of the Watergate break-in, but neither McNamara nor I took that idea seriously. Mumford looked unimpressed with our response but we ignored his suggestion anyway.

Now that the dust had settled, the truth was before us: an FBI report from Washington. In all the confusion over the robbery, we had ignored a simple but important fact – McNamara had faxed over the papers to Washington to get their cipher unit working on decoding the damn thing. And that is precisely what they had done.

The game of cat-and-mouse was over for the minute. By taking pages and paragraphs from the code, you could figure out which words and letters were part of the deciphered message. The bottom line is that, if we'd had more time and better concentration, we might have figured it out. The others might have anyway, especially Mumford because he was a spy. That was his day job, I thought.

Anyway, the Washington Bureau report boiled down to a lot of blah and one key phrase. We had an address in Houston, which

# The Case

McNamara checked out using one of the many FBI computer systems at his disposal. The place was a house owned by a Mrs. Constance Glenn. Before we headed to the airport, we grabbed our things from the Vacation Villa and Phil contacted the local Texan cops for background info and to alert them to keep an eye out for any suspicious movements. And, no, they shouldn't move in and do anything. Just monitor and keep him informed.

Back to the International Airport for us and a flight to Houston.

"Bet we find another code to decipher," said Mumford when we were standing in line waiting to buy a ticket from the United sales desk.

"Doubt it," I responded. "It's more likely to be something different, surely. Otherwise, what's the point."

Mumford nodded and we both realized he was just trying to think of something to say.

"But I'll take fifty dollars from you if you like," I added because I liked him and didn't want him to feel out of sorts. Mumford smiled and we shook on it.

No surprises here, but the flight was uneventful. The most interesting news was that I didn't spill my coffee and Mumford didn't spill his English breakfast tea. Phil didn't order a drink at all.

WE TOOK A little over four hours to reach William P. Hobby Airport, south of the city itself. By the time we left the terminal, it was nearly five, so we hopped into a taxi and made our way to Mrs. Glenn's house on South Wayside Drive between Allison Road and Stonhom Street.

This was an unassuming place with a few steps up to its front door. The street itself was less than a mile from the airport so there was a patina of diesel fumes covering everything. The steps, the walls, the sidewalk. Everything. You could almost taste it in the air. As the taxi drove away, we were left standing in front of the building, curtains shut on the first floor and upstairs too. Bit strange.

Phil tried to peer into the front window in between the cracks in the curtains, but all he could see was the inky darkness within.

"I'll try the back," said Mumford and vanished round the side of the house. I was left standing by the front door doing nothing. No harm, no foul.

I put my ear to the door to see if anyone was inside, but I could only hear bupkis. As I leaned further into the soot-drenched wooden door, I realized there was movement in it. I pulled it towards me and, hey presto, it was open. I called McNamara and he went to get Mumford. They both reported nothing untoward in the backyard.

We opened the door and looked both ways down the street. There was no one in sight. We pulled out our guns and went inside.

The hallway was dark, but not so dark we couldn't make out two rooms coming off it, along with a set of stairs heading upwards. I gestured I'd take the stairs, Phil went straight ahead into the kitchen which left Mumford to check out the living room.

Sneaking up the stairs, my biggest concern was which steps would creak loud enough for Glenn to hear me coming. Or anyone else. But for some lucky reason, no step gave me away. There was a small landing to receive me when I reached the second floor and three doors, all open. Two led to bedrooms and the third led to the head.

A cursory run-through showed the lights weren't on and there was, quite literally, nobody home. But every room had been turned upside down. Total chaos. Every drawer pulled out and upended. Every wardrobe door had been opened and the contents strewn on the floor. Both mattresses were leaning against the walls. The level of thoroughness showed professionals had been at work here.

I sauntered downstairs and went into the kitchen. Phil had already walked through it into the living room and I followed through myself to find the same chaos with Phil and Mumford standing, guns holstered, looking around and staring at the sea of paper, cutlery, crockery, and anything else which had been thrown out of the way during the search.

The one thing missing, even though there was a huge amount of tidying up to do, was Mrs. Constance Glenn. We would have noticed her even if she had been under a mattress.

The light was failing and either our predecessors had got what they wanted or they had failed and had given up. Either way, we had no clue where to go next or where Connie Glenn could be found. So we went back to the airport to sample the delights of another Vacation Villa.

This one was worn out and tired, real tired. The wallpaper was peeling off the walls like the glue had decided it had had enough and just wanted to get the hell out of Dodge. And who could blame it?

THERE WERE BRIGHT orange and red lights festooned around the hotel bar and we propped up the counter to stop it running away. I bought the first round using the fifty I took off Mumford. A bet's a bet.

The only other person at the bar that night was a hooker with more wrinkles on her neck than on an elephant's scrotum. She was fifty if she was a day and had a tattoo of a rose etched into her cleavage, but it wasn't even and looked like it was heading away from her heart because of some long-forgotten argument.

We gave her a Jackson just to leave the bar which she took a little too quickly and with no attempt to haggle. Was probably her best night of the week. And she stank of sperm and body odor. The fishnet tights and shortened leather skirt finished her look. I was glad when the skank left us alone and walked out the bar.

We sank two beers and downed some bar snacks but based on the front of the house, no one was brave enough to try anything concocted behind the scenes in the kitchen. Pretzels, peanuts, and olives were all we could bring ourselves to eat in this fine establishment.

Talk crossed many directions and all the roads led back to Mrs. Constance Glenn and her ransacked home.

"Sure was a professional job," I pointed out and the other two nodded in agreement. "But who was it? Who would have the balls to rob the FBI?"

"There are plenty of countries who'd be happy to rip the US of A a new asshole," commented McNamara and, although this was true, there wasn't a likely candidate.

Mumford noted, "The Russians would have done more than take a few pieces of paper… unless they photographed it all instead…" and as he trailed off stuck in his thoughts, McNamara's eyebrows rose as he said, "If they were only photographing records then why steal any at all? Why not just quietly take photos of everything they wanted? Whoever did it wanted us to know they'd done it."

"Because they don't give a shit who knows it," I added. "And who doesn't care what the FBI thinks?"

This question hovered in the air for a few seconds until Mumford gave the answer we were all thinking.

"The CIA of course."

That uncomfortable idea lay sticking to the bar counter for the rest of the evening until we called it quits and went back to our rooms to get some shut-eye before we regrouped to find Glenn and the missing package in the morning.

# 33

THE NEXT DAY, we went back to the airport itself for breakfast because we couldn't face eating in that dive. Then we hightailed it back to Glenn's house to see what, if anything, we had missed. We knew we had to tread carefully because we could have been under surveillance ourselves.

The plan was to go through room by room, all three of us. Nothing was to be left untouched. Everything would be checked. Phil called his office and got them to deliver packing crates so we could tidy as we went to give us a chance of reviewing anything later on without having to hear the deafening sounds of planes flying over our heads every minute.

We started in the kitchen. Every pot, every pan, every knife carefully examined and put away. Then we started on the furniture. We took the cupboard doors off their hinges and then took the cupboards off the walls in case something was hidden behind them. Nada.

The bedrooms would be the hardest to deal with because of the sheer volume of crap, so we went to the living room instead.

Again, we filled boxes with the paper strewn on the floor and we packed away the plates and ornaments from the sideboard. Then it was time to gather up the shreds of cushions that had been liberally slashed to investigate their innards. But still there was nothing.

Then it was our turn to upend the sofa and rip it to pieces. We cut through the frame just so's we could check there was nothing hidden between the stitched-in cushions and the base. Although we had no idea what we were looking for, we also knew a professional team had been through the place. If they hadn't found anything, we would have to work very hard to get it ourselves. We also knew they might already be heading into the wide blue yonder with whatever Glenn had been storing. But at that point, we had no idea which way the wind had blown.

Phil, Mumford, and I were left standing in an empty room, save for the sideboard and a drinks cabinet. The TV's chassis lay on its side near the front window, but that was all that was left. Mumford shrugged at Phil and they both attacked the drinks cabinet structure. First the door, then the frame, until there was nothing left but a pile of wooden pieces in a box.

Meanwhile, I stood there thinking and looking; something felt wrong. Not just that we were destroying someone's possessions. I got over that after about five minutes. There was something wrong with the room.

THE KITCHEN WAS a normal kitchen. I mean, there were kitchen things in it and you could imagine someone cooking and eating in it. But the living room was wrong.

Standing there while the others hacked apart a perfectly ordinary piece of furniture gave me the time to reflect on how the room felt strange. Then it hit me. The carpet. Each bedroom had one piece of carpet, along with the landing upstairs and the hallway next door. But there were two pieces in this room. Both sections were the same color but one was ever so slightly darker than the other. The smaller section near the sideboard was darker, like a newer piece would be.

Just then I knew. We had been looking in the wrong place. We needed to go below our feet. I ran over to the darker carpet right by the wall and dug my fingers into the gap between the carpet and the wall. And pulled. The carpet came up in my hand to reveal the floorboards beneath.

Phil and Mumford had come over and were looking over my shoulder. As I carried on pulling at the carpet, a rectangle cut out of the boards was exposed, which had been replaced by a metal lid. There was a cut-out rectangle of carpet pad on top of the lid.

I picked up the carpet pad, threw it to the other side of the room, and grabbed the tin out of its hiding hole. I flipped the lid open and inside was an attaché case. The case was locked tight. We agreed the best thing was to keep it locked because whatever was inside was so important that people had been killed for it. Glenn at least.

The black case was heavy and we decided the best way to deal with the situation was for me to drive the damn thing all the way back to New York. The main reason was that whoever had bumped off Glenn and failed to find the case would check out all the airports in the city. This way we could limbo below the line and get the package over to Don Michael while making the least fuss.

I hired a Chevy from a car rental at the airport and placed the case on the front passenger seat. We all shook hands, and I hopped in the car and headed out of the airport complex to get on the I-45 as soon as possible and head north as fast as the speed limit would allow.

I turned the corner and almost smashed straight into two parked cars across the street amid a hail of bullets.

# LOS ANGELES 1951

■ ■ ■ ■ ■ ■ ■

# 34

A WARM WELCOME and a hail of bullets. That was the furthest thing from my mind when I moved to LA several years before I turned my back on the West Coast after my army days.

I'd headed for the sea and figured Santa Monica was as good a place to hang out as any, but the sharp reality of my decision sent me to New York in the end; about as far from LA as I could be but still work on American soil.

As ever, I set myself up in a serviced office with a secretary to keep me in check and advertised in the local papers. Amid ambulance chasing and hanging out near the divorce courts, now and again, I would be thrown a more interesting crumb of work from my adverts in the free press.

I received a cold call off my advert asking whether I'd be prepared to spend a weekend in a hotel room with a friend who needed looking after. The deal was simple. I stay with the guy all the time and, in return, I get double my normal rate. What's not to like, right?

As a professional private eye, I suggested that we meet up to discuss details – and I also wanted half the money up front in case the proposition turned out to be a scam.

"You can come to our offices later today, if you like."

"Sure thing. When and where?" I was given the directions and, half an hour later, I headed off to their building on the corner of

Alpine Street and North Hill Place, not quite in Chinatown. The voice hadn't sounded Asian but sometimes you can't be sure.

"Our friend needs taking care of, you understand."

"Sure thing," I said not really caring about the guy nor understanding.

"And you must meet him on his boat, of course."

"Boat?" I asked as the hairs at the back of my neck stood on end. Suddenly this didn't sound the meal ticket I was hoping for.

"Yes, his boat. Mr.... er... Mr. Larsen needs taking care of."

"So you said. Is there anything in particular I need to know?"

"You don't need to know anything. You just need to make sure he stays out of harm's way in the hotel we will choose for you. Keep him in the room, keep him happy, and hand him over to us after you spend the weekend with him. That's all."

I nodded and smiled, not entirely liking the idea but thinking of the smell of that money. I forgot to mention that the guy I had met had blond hair, blond eyebrows, piercing blue eyes, and a pointed nose. The meeting room we were in could have been rented by the hour, but at least the guy had greenbacks.

The upshot was that the day after I handed back Larsen, I'd come back here to get the other half of my payment. As I had enough cash on me to keep me going for a long couple of weeks, all this seemed perfectly fine. Apart from the boat that is.

WHY WAS I so concerned about the aquatic nature of the start of this job? Simple. I hate boats. I don't like the way they bob and weave in the water. I dislike their movement.

There I was, stood in a small boat moored next to Island White, a feeble lump of rock in San Pedro Bay, just east of Long Beach Bay. I clung to the side like there was no tomorrow as Larsen, wearing a life vest, was manhandled from another small boat. Although it was pitch black – there were clouds in the sky making it hard to see by starlight – I got the sense it was Latinos handing him over. I paid no real attention, as I was only trying to get a bearing on what I was letting myself in for.

Larsen had a waterproof jacket covering his head to help keep him dry, so I got little chance to see what he looked like until our tiny dinghy got back to dry land.

We were whisked into a chauffeured Ford and I got my first opportunity to get a look at him.

Larsen was in his late forties, maybe early fifties, and had blue eyes, as piercing as Kurtz in whose office I had spent a few minutes just the other day.

I watched Larsen stare out of the window as we drove through town and out to the suburbs of San Pedro. There was a sadness in his eyes. I assumed he was happy to be in LA, but I had no reason to assume that.

The hotel itself was a flea pit, but we were assured the concierge had been paid well by Kurtz, so if there was anything we needed – for *we* read Larsen – then I placed a call and it would be found for us.

Our room was on the third floor, out of the elevator, turn left and round the corner, keep walking to the far end and ours was on the right, number 313.

When the bellboy opened the door, I knew we were in for a joyous time as there was only a double bed visible. He showed us round the suite until I gave him a five-spot to leave the room. And when I call it a suite, I'm merely repeating the phrase the boy used. There was the bed and a large space with two easy chairs and a couple of wardrobes. That was it. I'd assumed we'd be in separate rooms, but I was so wrong.

The first thing I did after the boy had pocketed my money was to split the double bed back into two singles with at least two feet between them. If I would be sleeping in the same room as Larsen, I saw no reason why we needed to be in the same bed as well.

Larsen took his small bag and hung up his scant clothing onto hangers in the cupboard. A couple of pairs of pants, the odd shirt, and a spare jacket. All light materials; some looked like linen.

Meantime, I sat in one of the chairs and watched him, trying to gauge what this guy was about. Larsen had a deep tan – he had spent time in the sun – and I mean a lot of time and a lot of sun judging by his blue eyes and blond hair. This was a man with solid

European ancestry, not Mediterranean but northern European. Not the kind, to be sure, of people who'd be into tanning.

So that showed me he had spent many years in sunny climes. Given he'd arrived in the City of Angels by boat, I guessed he'd come straight from South America somewhere.

Larsen finished putting his things away and sat on his bed, legs crossed. I smiled at him.

"My name's Jack Adkins, but you can call me Jake."

He nodded but said nothing.

"I know your last name is Larsen. May I ask what's your first name? What should I call you?" He smiled and nodded, but said not a word.

I smiled back at Larsen and tapped my fingers on the armrest rhythmically. Larsen just sat there and stared at me.

"You don't say much, do you?" I asked after a minute or two.

He shook his head and smiled, so at least I knew he could understand me, even if the guy was taciturn.

"Okay, buddy. If that's how you want to play it, but we will be spending several days together in this room and time will go pretty slowly."

"Don't call me buddy," were the only words that shot out of his mouth. And they came with a thick European accent, which I couldn't quite place because I had only four words to work with.

"That's okay. What would you prefer I call you, Mr. Larsen?"

"Mr. Larsen will do fine."

"Bit formal wouldn't you say?"

"It'll help remind you that you are my servant and not my friend, Jake. I only let my friends speak to me – how you say? – informally."

"Okay, Mr. Larsen, no worries."

Lovely that he saw me as his servant. Obviously, my billing hadn't been explained the same way to him as it had been to me.

"Is there anything I can get for you right now?"

"No, nothing. I'd like some peace and quiet and *Die Zeit* in the morning."

"What suit?"

"Huh? No, *Die Zeit*. It's a newspaper."

"Oh, my mistake. Say it for me again." And Larsen did so I could get the name in my head long enough to call down to the concierge to get it organized.

Then I watched him lie down on his bed with his hands behind his head and stare at the ceiling. I gave him the silence he had requested. For an hour.

DURING THIS TIME, I got to think about Larsen. There he was, lying on the bed, a middle-aged man with a receding hairline, black-to-gray in color, and a dark tan. His hands looked like they had never been used before. The nails were cut short and well-manicured. He had not seen a hard day's work in his life. Whatever he was up to before he landed in the US was not manual labor.

As for his clothes, he had a cream linen three-piece suit, which made him look crumpled. Like he'd been thrown on the bed in a messy pile, but I guessed that linen was precisely the right material to have in a suit if he'd been spending his time in an Amazonian jungle. Or whatever.

The more I considered his name, the more I realized it couldn't be real. I worked out Larsen was a Scandinavian name. I couldn't say if it came from Sweden or Denmark, but I knew it was Scandinavian. And Larsen had asked for a German-language newspaper. What Swede would read a German paper when they had been living in South America for many years? Made no sense.

Or rather, it made no sense if I believed he was from Scandinavia. However, if I thought he was German then his choice of paper made sense and his name was plain nonsense.

He was a German who had spent many years in South America. Now you don't have to be a tremendous student of history to know it had only been six years since the end of the war and many of the old German soldiers had fled to Bolivia, Argentina, and Peru before the Nuremberg trials began. And when I say soldiers I mean the high command and members of the elite SS.

So Larsen – or whatever his name – was most likely a Nazi. A goddamn Nazi. I was being paid to nursemaid a fucking Nazi. My dad must have rolled over in his grave.

He'd joined up when Pearl Harbor was attacked and spent three tours in Europe. Dad was a Marine, a Red Beret, and he was one hell of a fighter. He didn't talk much about his time in the army, but the way his eyes glazed over, you could tell it was tough out there.

I was named after my old man, but I refused to be called Jack Jr. Even from an early age, I wanted to be my own man.

He was in one of the early landing vehicles during Operation Barbarossa and then fought his way through the soft belly of Europe and into France, then into Germany. We received a letter from him when they first entered German soil and were on the final push to Berlin.

# 35

JACK SOUNDED UPBEAT and earnest, as he always was. My mother told me he had always been a serious man, which was one of the things that attracted her to him. She'd had a string of fellas who'd been flighty, to say the least, from the odd story she'd shared about her younger years.

There was one more letter that arrived from him after they reached Berlin. After that furor, his unit powered through into Poland and was one of the first to get into the camps, just ahead of the Russians. It was hard for us to tell if they were more concerned with liberating the people in the camps or merely wanted to beat the Russians at something. My old partner, Ed told me he didn't believe anyone cared about the Jews, it was only ever about the power struggle between the Russians and the Americans.

I don't know either way, but I do know the last letter was posted the day after he'd been inside Belsen. It was a dark, moody letter, in which he decried the whole of humanity and all the evil that human beings were capable of.

The next day, he stepped on a land mine and his body was splintered into a million pieces. We got a letter from Uncle Sam in the fullness of time telling us how sorry he was that a land mine had killed Jack Adkins Sr. Uncle Sam wasn't as sorry as I was though, despite the kind words in the letter.

In case it's not obvious, I figured that the land mine had been placed there by the Germans and I blamed them entirely for his death. And here was Larsen, a German who was secretly entering the country a few years after the war having spent the intervening time in Bolivia or wherever.

The only believable conclusion was that the guy was a Nazi. And that didn't sit well with me. Not at all. Not the way Jack died. I could feel myself tense my back molars, not grind them, but the pressure on them massively intensified due to my jaw muscles. This German Larsen was no friend of mine and I was stuck in the room with him for at least two days. Two long days.

And then I thought about the implications of Larsen's arrival in the US. Why was he here and why now? My employer was not a government department. You can tell government men by the way they walk and the shoes they wear – and their hair length.

That meant Kurtz was from the private sector. And what would a company want with an old Nazi with not much personality? Made no sense.

Perhaps he was one of those charismatic dudes, who only lit up a room when he switched on but kept himself to himself at all other times. Maybe he was here to give a speech to the company, and they didn't want to make a big song and dance over his arrival.

Or, more likely, because of his past, Larsen couldn't get a visa to enter the country in the first place.

Alternatively, maybe Kurtz was just his benefactor, and the guy needed to come to the US for medical attention. That he only wanted to lie down and do nothing showed a certain lethargy in his character. Or he was just bored being in the same room as me. Both options were possible.

If he was ill, what was I going to do if he took a turn for the worse? I mean, it's not like we could take him to the nearest ER because he wasn't really in the country, if you see what I mean.

I could call down to the concierge, but there was little he could do, I guessed. Truth was, there would be some quack Kurtz had lined up, ready and waiting, in case something occurred. But at that point, I had no idea what the deal was.

"Tell me, Larsen, what are you doing here?"

Larsen opened an eye and stared at me then shook his head and closed the eyelid again.

"Look, we will be together for the next couple of days, the least you can do is talk to me a while."

Larsen snorted but said not a word.

"Jeez," I said under my breath.

"Leave your messiah out of it, boy."

I raised an eyebrow at that unexpected interjection.

"I do not need to hear your prayers to your god, thank you very much," he added. Well, at least I'd got him to talk to me.

"Excuse me, sir."

"Indeed."

"I'm just tired of the stone-cold treatment."

"Understand, boy. I have spent much time on my own and I tend not to play nicely in the playground anymore."

"*Da nada*," and we were silent for a spell. This period of unspoken time didn't feel like it was forced on me but was a mutual respect for each other's thoughts. After a few minutes, I killed the silence dead. "I'm sorry if my American ways annoyed you. We're quite chatty is all."

"It does not annoy. I just find them tiresome."

"Thanks for your honesty," I replied, trying not to lace my response with the sarcasm it deserved.

"You can rest assured that I am always honest. I do not waste my time with lies. They exist so that weak men can be guided by the strong in the absence of self-evident facts."

Now that was a phrase that tripped off his tongue with consummate ease. That was part of a much longer speech, which he'd given before or was planning on giving fairly soon. He sure was the friendlier type of Nazi. Despite myself, I warmed to his frankness.

In a business where you spend all your time second-guessing what everyone is saying to you, Larsen's straight-talking was refreshing. I might have only been in the business a couple of years but I'd had it up to my neck with the bullshit people come up with to hide what they're doing or hide what they really think. So an honest Nazi appealed to me in that room on that day in Los Angeles.

"I assume that Larsen is not your actual name then."

Larsen smiled and nodded.

"Is there a false first name I could use instead of a false last name?"

"Call me Herman. Many people do even though it's not my name." Now it was my turn to smile.

"Okay, Herman. I shall do so." I was doing my best to keep our conversation factual and to the point. Herman didn't like small talk as it rubbed him up the wrong way. Who could blame him?

He settled back onto his bed, closed his eyes again, and covered them with one of his arms as if to fend off the light of the day.

I let the silence hang in the air again because there wasn't much that I wanted to ask him, which I thought he might answer. 'Are you, or have you ever been, a member of the Nazi Party?' appeared on the visa waiver program form in the 80s, but it's not something you should ask someone you think actually was a member of the Nazi Party between 1933 and '45.

"Tell me," said Herman breaking the silence in the room.

"What?"

"You are being paid to sit with me, correct?"

"Yes, Herman. That's what I'm being paid to do."

"And do you know why you are doing this, beyond the money of course?"

"No, Herman. I do not. I have some ideas, but I have not been told what you are doing in this country."

"It is best if that situation remains. Best for you and for me, that is."

"Shame, I'm intrigued to find out, Herman."

"I am sure you are, Jake, but this will not happen."

"Figured. Never mind."

"The money will have to be sufficient for you."

"I reckon it will have to be, Herman. It'll have to be."

Herman smiled at me and sat up.

"Is there a drink I could have?"

"Sure thing. What'd you like? A coffee, a soda, or some liquor?"

"Oh, a coffee was all I was thinking of."

# 36

I GOT UP from my chair and went to a coffee machine, placed in the room by the hotel staff. There were ground beans, mugs, and in the fridge minibar was some milk. Five minutes later and there were two strong cups of java being sipped by the pair of us.

"So tell me, Jake."

"Yes?"

"What if I doubled your bounty, would you help me leave this hotel and go off for an hour or two?"

"That's a mighty fine proposition, Herman. Mighty fine." My mind raced, weighing up the risks and the rewards; double the very high existing fee and take the consequences from Kurtz.

"Herman. No disrespect to you at all, but I think I will have to say no. I've already made a commitment to Mr. Kurtz and I don't believe I should go back on my word." The truth was I was afraid of what Kurtz might do if I failed him.

"Jake, I respect a man who believes in keeping his word. If you don't hold onto your word, you have nothing. You are no better than pond scum. Absolute scum."

Herman stared at me with those piercing blue eyes. If he had been testing me then I had passed, but he continued to unnerve me, nonetheless.

I thought I'd be a bit fresh and see what happened, partly as a defense mechanism because of how he was making me feel. I'm a child at heart.

"So do you have anyone back home?"

"What?"

"Back home. Is there a wife, girlfriend? Children perhaps?"

"What an impertinent question."

"No offense, bud, I was just wondering if you were missing anyone, is all."

"Oh, missing people. No, there is nobody back where I live. Not anymore."

"Was there a someone, then?"

"Yes. There was once. Two years ago, actually."

"Oh?"

"Yes. Her name was Selena Cabral, and she looked after my needs for three years."

"All your needs?"

Herman squinted an eye at me and smiled.

"Yes, Jake, all my needs. She cooked and cleaned and washed my clothes. She conversed with me and she slept with me. All my needs."

"What happened to her? You speak of her in the past tense."

"I did because Selena is dead. Would you like to hear the story of her passing?"

"If you're willing to tell me, sure."

"Then I shall. I first met Selena three years ago. She was my housekeeper. As I told you, she cooked for me, she cleaned my house, she shined my shoes. Her job was to look after me and to make sure I wanted for nothing. And she was very good at her job. I was fully satisfied with her work."

"What I have not told you was that she was young, barely twenty years old with round breasts, long black hair, and a full mouth. Although she was not my type, you might say, I did feel a fascination for her. For her young body. So one day, after she'd completed the typing for me I'd left on my Dictaphone, I went up behind her and placed my hand on the back of her neck.

"She let me touch her neck and her face and shortly after, I had ripped off her clothes and took her from behind on the oak desk in my office."

I inhaled deeply, hearing Herman's tale, not knowing how much to believe and how much to trust the man, but he continued.

"From that point on, I would have my way with Selena once or twice a week. As I get older, I have found that my sex drive has reduced."

"Your libido."

"Yes, as you say, my libido. So it was never the case we spent much time having intercourse, but when the urge seized me and she was around, I would let my desires overtake me."

"Sounds perfect. No strings and as much of it as you wanted."

"Perfect indeed, but my prolonged time with Selena proved her undoing. By giving her my attention, I allowed my focus to slip somewhat with respect to the work she was conducting for me.

"I have already mentioned that she did typing for me. Well, she also looked after my filing and correspondence, along with the other more menial tasks I mentioned initially.

"This meant she gained an insight into my affairs that no other human has had since my wife… died."

Yet again, there was a silence in the room as Herman dwelt on the thought of his wife and her demise.

"Go on if you are able," I commented, hoping beyond hope he would carry on, but I was aware the man had bumped into grief over his wife's death all over again.

"What? Surely… Selena learned more about me than any other woman since the end of the war. She knew about my past and about what I was doing and where I was going. And that would have been acceptable because I had learned to trust her.

"Of course, that trust came at a price. Selena dropped little ideas into my lap about what she knew and what action she would take on the basis of that knowledge. And this was when we started to have problems between us.

"On each occasion when she threw out these thoughts, I would make it clear to her there would be terrible negative consequences for her if she acted on these notions. I hoped she believed me and understood these were not merely empty threats.

"One day, I walked into my office to see Selena bending over the oak desk and, with her rump squarely in my line of sight, I knew I wanted her there and then. I approached her quietly to make the tryst more exciting but as I got nearer, I realized the reason she was bending over the desk was because she had a miniature camera in her hands and she was taking photos of my paperwork."

"I grabbed the camera out of her hand and threw it on the floor. At that precise moment, she wheeled round and I grabbed her arms to prevent her from assaulting me. Then I stamped on the camera and its film spewed out onto the floor, exposed to the light.

"I slapped her repeatedly about the face, but that made her angry rather than scared as I had hoped it would. So I tore open her blouse and ripped off her bra, slapping her about the face if only to make me feel better as it appeared to make zero difference to her demeanor.

"While still holding both her arms in one of my hands, I felt around on the desk until I came upon the silver letter opener, which Selena had used to open my correspondence for the previous eighteen months. I sliced her breasts and cut her left cheek from the corner of her mouth up to her ear. She screamed and pleaded, so much so that one of my attendants entered the room, but I told him to stay by the door.

"Then I tore off her skirt and cut off her underwear, so she was naked and bleeding before me, and dragged her quivering body so she was sat on the desk in front of me. I undid my trousers and went inside her one last time.

"Once I was done, I picked up the letter opener again and stabbed her in the vagina seven, eight, or nine times. I did not keep a close count. I did not care to count.

"My attendant took her bloody body from me. The next day I was informed she died of her injuries overnight and the following day, I had a new housekeeper. I only had to open my post once during this time.

"After that, I left my housekeeper alone, but allowed a woman to visit me to tend to my more personal needs…"

Herman was silent for a spell and I had no idea what to think or say.

"I'm not surprised you have trust issues," I said under my breath. Herman smiled and nodded.

"Yes indeed, Jake."

In the vacuum of this silence, there was nowhere I could think of taking a conversation where this man raped and murdered his housekeeper. And then decided to share the story with me.

The evening turned to night, and we hunkered down to sleep, although I only dozed because I didn't feel secure spending that much time with a man who killed his lover with his bare hands, more or less.

What we never got to the bottom of was what Selena was doing taking photos of Herman's letters. I didn't feel a strong urge to ask him, funnily enough, but the implication was clear – the guy was powerful enough to kill someone without batting an eyelid and without any consequences for his actions.

This old Nazi sure had some juice even to this day, and I figured the best thing was to let sleeping dogs lie.

Two days later, I got the nod and handed Herman over to Kurtz's people. After that night, he only spoke a handful of words to me. Perhaps that's why he told me his tale; so's I wouldn't be too curious and to stop me wasting his time yapping at him. He really didn't like small talk, for sure.

The day after Herman left my care, I visited Kurtz in his makeshift serviced office.

"Here is the rest of your fee. Count it if you like, but it is all there, every last dollar."

"Nothing personal, but I will. I've been stiffed in the past. I'm sure you understand."

"Naturally. One cannot be too careful."

I flicked through the notes in the brown envelope and, having checked that everything was kosher, I pushed the envelope deep into my inside jacket pocket.

"One thing before we leave."

"Yes, Jake, what is it?"

"Who exactly is Herman?"

"Herman? Who? Oh, Mr. Larsen."

"Yes, Larsen."

"He is a man you looked after for three days and is now no longer of your concern."

I looked Kurtz straight in the eyes and he stared right back at me and smiled. He wasn't giving anything away, but then, if I were him, I'd have stayed shtumm too. Let's face it, Larsen had a bad history when it came to employee relations.

# NEW YORK 1978

# 37

HERMAN THE GERMAN was probably the most dangerous man I had to deal with, even though by the time I met him his worst years were behind him. I always felt I had met a member of the SS high command, but I never found out who he actually was. In the end, he became nothing but a distant memory by the time my strangest murder case turned up at my door.

Marty had been poisoned, and the man sat in the chair opposite me wanted to know who had done it and why. Under normal circumstances, I'd have told him to go to the precinct house and ask his questions there. But this was different.

Why? Marty was a horse and the man sat in front of me was Phileas Bertram – or at least that was his stage name. PB was the ringmaster of a circus which had put up its tent on the outskirts of Coney Island and the following morning, Marty had been found dead having frothed at the mouth until it took its last breath. There was a bottle of poison in the stables so the cause of death was obvious. But they had no idea who had dispensed the fatal Socratic sauce.

I reckoned I could make some easy bread fingering the nag's killer without too much effort and have a bit of fun along the way. So, there I was in the middle of the ring, sawdust under my feet, with the cast of *Star Wars* lined up in front of me.

To say they were a strange bunch was an understatement. Every size of human being stood before me: tall, short, wide, narrow. Beards, mustaches, and clean shaven too – and that was just the women. Other species were represented: chimpanzees and miniature ponies at least. I was informed the rest of the menagerie were in their cages and available for my inspection whenever I was ready.

"Okay, everyone. My name's Jake and as PB has explained, I'm here to find out who gave Marty a fatal dose," I said in a loud voice hoping they all could hear me. I wasn't used to bellowing in front of such a large crowd. There must have been forty, fifty, maybe more, people in the ring. Then I lowered my voice having got their attention.

"Chances are someone standing here today did for Marty. By the time I'm done, we'll have you caught."

There was a general murmuring and shuffling of feet on the sawdust, which made the footfall sound muffled yet sizzling. Besides, no one likes to be accused of murder and I knew that. A quick survey of the faces gave me a head start to pick which groups I should interrogate first.

"If anyone saw anything, or thinks they might've seen anything that'll help us catch the felon, just tell me. My door is always open – especially as I don't have a door."

The attempt at levity fell flat, but it didn't deserve a big laugh anyway, so I let it go. There was nodding all round and several people peered at each other from across the ring. Three clowns had made eye contact, for example, with four midgets and I figured they'd be a good place to start. As expected, no one came up afterward and offered an eyewitness account of the slaying of Marty the horse.

After they had all shuffled out of the tent, I turned to PB, who was looking at each of his staff with deep distrust.

"You shouldn't stare at them like that."

"Why not? One of them bums killed my Marty."

"Sure thing. But unless this becomes a remake of *Murder on the Orient Express*, all but one had nothing to do with the death. You'll need them to continue to trust and follow you, wherever you guys take this carny."

"Good point, Jake. For the record, though, we are a circus, not a bunch of carnival performers."

"Whatever floats your boat," I responded, and shoving my hands into my pants pockets, I wandered off to speak with a bunch of guys whose shoe size was well into double digits.

I left the main tent and wandered around the collection of small marquees about two hundred feet away from the entrance where the performer's camp had been set. I spotted Larry, Curly, and Moe stomping into a red and yellow striped affair and I figured I'd follow them.

By the time I passed by the flap and entered, the three amigos were practicing pratfalls. The regularity and lack of communication between them made me think this was their standard warmup routine.

Most interesting of all was that, even though I had appeared, they plain ignored me and carried on pushing each other over and knocking hats off.

I waited to see if this would be a permanent state of affairs and, after two minutes, I got bored and coughed.

"Hi there. I need to take a few moments of your time. It's about Marty."

"The nag's dead. They die all the time. It's in their nature. Why are you in such a twist over this one?" Larry queried.

"I care about Marty because PB cares about Marty. Anyone got any idea who wanted the beast in the ground?"

Larry sideways glanced at Moe, who stared at the ground while Curly stared at Larry, eyes wide open, as though he wanted to encourage Larry to say something.

I moved a step towards Curly.

"What d'ya think?"

"Me? I know nothing. I have known nothing. Right now, if you come back tomorrow, I'll know nothing then too."

"You're a real know-nothing!" quipped Larry, and they all chuckled as though he'd referenced a private joke they were excluding me from.

"Funny, but someone forced a defenseless animal to a slow death and I doubt if that was out of malice towards the horse."

"Yeah, Marty was PB's pride and joy, so he was," Moe commented, letting the words trail off into nowhere as the three contemplated Marty's final hours.

"So, would I be right in thinking the perp was more interested in attacking PB than the horse itself?"

"I reckon so," added Larry, whose piercing bright blue eyes were a remarkable contrast to the deep browns of the other two in his act.

"Okay then. Who had it in for PB?"

That question generated zero response, but I had to ask it anyway. Trouble was I also understood it would be tricky for me to get them to talk again now that question was hanging in midair.

"Did he have any enemies outside the circus?" I prompted.

"No one outside the circus, for sure," offered Larry, but again his voice trailed off. What was unsaid had more significance than what had actually been said. If I believed Larry, then his enemies were inside the circus and no further.

"How do you guys get on with PB?"

"Mighty fine. We get on mighty fine," asserted Larry, who was their spokesman, perhaps because he was at least one foot taller than the other two.

"And does everyone get on well with PB?"

They looked at each other and Larry turned his head and looked at me. Then Curly elbowed him in the side to encourage him.

"Wouldn't say everyone, would we?"

Heads shook aplenty.

"Why's that then?"

"Well, since the start of the season, there've been a few tensions between some of us."

"Tensions? What sort of tensions?"

"PB has been trying to make a few changes to the running order of the show and not everyone's been cool about it."

"Whose noses have been knocked out of joint?"

Larry smiled and then Curly elbowed him again. There was no turning back.

"Miriam and her elephants, the dwarves, Hercules the strong man for starters. Others as well. We've had five minutes shaved off our act so that there's more time for Theresa and Marty. We haven't complained or nothing but we haven't been happy either."

"Why give the animals more time?"

"PB says the paying public prefers primates over people."

"Perhaps, perhaps," I murmured under my breath and all three laughed because I had noticed the alliteration.

"Thanks, you've been very helpful."

"Pop by later if you like and we'll throw a custard pie in your face."

"I might well do that," and I wandered off to find someone else who'd talk about mighty Marty the magnificent mare.

Two tents further down were the midgets, Huey, Louis, Duey, and Uncle Scrooge. They were sitting around, smoking, and drinking coffee on their little chairs. Even though I wasn't supposed to laugh, I had to bite my lower lip because they looked funny. Plain funny.

Whatever my thoughts on the little people, they were welcoming and offered me a cigarette and a mug of java. I accepted the drink and rejected the smoke.

This time I started with some general chat rather than going headlong into the main bout. Huey and Louis were the most communicative, but Uncle Scrooge also spoke plenty. Conversation twisted and turned and I steered the topic over to Marty.

"Tough break for the nag, wouldn't you say?"

"Sure thing," replied Louis, "but he did have it coming to him?"

"Say what?"

"Yeah, the beast had thrown a couple of riders the past week so I wouldn't say anybody was surprised to see revenge served cold."

"Who had Marty thrown then?"

"There was Theresa and Hercules, but not at the same time."

"Theresa…?"

"PB's girlfriend. And she's a trapeze artist too."

"And Hercules?"

"Would you be surprised if I told you he was the strongman?"

"Probably not. I don't surprise easy." I took another sip of my coffee.

"Would either have been mad enough at the nag to have killed it?"

All four of them sat and pondered that question. Then I realized they all had the answer but weren't prepared to say it out loud.

"I'm not here to rat on you. Whatever you say, stays with me. I'm here to find out about the nag, then I'm gone."

Duey piped up. "The trouble is that Theresa has a fiery temper on her and Hercules could strangle that mare with his bare hands. So it's anyone's guess which one of them woulda done it."

"Makes sense. But tell me, I can understand why a trapeze artist might start their act on a horse, but what was Hercules doing riding on Marty's back?"

"He likes horses," was the depressingly honest and obvious reply from Uncle Scrooge. I only named him that because he was about six inches taller than the rest of the bunch.

"Figures," I laughed, and they chortled back at me, which eased the tension that had been building up ever since I mentioned Marty.

"So tell me, how long have Theresa and PB been an item?"

"Most of the season. He hired her about five months ago and we reckon they shared a bed within a week or two," answered Louis.

"Some of us think he only hired her so he could shtup her," added Huey.

"But either way, we needed a new leading lady for the trapeze," contributed Duey.

"And why was that?"

"Because we buried her predecessor in Newark," Uncle Scrooge informed the tent. Served me right for asking such a dumb question. I was hoping I'd hear about a bust-up and how the last high-wire act had wanted to get revenge for being sacked. But a broken neck was a broken neck.

"Tell me about Theresa, then. What's she like?"

Uncle Scrooge snorted. "Great tits."

Duey added, "One of the few good things about being this height is that I can stare at her crotch and she never notices." They all chuckled at that. Me too.

"Seriously, what's she like?"

The guys settled down after a short while and they inhaled deeply on their smokes.

"Her biggest problem is herself," said Louis, with a somber air I'd not seen from him before.

"The trouble with Theresa is that she takes herself extremely seriously. Now, she's up on a high wire hundreds of feet off the ground, so I get why she'd be deadly serious about her act. If I was dangling from just my ankle up there, I'd be taking it serious myself."

"But…?"

"But she's like that on the ground too. She thinks her trapeze act is the most important part of the show and looks down on the rest of us."

Duey smiled. "And we don't need people looking down on us any more than they have to." Again, a bunch of chuckles ensued, although I didn't join in this time because it wasn't that funny and I wanted the midgets to stay focused.

"And what's that got to do with Marty? I don't get it."

Huey looked at me and shook his head.

"You don't get it? Bud, why's PB hire you if you can't understand the simple stuff?"

"Explain to me then."

■　　■　　■　　■　　■　　■　　■

# 38

"OKAY, MAC, THIS is the story. At the start of every hire-wire act, you need a gimmick to get from the ground to the wire. Some use a trampoline, others just climb the pole. Theresa would ride round on Marty to make the audience think she was a horse-riding act and, just when she'd finished a couple of jumping tricks, she'd stand on his back and leap up. She was on a wire and that'd make her fly up into the rafters. Looked real cool and almost always got a gasp from the paying crowd. Then she'd undo the harness that got her up there and the real act would start in earnest. Nice touch."

"And without Marty, her big intro has been ruined."

"Now you're getting it, fella."

"If it's all about the high wire then why hurt a horse? Why didn't they take out Theresa? There must be loads of ways to knock out a high-wire act, for sure."

"I dunno nothing 'bout that. There were a lot of people who resented Theresa enough to want her act ruined to teach her a lesson. I'm not sure anyone wanted her dead. That's a whole different ball game. We're not a sideshow carny, you know."

"Would you say the resentment towards Theresa began when she started in PB's bed or when the schedule for the show got rearranged?"

"Hard to tell, bud. The two things happened within a day or two of each other, right?"

Louis looked at the others and they all nodded in agreement.

"Thanks. You've been a bunch of swells." I exited stage left followed by a bear.

For a second, I took a step back and considered what I'd got so far. There were two horse lovers – Theresa and Hercules – as well as the rest of the circus and anybody who walked past the place and had it in for horses. The final group was an unlikely source and, even if the perp was from outside, I'd never be able to find him. PB would need to call the cops out.

My best guess was the motivation was jealousy because of Theresa's relationship with PB or due to the extra time her act was getting. Or both. If Hercules would kill a horse, surely he'd strangle it with his bare hands and not find a bottle of poison and assassinate the ass that way. The easiest way to check him out was to visit him and that's where I went next.

THERE WAS NO one in Hercules' tent so I smooched round and asked a bearded lady if she'd seen him and she pointed to an enormous tree of a man the other side of the tents. Now, you might think if there was a bearded lady, this place was far more a freak show than a circus. And you'd be right if it wasn't for the fact she happened to have too many hairs sticking out of her chin. Menopausal women of the world be warned.

Trudging over to Hercules, I watched him lift a car onto its side and over onto its roof. He'd done this many times before because the bodywork was beaten badly and no one else was acting like anything was out of the ordinary.

"Hi there."

Hercules stared at me like I was shit on his shoe. Probably how he looked at most people most of the time. The guy didn't appear to be the life and soul of any party.

"How's it going?"

A stare and he rolled the car back onto its tires.

"I am listening."

"Okay… I'm talkin'. Who d'ya think did for the horse?"

"Not for me to say. Not at all."

"Does that mean you know something and don't want to say?"

"Not for me to say."

"Why's that?"

"I am only the strong man here. No one wants to hear what I say."

"I do. I'm asking you to say what you think. So what do you know? What have you seen?"

"There is unhappiness in the circus."

"Why?"

"Most of us have lost show time."

"Since Theresa turned up?"

"Around that time but it is not Theresa's fault. She is a beautiful addition to this show. She is a light in the dark of the night."

"So whose fault is it then?"

"Not for me to say."

"And who'd be so angry about it they'd kill a horse over the matter?"

"A crazy man. A crazy jealous man."

"Do you know who that man is?"

"Not for me to say."

I sighed. Reticence is a mighty fine attribute but constantly pleading the fifth was another matter entirely. I played twenty questions.

"Was it a show member?"

Hercules nodded, realizing I had changed tack.

"Were they female?"

A shake of his head.

"I have to go now." And with that, he walked away from me, leaving the car where it was and me with my hands in my pants pockets and a quizzical expression on my face.

"What the f…?"

A woman strolled past wearing a silver leotard with a jacket over her shoulders. The contours of her body, of her breasts, were more than visible to anyone who turned their head in the right direction. And my head turned. She was hot.

She ignored the fact I was gawping at her like a Hanna Barbera character and carried on into a tent. I continued to stand there like the fool I was for a few minutes and then I wandered around the tents trying to find someone to interview. I had lost all my concentration with one look at those nipples. Man, oh, man.

WITH NO CLEAR idea which way to go, I walked from one tent to another, hoping to find someone interesting to talk to. Half an hour later, I found myself stood right in front of the tent into which that silver leotard had disappeared.

Before I unzipped the entrance flap, I could hear a variety of noises coming from inside. No imagination was needed to work out what was going on the other side of the tent wall, but I opened the door anyway.

Sure enough, there were two bodies on a bed. Lying on the floor between me and the bed was a silver leotard and the jacket I had seen hanging over those shoulders. Between the sheets were an unbelievably hairy back and broad shoulders in the form of Hercules and the unknown woman herself. At least, she was unknown until Hercules moaned, "Oh, Theresa!" several times. Being an arch detective, I realized those nipples I'd imagined touching from earlier on belonged to PB's girlfriend.

Then there was a stronger realization that Hercules was humping PB's girlfriend, and this was not the situation I should stand and watch.

A cough escaped from the back of my throat and Hercules turned his head to see me staring at him.

"Don't stop, you hairy fucker!"

Theresa had yet to notice my existence and who could blame her? There was a beast of a man thrusting inside her and she was enjoying it.

Because the strong man had shifted his position on the bed, the sheet slipped off and landed on the floor. Theresa's legs were wrapped around her lover and her breasts were jiggling in front of me. All's I could do was stare at those nipples, wobbling under Hercules' hirsute torso.

Once Theresa's head stopped leaning back in absolute ecstasy, she spotted me in the corner of her eyes and shouted, "Get out of here you pervert! What the hell do you think you're doing, you freak?"

As I swiveled on my heels to leave, I saw her fighting with Hercules to grab the covers to hide her embarrassment. The nipples vanished behind a pillow and, even though Hercules had got off her, I still couldn't catch sight of her bush. That second pillow was now my arch enemy.

# 39

THIRTY SECONDS LATER, Theresa came out of the tent, leotard on, jacket buttoned all the way up. Her cheeks were red, at least the ones on her face. I tipped my hat and introduced myself.

"What do you want, you peeping tom?"

"Does PB know about you and Hercules?"

"No idea. And it's none of your business anyway."

"You're right you two screwing each other is of no concern of mine – unless it has something to do with Marty's death."

"This has nothing to do with Marty. How could it?"

"Don't ask me how. That's not my problem. I'm just trying to figure out who did for the nag. And the best way to solve that conundrum is to work out why the nag had to die. Any ideas?"

"I loved that horse. He was steady and soft to the touch. If you think I had anything to do with it, you are so wrong. My act has a gaping hole at its start."

Not the only gaping hole we've seen in the last five minutes, I quipped to myself.

"Can you think of anyone who might have wanted to scupper your act then?"

Theresa had calmed down and, judging from her expression, she was prepared to contemplate the answer to my question.

"Not off the top of my head. I mean, there were quite a few people whose noses were out of joint because my act had gained four minutes and theirs had lost time. Do you think that had something to do with it?"

"Hard to say for sure, but annoyed people end up doing bad things. Is there anyone who was particularly annoyed by the change in the timings?"

"Not that I was aware, but most of the other acts won't talk to me."

"Because you were sleeping with PB?"

"Kinda. Mainly because I was also with Hercules and they think PB will go ape shit when he finds out."

"Are they right?"

"Probably, but I'm having fun on the rollercoaster until the train derails."

"Makes sense but when you piss people off, they're bound to react, right?"

"Yeah. I don't bear them any grudges. They're just following their hearts, same as me."

"But your heart has quite an appetite, doesn't it?"

"That's quite a mixed metaphor, but I know what you mean. I am insatiable. Always have been, always will. I hope."

"So do you reckon the murderer was jealous of your extra four minutes?"

"Most likely, yes."

"And would you say the best way to get back at you was through the horse?"

"Why not? I loved that horse." A tear appeared in the corner of her left eye and I believed her.

"But surely, there are easier ways than poisoning a nag. I mean, you're on a high wire. Isn't there a cable that could be weakened to exact a revenge on you, you know?"

"What a gruesome thought. Yes, most of the acts at this circus face death every day: there's a lot of risk in what we do. But there's an unwritten law. Circus folk don't attack other circus folk. We don't do that."

"But you'd happily kill a ride?"

"Not happily, but murdering Marty would have been an option for someone."

"I see. And how do you know the jealousy was aimed at your extra four minutes of fame and not, say, because you were putting out with PB and Hercules?"

"I have appetites that need sating. Don't judge me."

"I'm not judging; I'm merely enquiring. You've said you reckoned Marty bit the dust because of the extra time, but how do you know there isn't a lover scorned in this circus instead?"

"Well, now you put it that way, I don't suppose I do know that."

A whole world of possibility opened up to me. A vast expanse of unknown was engulfing me and I needed a break. So I looked down to see if I could catch a glimpse of those nipples, but Theresa's jacket was still firmly buttoned up. The only thing the material revealed was her overall, curvaceous shape, but no specifics. Nothing I could attach to my imagination for later. Shame.

My eyes returned to Theresa's face.

"Like what you see?"

I felt an intense embarrassed glow overtake my cheeks.

"Sure do. Another time and another place and who knows what might have been, but I'm working now and that's the end of it."

Theresa licked her lips and put a thumb and finger ever so gently onto either side of my left jacket lapel.

"When this is over then, don't forget I'm here. I do have an appetite that needs to be sated…"

Insatiable. Literally.

While this conversation was helping me get in the sack with Theresa, it was doing nothing about uncovering who killed Marty. I tipped my hat and walked away from the tent with its sweet stench of sex behind me and the alluring hips of that high-wire temptress.

Meantime, Hercules was nowhere to be found. He'd thrown on his breeches and run out the door without even flipping a look in Theresa's direction. For a guy as strong as cheap cologne, Hercules wasn't living up to his namesake.

Best course of action I could figure was to skirt round to PB and see what he made of all that was going on in his circus.

Back in the main ring, PB was directing traffic as acts came, rehearsed, and left. I sat on a seat and watched the show for free.

What I had discovered was close to bupkis, but the piper deserved to hear the tune I'd written.

"Jake, how's it going? Found anything for me yet?"

"Not quite, PB." I stood up and ambled over.

"I've been discovering all sorts about the circus, but I'm not sure I'm any nearer to finding Marty's killer."

"What you got?"

"This place is a seething mass of jealousy, that's what. Wherever you turn, there's someone else looking to stab you in the back. How do you survive here?"

"You get used to it, Jake. These people are show people and that makes them mighty special."

"I've also found out some info on Theresa…" I trailed off because I felt the guy should know about his girlfriend, but I wasn't keen on being the one to tell him. Over the years, I've noticed how people shoot the messenger when it's bad news and ignore him when the news is good.

"Has she started back with that gorilla, Hercules?"

"You knew?"

"Given the amount of noise those two make, who doesn't know?"

"And you're okay with that?"

"Course not. I hired her because she has a great ass and a fabulous pair of tits, but I doubt if one man will ever hold her attention long enough to keep her. The way I see it: I share Theresa with Hercules and whoever else she fucks in the cast and crew. Chances are we are not the only ones. That girl has appetites, you know."

"Sure thing. Trouble is the motive for the killing is either your relationship with Theresa or because you gave her four extra minutes and the other acts have suffered."

"Listen carefully, Jake. The other acts haven't suffered. If I didn't add more time to Theresa's act then we'd have less money in the till. People have been lining up to see those tits and that ass soaring above their heads. If Theresa goes then this place is done for. Have you any idea how hard it is to keep a circus alive nowadays? Everyone stays home and watches TV."

"Have you told the cast what you've told me?"

"Yeah. It's only fair they understand what's going on. We're all trying to scratch out a living."

If PB was being honest with me then the extra four minutes had nothing to do with Marty's death. And if that was so then the motive was about getting back at Theresa.

Fate stepped in to relieve me of the burden of thinking. A lion dashed through the ring, chased by his handler and followed by a crew member with a rifle. My money was on the guy with the rifle.

Sure enough, a single shot rang out, and I saw the lion collapse on the spot with a tranquilizer dart embedded in his torso.

The handler, whose name I later found out was Bruno, had wrapped his arms around Clarence and was sobbing at the lion's fall. Then he stood up and rushed at PB, who punched him squarely in the jaw. Bruno plummeted to the ground and stayed there, howling in pain and cupping his chin with both hands. PB could handle himself.

What had this to do with fate and Marty? Simple. When PB took Bruno back to his tent to make him take a rest, there was a spare bottle of poison visible to anyone who wanted to visit the tent.

This was the source of the problem. No one had visited Bruno in a long time and when Theresa appeared in the show, she paid Bruno much attention and popped by one evening a week or so earlier. Unfortunately for the pair, Bruno had been unsuccessful in satisfying young Theresa due to her enormous libido and, more significantly, because he failed to get a hard-on that night.

Bruno was an old-fashioned gentleman, who hailed from West Germany or Austria. He was far from pleased when Theresa finished herself off in front of him, left his abode, and had refused to speak with him since that night.

'Revenge is a dish best served cold' was Bruno's motto, and he lived that dream. In his befuddled brain that meant Marty had to die.

Good news was that PB paid me even though he solved the crime. Two days later I went back to Coney Island to see if I could get a piece of Theresa's ass, but the circus had left town and her silver leotard had gone with it.

# LOS ANGELES 1953

# 40

THE SOLUTION TO Marty's death fell straight into my lap, but there was one occasion when I was paid to commit a murder, not solve one.

Alice Lechuga entered my office looking like a million dollars or rather someone who had been short-changed a million dollars. The hem of her dress was unraveling and you could sense the general tiredness that permeated the very material of her clothes. There were no bruises, but her expression looked as though she had been pummeled repeatedly over several years. I thought this before she opened her mouth.

Her story was a typical sad affair. Alice got married young and regretted the decision within weeks of the ceremony. The husband was not a violent man, despite my expectations, but he was not a faithful man either and this was the cause of her problem.

Axel had a wandering dick, and he'd spend night after night away from home, sleeping with the single women in the neighborhood. This generated many a marital argument because soon after he strayed from his marital oath, tongues wagged.

Soon, the gossip was flying back to Alice, who confronted Axel about his extramarital encounters. To her surprise, he didn't deny her accusations, but reveled in them, proud as anything. Axel reminded Alice they were married and she couldn't get out of it and, no matter what she may say or do, he wouldn't agree to a divorce. Either she accepted how he behaved or she didn't, but he wasn't changing his ways for her. She didn't satisfy him enough sexually and that was the end of the matter. Or so he thought.

That was four years before and nothing had changed. Now Alice had suffered in silence but she would not take it anymore. She knew she'd burn in hell for an eternity, so she thought, but if she couldn't get a divorce then he would have to die.

At this point in the proceedings, Alice pulled out a large manila envelope from her bag. Inside the bag was a large amount of cash. She had saved money from her housekeeping allowance and, quietly and secretly, had stashed it away until there was nearly five hundred dollars. Enough for me to buy a new ride.

"What do you want me to do in exchange for that money, Mrs. Lechuga?"

"Call me Alice. And I want you to kill my husband."

"Alice, do you understand what you have just said is a criminal act and you could go to jail for a very long time?"

"Do you realize that unless you report me to the police right now you'll be guilty of conspiring with me to kill Axel?"

"Well put. Does he have to die? Can he not be hurt until he agrees to a divorce?"

"No, I want him punished. He must suffer as he has made me suffer."

"And you think I'm the best man for this job?"

"I don't know, to be honest, but you come recommended by a friend of a friend which makes you the best chance I have to be rid of that man."

I thought for a minute because I'd never been paid to murder before. Sure I'd killed in Korea, but that was different. I was mighty tempted by the dough, and the cash could be useful seed capital to head east at some point.

The clincher? The pitiful, distraught face sat on the other side of my desk. At that moment, I'd have done anything to bring relief to that pained expression, that anguished howl of a woman.

"We will not meet here again, understand? And you will not be a client of mine during the process either."

"I got it."

"After it is over, we will never see or communicate with each other again."

"Sure."

"Most important is that we don't write anything down. You will tear up any piece of paper you have with my name or number on it. I will take no notes. I am saying this because there must be absolutely no trail of evidence that connects us. Nothing.

"What we are embarking on is a very dangerous state of affairs and each needs to be protected from the other in case the police investigation uncovers you or me as being involved. Understood?"

"Why yes, Jake."

"Good. I am going to take most of the money now so we won't have any problems later with the financial side of the business."

"Okay, but..."

"Don't worry, Axel will be dead within a week. I don't welch on a deal and there's no way I'm gonna want this matter to hang around me any longer than it needs to. The more time I spend on it, the greater my chances of getting caught."

Alice then gave me loads of details of where Axel worked, what he did and didn't like, and as much as she knew of his paramours. After an hour we were through and I detailed an arrangement for the two of us to contact each other. She cried some more and we shook hands. Not quite a blood pact, but sufficient for our needs. Now we both knew a deal was a deal; we were committed.

THE WAY I figured, Axel was a slimeball and probably deserved to die. The memories of the horrors I'd seen in Korea were still relatively fresh and my respect for human life had yet to be fully rebuilt.

With Axel's office as my starting point, all I had to do the next day was to follow him from home for a while and get used to his movements. My plan was to find a slot when he was alone and then do the deed without any witnesses.

The majority of the day was spent in his office, which meant most of my time was spent in my car, scrunched into the driver's seat with my knees embedded in the steering wheel. There was nothing else I could do. I needed to be ready, with only a few seconds warning, in case he flew the nest. But he didn't. Not on Tuesday, nor the Wednesday. I was wondering if Alice had been making the whole thing up when I got a break on Thursday. Until then, Axel had worked late, driven home, and spent the rest of the evening with Alice. Then repeat.

Thursday, he left the office around four and took a left, rather than his usual right, out of the car lot. As soon as I saw that, I knew this would be an interesting afternoon's drive round town. Ten, maybe fifteen, minutes later and he stopped in the middle of a residential street; we'd been driving through the burbs for at least five minutes by then.

He parked outside a rundown house with a tired picket fence and long grass for a front lawn. Straight to the front door and a confident rat-a-tat-tat with his knuckles to announce his arrival. No doorbell for Mr. Lechuga.

A half a minute later, the door opened and a woman's head popped round to see who was there. A smile, a grab of Axel's hand, and he was dragged straight into the house, swallowed up by that briefly open door. I glanced at my watch to get a sense of quite how long he was inside, but after the best part of an hour, truth was that I got bored.

The private eye manual told me to stay put and wait for Axel's return because there was nothing I could do with what he was doing inside that fair maiden's home. But I went for a look-see, anyway. Like I said, I was bored.

I scouted round to the back of the property and squatted by a tree so I could get a crafty look into the kitchen. Nothing. More scurrying and a hedge gave me cover to crouch and stare into the living room.

To my surprise, I saw the two of them on a sofa. I'd assumed they'd have gone straight upstairs to bed, but yet again, my knowledge of human nature failed me. To be more precise, I saw Axel's ass cheeks moving in and out, while his pants and shorts dangled round his ankles. Meanwhile, the owner of the house had her legs akimbo with her panties hanging like a thread off one ankle while her hands gripped tightly to Axel's ass. I caught sight of one wobbling tit but most of the time, Axel's body got in the way of me seeing anything more. She had long dark brown or black hair, which engulfed Axel's head from time to time.

They carried on like this for several minutes until Axel arched his back and halted immediately afterward. He fell off her and turned to land on the sofa, legs outstretched, spent. The woman let her legs fall to the ground and also just sat there, stretched out.

A minute or two went by with nothing but two naked people resting after an exhausting fuck. Then I noticed that Axel's hand wandered towards the woman's crotch and he started to finger her without moving the rest of his body. She edged her body towards him – only an inch or two, mind – to make things easier for him, and then she raised her hand and used her fingers to manipulate his dick. You didn't need to be a sex counselor to understand they were about to embark on round two.

I stuck around for the second show but when the third show started up, I realized this would be a long night, so I returned to my car and drove round until I found a store to buy more cigarettes and a bite to eat.

Sure enough, Axel's car was still parked where he'd left it. Presumably, they either reached round seven, or they had something to eat themselves because he only left a few minutes before midnight. This much sex with his mistress explained why he had no energy to do anything with Alice.

When Axel left, he drove straight home and stayed until the morning when he got up and headed to work, like normal. Friday was a repeated sex session, but he played the family man at the weekend. Monday, Tuesday – mistress – Thursday through to the Sunday night: Alice.

As Alice had said, there was no discernible pattern in his movements. Chances were he'd get a call from the mistress and hightail it round to get himself some love action and spend the rest of the week pining for her and recharging his energy.

The best opportunity I had was to take him out on his way to or from the mistress. The latter sounded a better plan because he never left before eleven at night and there would be few people around then. Also, the guy would be extraordinarily tired and his reactions would be slower. This would give me the advantage of surprise and speed. My odds were improving all the time.

Before I carried out my plan, I wanted to find out a bit more about the woman he was banging, other than she had long black hair and a sexy bush. And I am glad I did.

# 41

THE FIRST TRICK when you want to learn about a total stranger is to use the phone directory, a book containing a list of people's names, addresses, and phone numbers. You can sit down and stare at the damn thing until you spot the address you've written on your scrap piece of paper.

Two days of staring at lists of addresses delivered me my answer; the dame was called Angie Greene. To the ordinary detective, that would be the end of the discussion, but if you live in LA, you need to know about the local rackets.

Mickey Cohen had been in jail for almost two years but his reach stretched way beyond his cell door. Mickey controlled almost all the organized crime which took place in the city, although I'm pleased to say I never met the guy.

Ever since he'd gone inside for tax evasion – like Capone before him – day-to-day matters had been handled by others, but he still pulled the strings. His number two, Frank Bompensiero had taken over the operation, and Bomp, as he was known, kept a close eye on all of Cohen's empire, including the girlfriends of the key members of the family. If you lived in LA and you mixed in certain circles, as I did, you understood how the wheels of the city continued to turn. And I knew Angie was one of Bomp's skirts.

These facts added up to a whole new way to kill Axel and I wouldn't need to be anywhere near him when he visited Satan. And that's exactly where he'd be going.

Axel worked at a company that sold water purifying units. Big whoop. The interesting thing about this dull product was that sewerage plants used them so they were big business. In a city like Los Angeles, water was more valuable than oil, so if you could clean up the equivalent of oil then you ruled the roost.

Mickey Cohen's mob had its octopus arms all over the sewerage business and anything that can create clean water would have been on their watch list. And this gave us the connection between Axel and Angie; they would have met through some mobster who knew Bomp.

Angie was something special: a real moll's moll. Rumor had it she grew up in Chicago, had mixed with the gangsters on the wrong side of the tracks, and had gone further west to Vegas to hustle her way through the Flamingo and as many johns as her body could muster. And then onto the west coast where she buzzed her way around many a barfly until she settled in LA and met Bomp and his merry band. The rest, as they say, is history and takes us to about five minutes before Axel bumped into Bomp's gal.

Later, I heard Axel was invited to a mob party because he was supplying them with a hundred plus machines to clean sewerage plants across the LA area. Like everyone else there, he drank a large number of vodka martinis and supped from many a young lady, hired for the night to keep the broadly male attendees physically content. Angie was primarily there for Bomp but, obviously, she strayed off the script when she met Axel and left the party early with him to squeeze his wallet dry.

LOVE BLOOMED FROM this chance encounter – or at least lust flourished, which is nearer the truth. They enjoyed each other's bodies and had fun together. Angie had more to lose as she was seeing Axel behind Bomp's back, but Bomp was only concerned she was there when he wanted her. And that was every other Friday evening when the mobsters took out their girlfriends instead of their wives.

The rest of the time Angie was free to do what she wanted and Bomp kept her in the lifestyle to which she became accustomed. She was no better able to look after these nice new expensive things than when she was a five-dollar hooker. That explained the rundown shack she called home.

Perhaps the most remarkable aspect to their affair was Axel's ability to carry on doing business with Bomp while fucking the guy's girlfriend behind his back. Part of me always wondered if Angie didn't so much bump into Axel as much as she was placed there strategically by Bomp to keep an eye on an important asset for the water purification plants. No disrespect to Axel, he was a fine-looking guy, but nothing that special to write home about. Just another Latino on the cusp of going to seed.

The other fact worth remembering was that water purification was – and is – much more than an industry utility. In a city like LA, the entire area lives and dies on how much water gets transported into the city. Whoever controls the water, controls the city completely. Mickey Cohen's stranglehold on LA came directly from his management of the clean water supply, so Axel might have had a slight paunch and be shtupping his girlfriend, but Axel also held the key to millions of extra dollars of revenue. For a man like Bomp that made Axel worth keeping alive. At least while the water kept flowing.

Rumor around town was that Bomp had expanded Mickey's empire in two ways. First, he'd leveraged many of Mickey's Hollywood contacts to increase the volume of cocaine and heroin transported into the city each year. And the dealers were household names. Genius.

Second, Bomp had maneuvered mob guys into key positions in the water utilities and purification plants. In hindsight, this was when the Mafia took a real stranglehold on the most powerful state in the union.

I reported back to Alice so she'd get ready for the next, and much more dangerous, phase of the operation: the murder itself. We had agreed that if I needed to speak with her, I'd drop a five-dollar bill inside her morning paper once it was lying on her doormat.

Then Alice would make her way to a coffee shop across town. We'd choose a different place each time we met so there'd be no pattern to follow and the cops would have to ask a lot of waiters before they'd find two who had seen us conspiring together before the job. Simple, elegant but hardly original. Like Alice herself.

*CAFÉ ROSETTA* WAS my choice for our first hook-up mainly because I'd never been there and I had found it by closing my eyes and slamming my finger down on its entry in the phone directory. Again, the randomness of the venue limited the chances of anyone recognizing us when we were there.

Sure enough, the coffee was decent, Alice arrived on time, and our booth was sufficiently comfortable and private for no one to pay us no never mind.

"How's it going?"

"All is fine, Alice. Don't worry."

"I thought, when you sent your message, that something was up."

"Oh no. Quite the opposite, really. First things first. I have seen Axel with another woman. You were right, he is having an affair."

"Sonofabitch."

Over the years, I've learned to let that information hang in the air a while because, like pigeon feathers, thoughts take a while to settle down after hearing those words. If you want cool heads, create a cool environment. So, I sat quietly for a spell, stirring my coffee to cool it down while hoping the same was happening to Alice's rekindled rage.

"Are you still interested in pursuing our… arrangement?"

"Goddamn right, I am. Son of a bitch deserves to meet his maker."

"Fine. In that case, I should warn you that soon your wish will be my command. When we leave *here*, there will be no turning back. Within twenty-four hours Axel will be no more, so if you are not certain, now genuinely is the right time to mention it. Tomorrow will be too late, okay?"

"Jake, I completely understand our situation and I thank you for trying to protect me from my own desires, but I want that man dead and I want it to happen as soon as possible." These last words were barely audible. Alice's voice had lost all its power and, through gritted teeth, all I could hear was a hoarse whisper.

"Good. Then you can expect a call very shortly when I will collect the second installment of my money." To save problems later – like Alice deciding she didn't want to pay me after all – I'd taken three-quarters of my service fee up front. But that still left a sum to pick up after the deed was done.

Last, I gave Alice the random venue for our next rendezvous and as she'd arrived second, I stood up, pecked her gently on the cheek, threw down enough greenbacks to cover the check along with a healthy tip, and walked out the *Café Rosetta*, never to see it again in my life.

One thing, as I bent down to kiss Alice on the cheek, I inhaled her perfume, which was divine. With that, my nostrils flared, and I inhaled her scent deeply and wanted more. But this was not the time and certainly not the place. Quite sensibly, I didn't look back.

My plan was simple, which meant there was little to go wrong and, even if it did, I had a perfectly serviceable plan B.

Plan A was to drop a line to Bomp and tell him what his water cleaning pal, Axel was up to with his moll. I figured this information would be enough to get Axel clipped by Bomp's gang. Plan B was the original idea; I'd take the guy out myself.

NOT FOR THE first time in my life, I headed for the Italian quarter to find a guy called Giuseppe. The inevitable consequence of the journey meant I was stood in a small room, while a guy with olive skin and way too much grease in his black hair eyed me up and down with total disdain in his expression. I didn't mind because I wasn't going to ask him for a favor, so I was safe.

"What did you say your name was?"

"I didn't. I'm just a fella who wants to share what he knows with people he thinks should hear what he has to say."

"And that would be me, would it?"

"Hope so. I reckon it is, yeah."

Steely eyes stared at me as the goon tried to figure out if I was a stand-up guy or a tire kicker.

"And what do you know you think's so important?"

"I know who Angie Greene is fucking and I'm not talking about any Italian man, if you get my drift."

The dude sat up straight in his chair, partly because I had referenced the great man Bomp himself and partly because of the incendiary implication of my comment. I offered more details so he believed my claim and I could show I was to be taken seriously.

"And why do you feel the need to give up this information without even asking for a payment or nothing?"

"Don't like the guy she's with and I'm hoping he might meet with an accident sometime soon."

He nodded, understanding my motivation easily, and then we parted company. Job done.

Two days went by and I carried on my surveillance operation, following Axel from his office back to home and on the second day, he scooted round to Angie's for a quickie. Apart from that, nothing happened. I had hoped the mob would operate at a faster pace than this, but no joy.

In fact, forty-eight hours after I'd dropped the dime on him, Axel was still walking round town as happy as Larry. A very happy Larry, who was no doubt still hanging out with his friends Curly and Moe.

Plan B was looking like it would nudge Plan A out to touch. Sure enough, when Axel was continuing to breathe four days after my conversion, I knew I would have to kill the guy myself.

While not exactly the ideal solution for me, I had known this was a likely outcome the minute I agreed to kill him. After all, that was the original deal I'd signed up for.

# 42

I CARRIED ON following Axel for another day, hoping the mob would do the deed, but still there was nothing but a living, breathing water purification salesman. By Sunday night, I did some real planning and figured out that if I used a gun, I would have the age-old problem of trying to hide or destroy it. Neither appealed.

Then I went through the mental list of a killer's tools: blunt instruments, sharp instruments, heavy objects, and so on. I reached my conclusion before the thought process even started – that I'd need a decent pair of gloves to mask any fingerprints and my bare hands. Anything else would just be a piece of evidence to be found at some later date.

Armed with my conclusion, I watched Axel enter Angie's front door again around ten on Sunday night and I waited. Soon after one, Axel reappeared at the door and walked to his auto, stopping only to put the key in the lock, turn it, and crouch down to sit inside.

This was the moment I pounced. The car was parked away from any street lighting, precisely because Axel didn't want to be seen. So I grabbed him from behind, snapping his right arm around his back and placing my free arm around his throat. The sudden surprise of the attack meant Axel had no time to think about what was happening to him and I let go of his hand so I could exert more pressure on his throat with my arm. He gurgled and instinctively snatched at my arm with both his hands. It was getting harder for him to breathe.

I looked around the street and saw no one about but I still felt quite conspicuous. I dragged Axel by the throat, keeping my arm wrapped tightly around his neck. We slipped in between two trees by a nearby hedge. Then I got to work, pulling my arm tightly back to restrict the airflow as much as I could. The gurgling increased as did the ferocity of his scrabbling.

I punched him in the kidneys to reduce the amount of struggle inside him and his hands ending up resting on my arms instead of gripping them. The gurgling morphed into a rasping sound and my work was nearly done. One more squeeze and he ceased any breathing noises.

The driver's door was already unlocked and I only needed a minute or two to drag his sorry ass into his car and leave him slumped at the wheel. I hopped straight home, removed all my clothes, put them in a plastic bag, and tied up the contents. Then I showered, changed, and took the bag away from my apartment block and over to a building on the other side of the city to place it carefully in a pile of commercial trash. I'd studied the routes of various refuse collection companies and had memorized which collected early on a Monday.

Several hours later on my way back, I signaled to Alice that my end of the bargain was complete through the usual addition of a fin to her morning paper. When I got back to my bedroom, my alarm sprang into action and my night's work was done. I lay on the bed and grabbed a few hours' sleep before I headed off to our rendezvous.

*Café Olé* was yet another venue with a dumb name and a reputation for decent coffee. By the time I arrived, Alice was already sitting in the booth with a drink in front of her, perusing the menu for brunch. When I got to the table, she stood up and threw her arms around my neck like we hadn't seen each other for a decade. With her lips less than an inch from my ear, she whispered, "Thank you so much," and planted a kiss on my mouth while holding both my cheeks in her hands. The broad sure was glad to see me.

"Have whatever you want on the menu. My treat!"

I smiled and when the waitress came over, I ordered a coffee and a stack of pancakes. I wasn't hungry at all, but I didn't want to dampen Alice's enthusiasm either. There was a brightness in her eyes and a lightness to her voice I hadn't witnessed before. Being a widow was agreeing with her.

"Just so I know. Is it done? Have you…?"

"Yes, I have. The deed is done. You won't be seeing him anymore."

She smiled and her relaxed shoulders appeared to have another release of tension as she leaned forward across the table and took my hand, nice and casual as day. I glanced down and looked back at her face, but did nothing to stop this sweet-smelling woman from touching me. The truth was, I liked it. Her perfume was the same she'd worn that first day we met and it engulfed me in a warm glow, causing a little fizz of pleasure in the pit of my stomach. Or at least I thought it was my stomach.

OUR FOOD ARRIVED and she consumed her eggs over easy with vibrant energy while I picked at my stack taking only a mouthful or two. My appetite had gone from the moment Axel had taken his last breath.

We talked about the weather and Alice's house, but one thing we did not talk about was Axel. Apart from when we were eating, Alice held my hand and stroked my fingers during our conversation. Eventually, she stood up and came over to my side of the booth.

"There's something I want to tell you," she whispered after I had shifted over slightly to accommodate her full hips.

"What's that then?" I asked as she put her hand on my leg under the table.

"I've taken a room in a hotel round the corner. Do you want to come over and check it out?"

For a widow, Alice Lechuga was coming on strong and, despite my lack of interest in food, my other appetites appeared to be working just fine.

True to her word, Alice paid for the brunch and we stepped out into the sunshine, strolling along the street hand in hand. By the time we'd turned the corner, I had my left arm around her neck and her right arm was planted at my hip.

The room Alice had got was not just any room, it was a suite.

"This must have cost you," I said issuing a whistle of astonishment when we first entered the hallway and I closed the door.

"Sure did, but I can afford it now."

The furrows on my brow showed my lack of understanding. I couldn't see the connection.

"Why, darling, Axel had a life policy and I'll be able to claim it once the coroner reports misadventure. The only way I couldn't get the money is if it had been a suicide."

She stepped into the bedroom, placing her clutch bag on a chair. Keeping her back to me, she turned her head towards me and said, with the sweetest voice imaginable, "Be a love and unzip my dress." And I did.

We frolicked in that room until nightfall, discovering every nook and cranny of each other's bodies. I lost count of the number of times my dick was inside some orifice of hers or another. Just didn't matter.

By the end, she put her clothes back on while I lay in bed.

"Stay until morning if you like, lover."

She kissed me on the forehead, left the rest of my money in an envelope on the dressing table, and walked out.

Over the next week, we met twice more, but we realized the only things we had in common were Axel and that we enjoyed fucking each other until at least one of us lapsed into unconsciousness. That was not sufficient to sustain any relationship. Mainly because she was rich enough to buy someone far more interesting than I could ever be. And we both understood that.

Besides, by the end of the seven days, I was getting an extremely sore dick and, when I visited my doctor, found she'd given me a dose.

Once I was cleared up, I left the City of Angels and headed east for the rest of my life.

# Baltimore 1968

# 43

MARTIN LUTHER KING and Robert Kennedy were both dead several months before I found myself in Baltimore. The mood in the country had turned a shade darker since Kennedy's brains were splattered on the floor and the tension in the black neighborhoods was palpable, at least on the odd occasions when I hit those ghettos.

Most of my time that long, hot summer was spent taking money from the bridges-and-tunnel set in Manhattan. You know the sort; worried about husbands and wives pleasuring themselves with younger alternatives during the summer of love, while hippies pleasured themselves with any orifice they could find on the other side of the country.

As luck would have it, I followed a john into the suburbs of Baltimore around July or August. I can't remember which at this point in my life. Either way, I walked past a cemetery near a park not far from the freeway when I realized I had no paper to use for my usual information retrieval technique of dropping a generous Hamilton on a dude. When the thought flashed across my mind, I was standing in front of a branch of the First Bank of Baltimore. The place had been open only a minute or two as I saw the time on my watch was nine.

Pushing the door open, I took my turn in line to swap out my larger notes for something more useful. As I settled into the wait, I popped my hands into my pants pockets because bank lines are plain tedious.

To relieve the monotony of the experience, the doors of the bank burst open and three guys with balaclavas shot straight in. One punched the security guard in the face as he was standing by the door, keeping the bank safe from robbers and other felons. The old man dropped to the marble floor like a sack of potatoes and one of the balaclava boys shouted, "Everyone, lie on the ground and do what we say or we'll shoot you in the fucking head!"

We all hit the floor as good as gold. Everyone was attached to their heads and wanted it to stay that way.

I made sure I was particularly still because I knew I had a piece in my jacket and I didn't want to go through the hassle of explaining that to a man holding a sawn-off shotgun, for that was their weapon of choice. And who could blame them?

While one of the jokers kept the barrels of the shotgun squarely on us, the other two vanished through a staff door, opened by a cashier on the advice of the leader of the gang:

"Open the fucking door or I'll put a hole in this bitch's head!" A clear instruction, easy to understand. The girl behind the desk made the right choice and buzzed the door open to let them through. Each of the guys was carrying a large black holdall and the third who stayed with us passed his bag over to one of the others.

"If they move, kill 'em!" said the one issuing the instructions and all the threats. I believed him and remained as still as physically possible.

I had placed myself on the floor so my head faced sideways and I had a clear view across the marble to the other side where the staff door was and, presumably, the safe beyond. This meant I could watch the two balaclava boys leave the place and close the door behind them.

While they were gone, the third guy stormed up and down the room, keeping the barrels of his shotgun trained on the citizenry who were eating dirt. He was puffed up with his newly-found power, but the dude knew how to hold a gun, so I was more relaxed than if I'd thought he was just another hothead with a weapon. Those guys are the most dangerous. They don't even know to keep the safety on unless they need it. Over the years, I've seen countless guys pour lead into their toes way earlier than they'd plug a civilian.

Right now though, there were many civilians inches from my head and I could hear enough whimpering and sniffling to know soon someone would try to do something very dumb.

Hard to say with all the commotion and shouting and tears, but I figured we'd been in this situation between five and ten minutes. By my reckoning, that meant the cops would surround the place any minute, which'd be a real test of these men. How would they handle that situation when it happened? We would have to wait and see.

As predicted, and there is always one, a member of the assembled throng made their move to be a hero. It was the old guard, who believed he should make more of an effort to protect the bank from these villains. His judgment was deeply impaired because, even though I've never worked in a bank, I knew the money was insured so there was never any need for heroics. Banks always get their money back. No one needed to lay down their life in the name of the First Bank of Baltimore and old Joe should have been told that during his innumerable training exercises.

However, Joe decided to have his glory day today and rolled over on his side and slid, as silently as he could, towards the main exit. He was not running away in slo-mo, but instead, his gun had fallen out of his holster and was lying by the wall next to the door.

Bully Boy might have been pacing up and down, but he was keeping a close eye on all of us and spotted Joe taking his tortuous route. Bully Boy walked straight over, kicked Joe in the balls to stop him in his tracks, and then smashed the butt of the gun into Joe's head. A red ripple trickled out of his skull and coalesced on the marble floor, forming an almost perfect circle of blood coming out of Joe's left ear.

This action sent the rest of the civilians into full panic mode, which was not what Bully Boy needed. To make matters worse, two events coincided with the butt connecting. First, the other two came back from the vault with their black bags now heavy with money, and second, the police arrived outside.

Now you don't need to be a trained psychologist to figure out what happened next. First, the folk with their teeth to the marble howled, cried, and screamed long and hard, because they were not used to witnessing such violence close at hand. It's one thing to watch footage of the Vietnam War on TV, another to see wood entering an old man's head only feet from your face. For the first minute or two, all you could hear was the wailing and gnashing of teeth.

Second, all the wailing stopped within an instant when the sound of the detective came into the building loud and clear through a bullhorn. "This is the police. We have the place surrounded. Put your guns down and come out with your hands up."

The answer to this suggestion was swift and clear, as well as being the number one cliché of all time for bank robbers. Bully Boy smashed a window at the front of the bank, pointed his shotgun out of the gaping hole, and let rip two short sharp blasts. Then he ducked back inside and hid behind the wall as a salvo of bullets from police guns showered into the bank, ricocheting around the place until all their energy had dissipated.

When I opened my eyes, I saw red dribbling off my eyelashes and I thought I'd been hit by a stray bullet, but I was wrong. This was someone else's blood. A civilian had been caught and was screaming in agony. As he was so loud, I knew he wasn't seriously injured. When you've been hit in a lung or the heart, you keep your thoughts to yourself as your last breaths ebb away. This dude was clutching his arm and rolling around.

Once the shooting died down, a woman took a scarf and tied it around the dude's upper arm to stem the profuse bleeding. If nothing else, the attention the dude received shut him up and let the rest of us think.

The two from the vault reappeared.

"What the hell is going on?"

"Cops."

"And why were they shooting at us?"

"I let them know we mean business."

"Brian, I told you not to shoot unless I gave permission, right?"

"Yes, boss."

The boss shook his head and Brian looked down at his feet. He had issues following orders. The boss was annoyed rather than angry like this was normal for Brian.

"You just oughtna done it, is all," the boss added, expressing disappointment in his voice rather than that initial anger. Besides, he needed Brian on side and the man was packing heat.

"What about the cops?"

"You keep an eye on the people and I'll have a look outside."

Brian did exactly what he was told and returned to pacing up and down near our heads, pointing the shotgun down but not toward anybody. I could see he had received some sort of arms training at some point; ex-military, perhaps.

Not that I've been in these kinds of situations many times, but one thing I have learned is when there are guys with guns and a lot of tension in the air always be wary of the one quietly fading into the background.

I had spotted that the third robber had remained completely silent on the way in, on his way out to the vault, and now he was back and standing near the boss and Brian. The dude stood there holding his shotgun with both hands, one on the barrel and the other near the trigger. He appeared less comfortable with his firearm than Brian, but this was not his first day with one in his possession. His eyes flitted from left to right and back again. The guy was stressed out of his brains. A small ripple of sweat broke away from his hairline and meandered down his forehead, along his nose, and dripped onto the floor. He was an accident waiting to happen.

The boss leaned against the wall near the front window and popped his head just above the line of sight to check out the police lines. His head bobbed straight back down. This meant the locals had come out in force and were pointing numerous pistols and rifles in our general direction.

While I was glad that the cops were taking an interest in our case, I was also aware that in their enthusiasm, the cops had already wounded one hostage. In particular, he was sufficiently close it could have been me with a hole in my arm and not him. This made me nervous, and I too felt a bead of sweat drip off my head, but because of my position, my bead fell off my ear, rolled along my neck, and landed on the floor.

A noise ripped across the silence in the bank. The boss, Brian, and Quiet Colin swung round pointing their guns every which way they could. The noise was emanating from a telephone on the cashiers' desk and, once he realized this was the source, the boss walked over and picked up the receiver.

"Yes? Everyone is fine, but you hit one civilian with your gunfire just now… Flesh wound I'd say… Yep… Sure… Now you need to listen to me. We will need a fast car and a clear exit route out of this town, you see? If we don't get that in the next hour then someone's gonna die. All we came in here for was the money and the only person stopping us is you. So listen up and listen good. Give us what we want or you will be on the news explaining why you let these good people get a bullet in the head. Capiche?"

Then he put the phone down as soon as his last word had been uttered to cut off any response. Nicely played. The phone rang again before the boss had time to walk away from it.

"Yes?"

"What do I get if we let him out? Food? You're fucking kidding me, right? We've only been in this place ten minutes and already you're worrying about the catering? Let me make it easier for you. The guy's not in any imminent danger. I'll let you send in a medic to check the guy's okay and patch up his arm then I'll let the medic out again. I've more than enough hostages, I don't need another one. That way, you know no one's about to die from one of your bullets and that I'm a stand-up guy… Okay, call me when you've got a medic ready."

The boss took Brian to one side and they whispered for a few minutes while the quiet kid looked on. Then he swapped over and, presumably, gave the same message to him too. Although I was straining to hear, they were too far away for me to catch anything but the odd word. To be honest, all I figured out were their names. The boss was Frank and the quiet comrade was Andrew. Apart from that, they could have been planning my birthday surprise, for all I knew.

# 44

FRANK AND ANDREW stared at us and Brian went back to his pacing. The guy was the most nervous of all of them and was the only one stupid enough to let his gun off. As soon as you fire at the police, you've added several counts to your charge sheet – and to the charge sheets of your accomplices too. I doubted Frank was too happy about that. From the phone interaction, I believed all he wanted was a straight in-and-out bank robbery. Managing hostages and fighting with the police were not on his to-do list. They wanted out and as quickly as possible.

Like I said, Brian was the loose cannon and he carried on walking one way, then the other, until he stood by the head of the guy with the bullet wound. First, he pushed the guy's side twice with his foot. Just enough to annoy, not enough to cause any more pain than the man was already experiencing. Then the tapping got harder. Hard enough so that the squeals got a bit louder and the noise made Frank turn round. "Pack it in and leave him alone. We need him as healthy as we can if he's going to be of any use to us in a trade."

Brian nodded, waited a minute, and started up again. Then he kneeled down next to the dude and poked him in the arm, somewhere around the wound. My head continued to face towards the fella so I had a perfect view.

The general poking around became more specific over the next two minutes until the woman on the other side of the fella to me couldn't take it anymore:

"For God's sake, stop it. He's hurting. Why don't you stop it?"

With that, Brian twisted round, raised his palm above his head, and let it swoop down across the woman's cheek. We all caught the slap. She whimpered loudly and I saw the bruise form on her face almost as soon as Brian's hand had left the vicinity.

Frank ran over and pulled Brian away, dragging him by the arm to the other side of the room. More blood came out of the guy's arm; Brian had made sure the wound was deeper than when the cops first did their worst.

The woman who had complained converted her whimpering into incredibly short bursts of breathing and we all sensed the stress of it all was transforming into a full-blown anxiety attack. Andrew came over and, flitting glances from one side to another, bent down to check her out. He helped her crawl next to a wall so she could sit up, isolated from the rest of us. He then rummaged around her clutch bag until he found a paper bag and gave it to her to breathe into – a trick he know doubt had picked up on Dr. Kildare.

Five minutes later and her breathing was under control but the whimpering continued unabated. To be honest, I think her reaction was the normal one. The rest of them were too petrified to respond in any visible manner. She had broken ranks and showed herself to be a human being. The others were living in pure survival mode.

After another few minutes, Andrew went over to her and made her crawl back to her original position next to Wounded Arm. As she crawled towards us on her hands and knees, her blouse hung low and I could see the flesh of her breasts hanging downwards, but they were hidden by a well-fitted bra. She lay down on her side, eyes red with tears, her hoarse sobbing the only sounds we could hear. Eventually, calm reigned.

This was punctured by the sound of the phone, which Frank answered as he was standing right by it. He agreed to let a medic enter the place and check on the bleeder. He promised the cops that the paramedic would be given safe harbor back, but the boys in blue wanted more reassurance than the word of a felon in the middle of a robbery. Frank agreed to let a hostage stand outside the bank until the medic had done his job. That way, if the medic didn't come out, the cops would have saved at least one civilian.

Frank chose one of the cashiers and grabbed her by the arm and lifted her until the middle-aged woman was back on her feet. She slid across the marble floor, propelled by Frank's urgency until they were right by the door. Frank opened it slightly and shouted that the woman would be the next person coming out of the bank. True to his word, he pushed her outside, while still clinging to her arm. If anything went south, he'd be able to grab her back inside.

But the cops were true to their word too. A paramedic appeared and came inside. Andrew checked the guy's bag for pistol-shaped contraband, but *nada*. He went straight over to Wounded Arm, ripped open the shirt sleeve, and checked out the damage. All the while, Brian kept both barrels of his shotgun trained directly at the heart of the paramedic.

Several bandages and gauze pads later, the man was patched up and was looking much more comfortable, mainly because he'd been given two codeine under close medical supervision. At least he'd be quiet while he was stoned.

Then the medic stood up and Frank took him back to the entrance.

"Tell them they can keep the old crone."

He pushed the medic out, who grabbed the old cashier and they both walked slowly away from the bank frontage.

"Why the hell did you let one of them go?" snarled Brian.

"To show goodwill. We will need some mighty happy cops if this is going to end well for us, y'know?"

Frank was right. The odds of them coming out alive were close to zero. Cops don't like being seen to lose to bank robbers; makes them look bad. So they are far more likely to shoot first and ask questions later if they feel like it.

The room descended into silence again as Brian paced back and forth, trying to suck in all his anger at what Frank had done. His temperament wasn't helped by the whimpering which erupted, now and again, from one or other of the women lying on the floor. The cashiers were suffering a double indignity; not only were they lying face down on the marble, but they also were wearing skirts and Andrew and Frank spent some time walking around us kicking our feet apart like they were in the army. Wearing a skirt was not ideal for that kind of behavior and most of the men stared right up the skirts of the surrounding women. At least I did, anyway. I watched the black stockings vanish into the inky darkness that was the gap between the young cashier's thighs, but that's all I could see.

Then Frank huddled with Andrew, they nodded, and the two left the room and headed back to the staff entrance and on to the vault, presumably. Again, our lives were in the hands of Brian, who was no more stable a personality than when all three of them arrived at the bank at 9:02 that morning.

He continued pacing back and forth like a caged animal in a decrepit zoo, long since past its prime. Then Brian twisted round and grabbed the younger of the two cashiers by the hair and dragged her over to the other side of the room, near the row of cashier stations.

Brian stood at ninety degrees to the group of people, huddling on the floor, so he could keep an eye on us with his peripheral vision. Meanwhile, he kept his grip on the cashier's head.

Then he threw her down and she crumpled on the floor like a polyester shirt. Brian bent down and took a handful of blouse in the same brutish hand – and pulled, tearing the fabric at the seams until he held a bunch of blue material and we could all see her back through the hole he had made.

The girl wasn't much more than twenty and she hid her head in her hands, cowering and crying. Brian slapped her hard on the face with the back of his hand, sending her flying across the floor as she slid along the marble.

While still pointing the shotgun at the rest of us, Brian stomped over to the woman and grabbed at her blouse again. This time she was lying on her back so he grabbed the front of her blouse and ripped it off so she was on the ground with her black bra visible, all lacy. She screamed and he pulled a bolo knife from inside his jacket and sliced at her, catching the surface of her breast, and a spew of red burst out of her. The cut wasn't that deep, but he'd picked one of the fleshiest parts of her body. The shock of being cut meant she fainted immediately.

A MASSIVE NOISE blasted around the room and Brian's body flew sideways, blood and guts splattering in all directions. Andrew was stood by the staff door, pointing a gun at where Brian had once stood. And then a shitstorm of police bullets rained down on us as the cops reacted to the sound of the gunshot from their positions outside.

Andrew hit the deck as soon as he realized that and ricocheting bullets pinged around the room, bouncing off the solid walls and floor, occasionally catching an arm or a leg. Thirty seconds later and the volley was over.

There were innumerable holes in the plasterwork and, unfortunately, many holes in the people too. I glanced down to make sure I was safe and looked around at the red pools dotted around the still breathing bodies near me.

Andrew picked himself up and grabbed the bags he'd dropped when he'd taken cover a minute ago. Frank appeared, and they looked at each other and then looked at Brian. He was groaning, bleeding out on the far side of the bank. Frank took a peek out of the window.

"Stay calm, everyone. The cops have stopped firing on us. Everybody stay down."

Firm words, low volume – just enough menace in his tone for everyone to believe him without question. He walked over to Brian, gurgling and drowning in his own bile. Frank pulled at the knife still in Brian's hand and tore the blade across his throat. Brian wouldn't be harassing cashiers no more.

Frank's eyes darted at Andrew and Andrew, in return, nodded in his direction to show he understood what had just happened and was cool with it all.

From nowhere, I heard the smashing of the glass in the front windows and the plop of grenades landing on the floor. I was certain I was a dead man, but this wasn't Korea. White choking smoke burst out of the tear gas canisters and I choked out the venomous air from my lungs as best I could. Three or four breaths later, my eyes were streaming with tears and a terrifying noise ripped inside the bank as the front door burst open and a SWAT team took over every inch of the place.

One of them grabbed me and dragged me out of the bank, pointing a gun at my head until he could tell I was one of the good guys. Later that day I heard Frank and Andrew got away. No real idea how, but there must have been some kind of rear exit because they sure as hell didn't leave with the SWAT at the front. They took the money too, apparently.

We were all checked by paramedics at the scene and those who'd been hit by stray bullets – about six of them and the first guy – were taken by ambulance for treatment. Despite the amount of blood spurting out of arteries and veins, it turned out no one was critically injured. In fact, if you were shot by the police that day, you were one of the lucky ones. Four years later, they each received about fifty to one hundred thousand in damages. I didn't even get a flesh wound. I've bled more when I've cut myself shaving. Damn shame I wasn't shot by the police that day.

# HOUSTON 1979

# 45

BACK IN HOUSTON, I was in a hire car, speeding out of Dodge when I received incoming from unknown assailants. First, I only saw gunfire, and I hit the brake and swerved sideways to avoid the two parked cars which had been positioned to take me out. As I fast-turned the steering wheel, I flopped onto the gear stick and hit my head on the passenger seat. Smart move because no sooner had I done that than a salvo of bullets whipped through the driver's door window and out the other side. Glass shattered all around me and the car came to a halt.

If I stayed where I was, I'd die so I quick-shimmied over to the passenger side because it was further away from the onslaught outside and I opened the door, slithered out, and lay on the tarmac to collect my thoughts.

Just like Frank all those years before, I peeped over the hood to check out the exact source of the gunfire. Six or seven semi-automatic bursts were coming from well-concealed positions for the shootists, from behind trees and hedges, cars, and even a bus shelter. Feeling around in my jacket pocket, I could tell I had about five spare bullets for my Magnum .38 snub nose and I knew I had a full clip. Without tremendous sharpshooting, I was about to be gunned down in a strange town, all for the sake of a case in the…

Then I realized something truly appalling. In my rush to exit the vehicle, I'd left the case in the footwell behind the driver's seat.

Sighing heavily, I rolled over to be near the rear of the car and opened the passenger door so I could crawl and grab the damn case. Meanwhile, bullets kept flying at a high rate and a high velocity. I got my fingers to the handle and yanked it over to my side and out the rear door.

I was pinned down behind a car riddled with bullet holes by six or seven professional hitmen intent on my demise. This would have been a great moment to say something like I saw my life flash before my eyes, but it didn't happen that way. My teeth started chattering and a bad feeling spread from the pit of my stomach and up my spine until it reached the back of my neck. My mouth went dry, and I swallowed hard hoping to find saliva in the far reaches of my throat. No joy. My heart pounded like it was about to burst out my torso and I thought about my poor mother crying at my funeral. Like that would happen.

Then I heard gunfire behind me and I knew they'd split up and set up a pincer movement on me. I only had seconds, perhaps a minute, and then this would all be over.

SOMETIMES LIFE CAN throw you a curveball, something you don't expect that pisses all over your day like there's no tomorrow. And sometimes the curveball can make you smile. This was one of those occasions.

With the gunfire behind me, a bullet flew over my head. I looked in the general direction of the newly arrived incoming and saw two faces I recognized, even from three hundred feet. McNamara and Mumford had heard the commotion and come to my rescue like the cavalry.

Due to the surprise factor and well-trained marksmanship, they knocked out three of the bandits in quick succession, almost before I'd turned round to see them arrive.

By the time I'd returned to face my attackers, two more had fallen, which left only the three lone gunmen perched in excellent hiding places.

I let fire a short burst at a hedge with a head bobbing up and down and an arced plume of red splayed over the top. One down and two to go.

Then McNamara and Mumford ripped out crossfire across the entire panorama enabling me to leap from my sieve of a car, roll on the ground and get behind a tree before the bandits could return fire. I hoisted myself up into the foliage and onto a branch hidden by the leaves. From on high, I spied both the marksmen, clear as day. I refilled my clip and took aim. First shot through the heart, second at the head, third back to the heart. Did that for both. Six shots used up and three corpses lying twitching on the sidewalk.

The Dynamic Duo ran up to my tree and I slid down. Then together we walked to each of the bodies to check for ID and to scavenge as we saw fit. We knew we had only a small amount of time before the local cops responded to an inevitable noise complaint generated by our battle. And we didn't want to be there when they arrived.

My first thought was for the case and I picked it up from where I'd left it by the rear passenger door. We wouldn't be getting the deposit back on that rental.

Having gone through every bloody pocket we could find, we were still none the wiser as to who the assailants might have been.

"Must have been CIA," said McNamara, "with this much ordnance and no identification at all."

"Yeah, your FBI always carry their badges. So do cops. Either it was the CIA, the mob, or maybe the KKK?"

I wasn't sure how exhaustive my list was but I knew I was close to the money. McNamara nodded.

"My guess is CIA. If it was the mob, it must have been an unauthorized hit else why would the don bother getting us to collect the package in the first place? He could have just sent his own men in to blast away."

He had a point, but he was silent about the KKK, which I thought was odd as he was a precise man for all of his relaxed demeanor.

"If it was the CIA, what do you think is in the case they'd want so much?"

Mumford was right. The CIA rarely attacked mob hired personnel – that was us, after all – carrying out illegal but domestic business. There must be something pretty important of a non-domestic nature to get this much attention from them.

THE CASE WAS in my hand and I noticed myself gripping the handle more tightly as the conversation progressed. The obvious response would be to flip the lid and see for ourselves, but I remembered the don telling me not to do that.

"If such an event occurs then I shall have no choice but to torture for pleasure and kill you for business," he'd informed me. And I believed him.

"How are relations between the US and the UK?"

"All fine as far as I am aware," replied Mumford to my question. I scanned both faces, trying to discern what thoughts were flickering behind each pair of eyes, but those same eyes stared back at me doing the same thing too. A visual Mexican standoff.

I smiled and shrugged.

"Beats the hell out of me. And if it was the CIA, what would the don have that was so important to them they'd shoot us in public?"

"Dunno, Jake, but we'd better get out of here before the locals show."

McNamara was right and his comment was prompted by the sound of sirens in the distance, getting closer by the second. We ran down the street – I followed the other two – until we reached a vehicle with both front doors open. They'd hot-wired the car as soon as they'd heard the gunfire. Nice.

McNamara jumped behind the wheel and Mumford rode shotgun, so I took the driver's side rear seat because it was the nearest.

Before I had closed the door, we were off, cornering loudly and hightailing it round to head away from the bedlam we had caused. The journey to the station took twenty minutes. McNamara tried to avoid the main drag, hoping not to be stopped in a stolen vehicle, which meant we missed the traffic too.

# The Case

The parking lot was vast, so we hid the car in plain sight in a long, full row and ambled into the station complex. We bought three tickets for the next train out of town; didn't care where. So we ended up getting on the 10:47 to Austin.

HUNKERED DOWN IN one of the compartments, we kept checking all around in case the CIA had followed us, but we had paid cash for our tickets and we were sure the car hadn't been spotted on the way over. After ten, fifteen minutes we relaxed and sat back in our seats.

"Reckon we're safe. At least for the moment."

"For sure. The don'll be pleased with us."

"You think?"

"We've survived, haven't we? And we've still got the case."

"True. Anyone got any idea what's in the case?"

I bridled again, because the don's words of warning were still ringing in my ears, but said nothing.

"No idea, but I'm more interested why the don wants the case. How often does the Mafia spend this much effort using outside help to get something it wants?"

"I know. I mean, the tentacles of his organization must stretch wide enough for him to have got hold of the case by the time Dakila Valdez got his grubby paws all over it."

"Yeah. If the don knew about low-level pond scum like that, you'd think he'd have been able to extract the case without the three of us needing to get involved."

"True, but maybe that's the point. That Valdez had possession of it points to this being a lot more complicated than it appears. We think the CIA wants the contents and instead of using his usual goons, here we are on a train to Austin."

"You think it's no accident we're here?"

"Has to be. Whatever is in there, the don trusted us over his own people."

"Do you think the FBI has an interest?"

"Hard to say. I've not seen it in any reports coming through, so it's not on general release. But that doesn't mean it's not on a watch list for the hierarchy. Bill Webster might have it as his number one priority, but I've not heard about it."

"All this cloak and dagger stuff makes me nervous. I've not heard the British Secret Service has an interest either, but the top brass tend not to broadcast these things. We're more circumspect than our American cousins."

"But if it's important enough for the CIA, why has no one got any idea about it? We are reasonably well-connected guys, but we've bupkis on this."

"Perhaps the CIA wants it because it's all about the CIA. Maybe it's like the Watergate tapes."

"Or just some incriminating pictures of the don with a male hooker."

That permeated our skulls and as each of us tried to make sense of it, McNamara shook his head.

"Sorry, I was only thinking out loud."

"Jeez, keep your thoughts to yourself in that case, bud," I wheezed. We all laughed because the truth was we had no idea. We hardly knew each other and the only connector between us was the don. The randomness had to be more than mere coincidence. There's never that much coincidence in life, which meant it had to be part of some plan.

"The don is a wise man with a tremendous amount of power. Perhaps he needed guys he could trust who weren't part of his empire to get the job done."

Mumford and McNamara looked at me and shook their heads.

"You are a dreamer, my boy, if you genuinely think that."

I knew I was wrong as soon as I'd said it, but that didn't mean I had any clearer idea what was going on. My thoughts flashed back to a week ago when I was sat in a casino waiting for Aaron to come up for air with Rachel and the world seemed a lot less complicated. His dealings with the local mob felt benign compared to the shit we were in and I wondered if the don had any connection to that deal. On that train, I felt as though he was touching every aspect of my life. Didn't sit well with me, like he was controlling my passage along life's rich pageant.

■    ■    ■    ■    ■    ■    ■

# 46

THE TRAIN PULLED into Austin and we waited at the end of the carriage to let most of the others off before we disembarked. This would give us the best chance to prevent anyone following us if we were at the back of the line. We couldn't see anyone hanging back so we jumped off after waiting as long as we could when the conductor got to the point of saying, "Get back in, guys, or get the hell off my train, but you're stopping us from moving!"

Said with a smile, but by the curl of his mustache, you could tell he was not a happy man. Goes with the territory, I reckon.

There we were on the platform, scouting round like three penned pumas with paunches. Out the barriers and onto the station exit to find the line for taxis. We stood in line like all the other schmucks and hopped into the one allocated to us.

"Where d'you wanna go, guys?"

"Airport."

"Gotcha."

We didn't utter another word until the cab pulled up at the terminal. Nothing we would say was for the driver's ears and Mumford's accent was too noticeable to allow him to speak out loud anyway.

Then we strode into the terminal and joined the line for the United sales desk. It was a long line.

"And what's your firm's interest in all this?"

Mumford looked at McNamara, staring into his eyes for a second.

"None I'm aware of, dear boy. What have you heard?"

"Jack shit. But you haven't mentioned how you got acquainted with the don, if you see what I mean."

"You are right. I did not."

Mumford let that sentence hang in the air with no attempt at elaboration. I saw McNamara grinding his teeth with annoyance.

"Perhaps it has something to do with oil or water interests?" I proffered to ease the tension between the two.

"There certainly are shared interests in those two commodities," he acknowledged but added not one jot.

"You can let go of your stiff upper lip, y'know?"

"I am aware, but I am not prepared to discuss this matter in public. So that needs to be the end of it until later."

We were at the front of the line but we only had enough cash to buy two tickets. Given the recent tension, we left Mumford to go back to the station and follow us by train as quick as he was able.

With the case still firmly in my left hand, I walked with the other two up to the departure gate where we said our goodbyes to Mumford. The chances were this wouldn't be the last time we'd meet. It never was.

I SCURRIED OVER to a food concession and grabbed a coffee, no milk, and I sipped it while we sat waiting for the plane. McNamara and I sat in silence for about fifteen minutes. We'd spent so much time together there was nothing much left to say and the only topic remaining was the damn case in my hand and we were none the wiser about that than when we had started.

The last swig of coffee hit the back of my throat and I thought about hitting the head before the flight, but the announcement came out of a speaker right above our heads and everyone stood up to get in line. So we did the same.

Then we were at the front and showing our boarding passes to the ground crew. We walked onto the tarmac, over to the steps, and up into the front of the plane. Our seats were in the fifth row so that made perfect sense. Just as we entered the fuselage, I turned my head back to the terminal and thought I glimpsed Mumford scurrying past to the back set of steps. Shook my head and craned back to check again, but if he was there, he had gone.

A man behind me tapped my shoulder and ushered me into the plane. Another peremptory check and then we made our way to our seats. McNamara headed in first to the middle seat and I took the aisle.

The seat belt sign was already on and the third passenger in our little row was already in by the time we turned up. So we both did up our belts and waited for the plane to taxi.

Ten long minutes later and the plane entered the sky and banked hard right before reaching its cruising altitude and the seat belt sign finally switched off. We had about three-and-a-half hours in that tin can before we hit the Big Apple.

"Back in a minute," I said heading straight for the john because I had been desperate to take a piss ever since that last sip of coffee.

I came back to sit down and before I did, McNamara stood up and hit the head himself. Then he returned and we both settled in. The in-cabin screen showed we had a little under three hours to go.

In only a short while, I'd be in LaGuardia handing over the case to Simone Lambretti. I hadn't seen her since our time together in Seattle when we were sitting on a tiger fur rug waiting for a pile of money for me to free her friend, Sally from a gang of bad guys.

MY PREVIOUS DESCRIPTION of our time on the rug had missed out a few details. When I said I had made sure there was a respectable gap between our bodies, I overstated the situation by several inches. In reality, I had dropped right next to her so that our hands touched. She had turned with her skirt hitched above her knees and I moved in to kiss her.

Simone responded in kind and, shortly afterward, we were lying on the rug with her skirt around her ankles and my pants unzipped near my knees. She rolled on top of me and kicked off her skirt. I undid her blouse and played with her breasts while she unbuttoned my shirt and then she lay down on top of me with her legs either side of my hips and we kissed some more.

Simone could tell I was getting hard because she must have been able to feel me pushing through my shorts and her panties. She sat up and, using one of her hands, she pulled down my shorts and dragged her panty gusset to one side so she could sit on me until we both came.

Afterward, curled around each other, we had enough time for cooing small talk. She was young, but she was legal.

"You are my little Fuckabubba."

"Watch it, Jacko." She nibbled my ear, while I put my hand in between her thighs again. Then I snapped out of my reverie and wondered why the don had allowed Simone to get so closely involved in his business. There had never been an occasion since I first met him when he'd have put his daughter at the center of his affairs. Yet he was the one who suggested Simone should be the point of contact. How did she get so embroiled in the family business? She had spent the whole of her life trying to avoid the Lambretti legacy. She had said as much to me when we were lying on that tiger rug before we put our clothes back on. The screen flashed we had ninety minutes to landing.

"Penny for your thoughts?"

"Nah, just daydreaming. It's been a long hustle, these last few days."

"Sure has. What do you reckon is in the case?"

"Not a clue."

"Me neither."

"Does your organization have an interest?"

"Could be. I mean, we have a huge number on our watch list. The chances are slender of any interstate bad guys getting up to something without our knowing."

"But which bad guys?"

"Well, there's Don Michael for the get-go."

"Yes, of course, but he has many business interests as we both know. And if it was just something within his organization what the hell are we doing here?"

"Yep, I know. Most of our attention nowadays is on the KKK. It's the only other form of highly organized crime we have if you ignore the likes of the… if you ignore the likes of the don."

"I met some low-order guys once. I was in the south but those dudes scared me more."

"Correct response. Bunch of motherfuckers. In the good old days, they were flag-proud Christians wrapped in a misplaced zeal for the Lord and the white man. Now they're a money-making mob who kill Blacks for fun."

"So what would a bunch of Kluxers want that is almost in the hands of the don?"

"Beats the bejeebers out of me."

The Klan and that the CIA were after the case and I shivered at the thought one might do the bidding of the other. Sounded a little too farfetched, even in a post-Watergate world.

The conversation died and we returned to our respective thoughts. One thing I knew the mob had dipped its fingers into was water. I remembered the treatment plants out in LA in Bomp's territory and just last week Aaron was involved with some mobster and what sounded like another water deal. Perhaps that was it, the missing link.

"We'll be landing in twenty minutes, so please return to your seats as the captain will shortly be switching on the seatbelt signs. At that point, the washrooms will be locked and will not be available until after we land."

Water rights in California. Is that what this has been about? I looked down at my lap and wondered if people had died over a drop or two of water.

And if I was right then was the don's guiding hand so strong as to steer the FBI, the CIA, and the British Secret Service toward his aims and goals? To be honest, I couldn't think of anything so mightily important where that could be true. The only idea that flashed through my mind was it had to have something to do with the president. Who else was so important to bring everyone together on this? If that was the case, I was in much deeper than I ever thought possible.

The tires bumped the plane onto the runway and we shot down the tarmac until we heard the air brake kick in and a few seconds later we had dropped to a taxiing speed.

We hung around near a gate for a lifetime and then trundled forward a few more feet until we were parked in the right spot. The seatbelt light pinged off.

As I stood up, I looked back down the plane and, again thought I saw Mumford in the sea of heads behind me. When I'd gone to the washroom, I'd had a look around and had not seen him. Curious, but I still wasn't certain he was on the plane.

The door opened and all the passengers shuffled forwards. Something about being cooped up in a plane makes everyone desperate for a dash for freedom. But the only way for us all to get off safely was for everybody to chill out. We took our turn waiting for some free space in the aisle to go towards the exit. Our lungs filled with the cold, fresh air of New York. Well, fresher air than the stale stuff we'd been gasping the last few hours.

Finally, we were at the front of the aisle and I turned left to disembark. A steward smiled and said goodbye and I smiled back. I looked out the door and made out Simone at the bottom of the stairs. The don had said she'd be there but I couldn't figure out how she'd made it onto the runway, but she had, all while wearing a black ball gown.

I smiled and she acknowledged me with a flutter of her eyelids and a half-nod of recognition. We were almost at the end. I knew I had to play it cool for a minute longer and everything would be all right.

Just as that thought crossed my mind, I walked forward, out the plane, and onto the stairs. My right foot planted itself on the top of the stairs but my left foot got caught on the rim of the plane's door. I was looking at Simone and not at where I was going.

I stumbled, lost my balance, and fell hard. Because I'd been staring at Simone, I had slowed down and a small gap had formed in front of me as the other passengers had carried on making their way down to the ground.

My body twisted as I fell to stop myself landing on all fours, so my left shoulder was the first to hit the metal steps. Then my left side and the rest of me followed – with the case, still in my right hand.

And that was the last time I held that case because, in an act of pure instinct, I let go of the damn thing and it bounced twice down the steps until… the lock broke and the case burst open. Paper belched out and sprayed upwards for half a second and, at that point, I thought I could rescue the situation. Instead, a gust of wind grabbed everything and blew the pages sideways.

Sideways into the open arms of one of the engines from our Austin plane, which guzzled up every sheet and mulched them into confetti.

# FLORIDA 1999

# 47

ALL THAT WAS twenty years ago and here I am lying in my bed somewhere in the state that became my home.

You're probably wondering what the hell happened once the papers flew away. Answer: a total shitstorm. McNamara watched me fall and assumed I'd been hit by a sniper. Too much training on his part, I guess. So he covered my body while trying to shoot any damn thing that moved. Crazy.

Simone turned around and walked immediately out of sight, vanishing into the darkness like any Lambretti would. I haven't seen her since that night but I can still recall her scent if I close my eyes and inhale deeply. The don? Now that was a man who was far from pleased.

"You are lucky to be alive," he told me in his study a few hours later, "but I believe the accident was truly that."

I nodded, unable to utter a single word because I couldn't think what to say to make the situation any better.

"The good news – and this is relative, you understand – is that while I may not have the package, no one else has either. So while I may not have gained, there isn't another soul on this planet who has profited at my expense.

"For this reason, and for this reason alone, I shall spare your life."

My eyes widened at the thought I was seconds away from death.

"But you need to be punished, nonetheless. So I am banishing you. I never want to see you again, understand?"

My head nodded consent.

"I don't want to hear about you, read about you or in any other way come into contact with you. This means you must never set foot in New York, Boston, LA, Chicago, or any other city I may visit. If, by some chance, you hear I am coming to the place where you live, you must leave immediately. Do you understand me?"

"Yes… yes, I do." A tear departed my left eye as the sorrow and grief implied in his words came through.

Just before he dismissed me, he sent his goons out of the room and we talked some more. He let me sit down and we shared a glass of Scotch. Don Michael told me he realized I meant no malice and he had respected the work I had done for him over the years. We spoke about the people whose lives had intersected ours and I gave him all the details about what had happened the last couple of days.

We shook hands and, just before he called his men back into the room, he opened his safe and passed me an envelope. He had kept his word and paid me what he owed and a whole lot more; hush money you might call it. What a mensch.

SO HERE I am in Florida – I'm not saying where in case the don is alive and hears. I picked the place because it has casinos, albeit illegal ones, and the weather is good most of the year. I found a secluded spot by a pretty lake, bought an acre of land, and built a wooden shack smack in the middle of it. I call it a shack but in reality, it's a large bungalow.

My investigator's license expired many years ago and, since then, I've spent my time pottering about the local community and dispensing advice to the few who'll listen. I mentioned the casinos; I enjoy spending a few bucks there as a way to relax and there's a cathouse next door where I relax some more. Never had a wife, never found the need for a wife. I still have my gun and I keep it in a box under my bed.

And I'm in bed now because my doctor explained that a lot of black coffee and no exercise gave me bowel cancer, which has eaten away at my insides. I shall be dead in a few hours because I have nothing more to do in this life and I see no reason to prolong my agony for the sake of saying I survived. Survived what, for Chris' sake?

Under my bed is my gun box, but under the gun box is a wooden floor. If you look carefully, you can see a rectangular edge in the middle of the floor under the bed. Touch the edge of that rectangle and you will feel the trap door. Open it, why don't you? Put your hand into the inky blackness. You'll need to lie down on the ground and stretch because the drop is three or four feet. Don't worry, it's big enough for you to jump down if it is easier for you.

At the bottom, you will find a metal box. It has a big fat padlock on it needing a key. If you ever find the key then you'll be able to open the box and inside, you'll find some paper.

This isn't any old paper. When I said I hit the head on the plane, I sure was telling the truth, but again, not the whole truth. I brought the case with me because I couldn't stand the thought of losing it so close to the end game. And even though there wasn't much space to maneuver, I prised the lock open and gazed inside.

There was an enormous pile of papers and I could only glance at them, but I understood pretty quickly what it was all about. The first ten or twenty pages had print and the rest were blank, presumably to give weight to the case. No idea why, but I took the printed pages and folded them into my front pants pockets. Then I shut the lid and locked the case again. Turns out I didn't do a very good job of that.

And the paper you'll find in that box is the paper I stole from the don's case. I've read it and reread it and the more I do, the more I understand why everyone wanted to get their hands on those sheets and why blood was shed trying to do so.

Want me to tell you? Let these be my last dying words: Los Angeles Water…

THE END

# THANK YOU FOR READING!

**Get a free novella**

Building a relationship with my readers is the very best thing about writing. I send weekly newsletters with details of new releases, special offers and other bits of news relating to the Lagotti Family and Alex Cohen series, as well as information about my stand-alone novels.

And if you sign up to the mailing list I'll send you a copy of the Alex Cohen prequel, The Broska Bruiser. Just go to www.leob.ws/signup and we'll take it from there.

Of course, if you prefer to jump right into the first book in the series then grab your copy of The Bowery Slugger now.

And you can always follow me on BookBub if you want a quick and easy way to keep up-to-date with my work at www.bookbub.com/authors/leopold-borstinski

**Enjoy this book? You can make a difference**

Reviews are the most powerful tools in my arsenal when it comes to getting attention for my books. Much as I'd like to, I don't have the financial muscle of a New York publisher. I can't take out full page ads or put posters on the subway.

(Not yet, anyway).

But I do have something much more powerful and effective than that, and it's something that those publishers would kill to get their hands on.

**A committed and loyal bunch of readers.**

Honest reviews of my books help bring them to the attention of other readers.

If you've enjoyed this book I shall be very grateful if you would spend just five minutes leaving a review (it can be as short as you like) on the book's page. You can jump right to the page by clicking www.books2read.com/thecase.

Thank you very much.

Leo

# SNEAK PREVIEW

In the first of the latest series from Leopold Borstinski, The Bowery Slugger…


The game of baseball has a long and fine tradition, dating back over a century when rival villages would resolve their differences with a bat and a ball. While similar in appearance to the British sport of rounders, baseball is an American game played under American rules.

Even though the rule book is thick, at its heart the game involves two teams: one tries to run round a square and the other tries to stop them. A member of the team who is aiming to complete circuits of the square must use a stick to propel the ball, lobbed at them by the opposition, as far away from the square as possible. That gives them sufficient time to run around the square.

The stick, or bat, is tapered and varnished to within an inch of its life so that the baseball travels unimpeded on its journey. The other advantage of this stick is that the wood, out of which it is made, comes from only the finest trees. Why should we care about such details? Because when you take a baseball bat to a man's skull, you can be certain you will cause him damage.

Fabian planted the end of his baseball bat firmly into the side of Sammy's cranium, causing a little rhythmic arc of red to appear from his ear. Fabian continued to clobber him with blows to his kidneys, chest, back and head. Power swings and a practiced eye ensured each swing hit its intended target with deadly force. At first, Sammy twisted himself into a ball, desperate to protect his sides and front from the rain of woody assaults smashing against him. Then the pounding took its toll and his energy waned until his body slackened and he ceased trying to defend himself.

"You'd better not get up from this, you *gonif*. Understand?"

Silence for a reply because Sammy lay on the ground, one leg twitching, with no other movement. Fabian poked him in the ribs once. Nothing. He took the hem of the guy's shirt and wiped his bat clean with it, like it was any old *schmatta*. He walked out of the alleyway, careful not to be seen by any passerby. Then Fabian slipped into the shadows of the Manhattan night.

Although he didn't waste time looking back on his life, if Fabian had bothered, he would have realized that night was precisely three years to the day after he arrived in the United States of America.

Fabian continued to flee the scene of his crime, slinking from one stall to the next as he made his way back home. The image of Sammy's skull, blood pouring out, lingered in his mind despite himself.

He pushed through the crowds south on Norfolk, turned right onto Heston and headed towards the Bowery before another right back onto Eldridge Street. His eyes stared a few feet ahead of his shoes, hat tipped forward to make it harder for people to see his face.

To grab your copy, go to www.books2read.com/slugger

# ALSO BY THE SAME AUTHOR

**Alex Cohen**

The Bowery Slugger (Book 1)
East Side Hustler (Book 2)
Midtown Huckster (Book 3)
Casino Chiseler (Book 4)
Alex Cohen Books 1-3
Cuban Heel (Book 5 - Due 2021)
Hollywood Bilker (Book 6 - Due 2021)
The Mensch (Book 7 - Due 2021)
Alex Cohen Books 4-7 (Due 2022)

**Stand Alone**

The Case

**The Lagotti Family**

The Heist (Book 1)
The Getaway (Book 2)
Powder (Book 3)
Mama's Gone (Book 4)
The Lagotti Family Complete Collection (Books 1-4)

**Jake Adkins PI (Due 2022)**

I Confess (Book 1)
Habeas Corpus (Book 2)
Luther's Diamond (Book 3)

All books are available from www.leob.ws and all major eBook and
paperback sales platforms.

# ADDENDUM

In 1917, TP O'Connor, the second president of the British Board of
Film Censors issued 43 categories of material that could not be
portrayed on British celluloid. All have been violated in this novel:

1.  Indecent, ambiguous and irreverent titles and subtitles.
2.  Cruelty to animals.
3.  The irreverent treatment of sacred subjects.
4.  Drunken scenes carried to excess.
5.  Vulgar accessories in the staging.
6.  The modus operandi of criminals.
7.  Cruelty to young infants and torture to adults, especially
    women.
8.  Unnecessary exhibition of underclothing.
9.  The exhibition of profuse bleeding.
10. Nude figures.
11. Offensive vulgarity, and impropriety in conduct and dress.
12. Indecorous dancing.
13. Excessively passionate love scenes.
14. Bathing scenes passing the limits of propriety.
15. References to controversial politics.
16. Relations of Capital to Labour.
17. Scenes tending to disparage public characters and
    institutions.
18. Realistic horrors of warfare.
19. Scenes and incidents calculated to afford Information to the
    enemy.
20. Incidents tending to disparage our Allies.
21. Scenes holding up the King's uniform to contempt or
    ridicule.
22. Subjects dealing with India, in which British officers are seen
    in an odious light, and otherwise attempting to suggest the
    disloyalty of Native States, or bringing into disrepute British
    prestige in the Empire.
23. The exploitation of tragic incidents of the war.
24. Gruesome murders and strangulation scenes.

25.	Executions.
26.	The effects of vitriol throwing.
27.	The drug habit, eg opium, morphia, cocaine, etc.
28.	Subjects dealing with White Slave traffic.
29.	Subjects dealing with the premeditated seduction of girls.
30.	'First night' scenes.
31.	Scenes suggesting immorality.
32.	Indelicate sexual situations.
33.	Situations accentuating delicate marital relations.
34.	Men and women in bed together.
35.	Illicit sexual relationships.
36.	Prostitution and procuration.
37.	Incidents indicating the actual perpetration of criminal assaults on women.
38.	Scenes depicting the effect of venereal diseases, inherited or acquired.
39.	Incidents suggestive of incestuous relations.
40.	Themes and references relative to 'race suicide'.
41.	Confinement.
42.	Scenes laid in disorderly houses.
43.	Materialisation of the conventional figure of Christ.

# ABOUT THE AUTHOR

Leopold Borstinski is an independent author whose past careers have included financial journalism, business management of financial software companies, consulting and product sales and marketing, as well as teaching.
There is nothing he likes better so he does as much nothing as he possibly can. He has traveled extensively in Europe and the US and has visited Asia on several occasions. Leopold holds a Philosophy degree and tries not to drop it too often.
He lives near London and is married with one wife, one child and no pets.
Find out more at LeopoldBorstinski.com.

9 781999 770594